A CARLOS VERGARA NOVEL

THE ARCHIVED

CITIZEN

First edition

Edited by June Colbert

Cover design by premiumsolns on Fiverr

Formatted by Saqib Arshad on Fiverr

Paperback ISBN: 978-0-646-86656-7
E-book ISBN: 978-0-6456139-9-5

THE ARCHIVED

CITIZEN

Hope wills out everything.

CHAPTER 1

BUZZ, BUZZ, BUZZ.

The alarm wailed for the third time. If there was a way to sync it with one's circadian rhythms, it still wouldn't help William. His sleep schedule had no steady pattern. His own body decided when he should sleep; he had little to say in the decision-making process. Three a.m.? Sure. Why not? Who needs four hours of sleep to function?

With his face stuck in the mattress and his right eye flickering for light adjustment, William Kepler—a born and raised Australian—contemplated throwing his phone into the wall or smacking his hand against the device hard enough, with the little strength he had in the morning, to shut the alarm up. His own body compelled him to not get up, or move at all. Too much effort. The warmth inside his bed enveloped him so tightly, memories of safe cosy days when he was a child played on his mind. He enjoyed the moment.

But no matter how blissful those memories were, the alarm continued to wail and vibrate next to him on the floor. Manufacturer's settings meant the phone rattled so intensely that the bed shook as well.

Goddammit... I always forget to fix the settings on the alarm... He sighed, bracing himself to move. *Here we go.*

He reached over his single bed for his phone, but his numb arm wouldn't obey. No matter how hard he tried to bend it to his will, nothing happened. He threw himself off the bed onto the cold-tiled floor. Within seconds, the warmth from his body dispersed, initiating a sudden desire to get back into bed. In spite of himself, however, he regained consciousness fast, grabbed the phone and turned off the alarm.

Relief! The sudden quiet, and the lumbar support against his back from his bed, tempted him to resume sleeping.

Buzz, buzz, buzz.

The alarm wailed again. He forgot about the second alarm. Not wanting to dawdle a second longer on the cold floor, he went for his usual morning ablutions, which involved brushing his teeth in a hot-timed shower, and listening to UNHINGED—a podcast about recent events where the news remained supposedly unbiased and uninfluenced by major corporations who liked to blast gargantuan propaganda agendas that offered very little in the way of truth or interest to anyone with a rational mind. Or so he thought, anyway.

The morning report touched on three major topics—The Living Smog, World War III, and Protesters—the usual updates on the current trends and any progress being made under the watchful eye of the government.

Two years had passed since the Smog—a mysterious toxic living smoky fog carrying a deadly contagion—arrived and moved from country to country, evolving and adapting to the ever-changing environmental conditions. No one knew how it came about but a combination of unprecedented air pollution and tumultuous weathering seemed to be the best theory anyone had at the time.

The initial response by all governments towards the Smog were respiratory masks, hazmat suits, and the Almighty lockdowns—not terribly effective in most instances. At least they were seen to do something until they made them permanent. After all, a population hiding at home and afraid of dying was easier to control. The permanency drained the energy of everyone stuck at home who wanted out of this mad confinement and longed to be free to pursue once again a life of unfettered bliss.

The desire for some kind of escape was only heightened by the rumblings of war between countries after the superpowers of the world had fallen from the world stage. The two superpowers were at each other's throats, neither willing to make the first move to test the other's dominance as news articles blasted headlines like 'WORLD WAR III - THE BEGINNING?', 'BATTLE BETWEEN THE SUPERPOWERS RAGES ON!', and 'SURVIVAL TECHNIQUES: YOUR TEN MOST IMPORTANT SKILLS IN A WAR'.

These headlines served one single and well-crafted purpose: to create panic. It worked. Within a short space of time, fear and panic ran rampant, as people sought shelter anywhere, and any way they could.

It did work, he thought as he was one of those people.

CHAPTER 1

And then there were the Protesters, running wild in nearly every world city now, demanding governments remove certain legislations that had been imposed when the Smog first appeared. Most of these protests ended in altercations with law enforcement officers, and both parties experiencing casualties.

'Don't know about you, Jordan,' the host said, 'but I'm growing fonder of the saying, "the more I learn about people, the more I love my dog".'

'I'm glad yours is still alive,' the co-host said, 'Many, including my own, were lost to the Smog.'

'I'm sorry to hear that. But let us hope that we all make it through these dark times.'

William stood still in front of the stream, letting the water roll down his body, as the warmth moved through his limbs.

Bing! The shower ended.

'Morning quota for water use has been met,' an automated voice said.

He sighed, unimpressed as always by the short time he was allotted for his morning shower. He knew he had to speak with his strata managers to increase his quota but procrastination got the better of him every time—things that mattered always found themselves put aside for those that weren't. He left before the cold air could seep back into the shower to steal his warmth.

Once fully dried and dressed, he moved onto the next important task of the day: to get coffee.

Coffee, coffee, coffee.

His mind ran the word on a loop as he made his way to the kitchen. His automated coffee machine finished brewing a pot of coffee for him—completed in response to his SmartWatch as soon as his tired body woke up. He poured a serving and sipped his coffee. The bitter sweet flavory coursed down his throat, and within seconds, the caffeine and sugar triggered a spurt of energy.

Ah, better.

He continued drinking when something heavy brushed his legs. He glanced down to find Ramses—his black and white cat—looking at him with his dilated eyes, which meant one of four things: poor sleep, hungry, not happy with William waking up late, or all of the above. He always assumed all options were the case for his cat. It kept him on his toes to look after him properly.

'What happened to you, bud?' William asked, as he picked his cat up. 'You don't look so good. Let's get you something to eat, alright?'

He placed Ramses on the counter and served a can of minced beef into a bowl. His cat gobbled it up as if it was his first meal in days.

William went to his second room where he had set up his work office, and logged into the network to see his schedule for the day. The operating system flashed onto the screen with a buffering icon circling clockwise. When it finished loading, his applications appeared for several seconds before connectivity dropped out with an error message indicating his network 'was not authenticated'.

So far, business as usual then.

He performed troubleshooting protocols, then spent more time restarting the laptop.

Well, not the start I wanted but I'm not complaining, he thought. A cheeky grin crossed his face, as no one was around to tell him what to do; like millions of others, he now worked from home.

'Hey Raj,' he texted his manager. 'Authentication isn't working at the moment. Just troubleshooting. I'll keep you posted when I get an outcome. Might have to call IT if it persists.'

'Hey William, it's all good,' Rajesh messaged. 'Let me know how it goes. Text me back in 15 minutes if it still continues.'

Sometime later, he regained access to the network. He pulled up his emails, looking over the important ones highlighted with a red banner. These mostly concerned applications of credit—overdrafts, credit cards, and personal loans— passing their expected deadline. He breezed through urgent emails and tidied up the non-essential ones like general communications from the bank, and alerts of mandatory e-learnings he had to complete before the deadline or he'd risk losing access to the network and a portion of his bonus.

Can't forget bonus. Need the credits for special things.

Once he'd tended his emails and compiled a list of credit applications he needed to get done by today, he established his connection to the queues and looked at the number of calls in each tier. There were three tiers.

The application and complexity of the enquiry would determine which level the customer would go to. Tier 1 handled new accounts and personal overdrafts, Tier 2 handled credit cards and personal loans, and Tier 3 handled everything else, particularly complaints. He saw the numbers in each queue. Tier 1 had 8 calls, Tier 2 had 12 and Tier 3 had 14.

CHAPTER 1

Watch them go up though. It's a Monday—busiest day of all. It'd be so much better if they could call on another day. I don't understand how people don't get it that they're not going to get a response right away at the start of opening hours.

He got himself ready, placing his wireless headphones on and setting himself to AVAILABLE to take calls.

Ping! A call dropped immediately into his line. He had little time to do anything except check the customer's ID status. The customer came through GREEN. Don't need to identify them. Wait time: 37 minutes and 12 seconds.

'Hi there,' he said, 'you're speaking with William from Pinnacle Funds. I do appreciate your patience. How may I help you?'

'Yeah, hi,' the lady said in a dismissive tone. 'I did a credit application for $30,000 and it came back declined. I want to know why, as this doesn't make sense!'

'Yes certainly, I can look into that for you. I'm pulling up your profile now.' The page loaded up with her information and everything she held with the bank. 'Just to confirm, I'm speaking with Mariam Tanz.'

'That's *Mrs. Tanz* to you.'

Batter up! We got an entitled one here, he thought.

'Certainly, Mrs. Tanz,' he said, keeping his tone calm and welcoming. He clicked on her profile and searched for her recent application. 'I have your application in front of me. Just looking at it now for you to get the reason behind the decline. Just to confirm you did this application online or over the phone with us?'

'Online. I hope you can fix this. I've been banking with you for over ten years. I have all my accounts with you. Even got my home loan with your bank. Not once have I ever been declined for any application. And now this happens.'

'I do apologize for what's happened.' He found the reason for the decline— the assessment outcome stated serviceability to be a likely failure. Not enough income to cover the request. 'From what I can see here, your application was declined because it didn't pass assessment on the basis of servicing. Meaning your financial position overall wouldn't be able to service the loan amount.'

'What do you mean? Do you see the income coming into my accounts?'

'I've yet to look but I want to confirm that with you. Your income is as listed $170,000 gross per year, you have three home loans—one being an investment loan. Total overall debt amount of $4.3 million.'

'*Those* are joint accounts by the way which I don't pay. My husband does.'

'I can see, and that has come through, however, contractually, you are attached to the loan which has to be reflected on your balance sheet. Also, you have a credit card of a limit of $12,000 and living expenses are at $2,300 per month not including debt payments, correct?'

'Yes.'

'Okay, with everything captured correctly, unfortunately, we'll not be able to continue with this requested loan amount and term. However, we can try to go for a lower amount and a different loan term, and I can help with that. Would you like to try?'

'No, I don't want to *try* that. I want to do the application for the amount and term I requested.' The woman was clearly not holding back her frustration. 'If I wanted to try for a lower amount, I would have *tried* for a lower amount. Now, I want this application to be seen by someone else, if you aren't able to help me.'

'Unfortunately, there isn't anyone else who will be seeing the application as you're in the department who handles credit applications, and you are speaking to a senior specialist, Mrs. Tanz.'

'That's freaking ridiculous. I want to speak to your manager then. I want to speak with them now.'

'I can get them to speak with you and arrange a call-back from them, however, that takes 1-2 business days for a response.'

'Are you not listening to me? I'm not going to end the call until I get someone to speak to me.'

'Mrs. Tanz, with the outcome, and I can see this has frustrated you and clearly you are dissatisfied. I will be lodging this experience and noting everything including your dissatisfaction with the outcome, so that when my manager does speak with you, they'll know what's exactly going on. Did you want a reference number for that?'

'I don't want a reference number. I want you to put me in touch with them because I want to speak to them now!'

'Unfortunately, that won't be possible.'

'This is ridiculous. I've been a loyal customer for years. You have all my business but if you're not going to help, it's simple: I'm moving banks and you can get lost! Now, do you want to be responsible for that?'

William paused, not wanting to give her an answer. 'Mrs. Tanz, did you still want the reference number?'

CHAPTER 1

'You know what? You can get lost. Fucking stupid, dumbass idiot.' The woman ended the call.

For a moment, William sat in silence. His heartbeat thumped in his neck and ears. He took deep, long calming breaths, which didn't work. The caffeine from the coffee had pushed him into system overdrive. Five minutes hadn't even past yet and he already caught his first verbal abuse for the day.

Talk about a great start to the day. If this is the starter... oh, I don't want to think about the rest of the calls.

He quickly keyed his notes into the system before leaving the profile, hoping he wouldn't have to revisit it. On the plus side, she hadn't given consent for a call-back or taken the reference number, so there'd be no need to call her for the complaint.

He reached out to his friend on ENSEMBLE—a messaging system for work.

'Hey Mal,' he messaged. 'How's your start to the day? Just got my first call. It was a complaint, of course. Gotta love it, right?'

'Hey!' she texted back. '😨 That's no good. Is it an esco call? My day so far is alright. No complaints yet! 🙏 It's still too early to say... I've had some good idle. 1-2 minutes between calls when I started but we'll see how things go later on today. It'll go quick once we reach lunch time unless it's like app after app after app, you know?'

His colleague, Marlene Morris, burst with bubbliness throughout her conversations, making use of too many emojis when chatting. She hadn't been in the department long, but she displayed an aptitude and was a quick study. Her shift had started two hours before his own.

'Nice! Nah, it wasn't an esco call. It could have been but the woman didn't finalize anything with me... Lucky for me. Hopefully QA doesn't pick it up. Anyway, I don't think I'm going to be getting idle any time soon. It's been a few months since we've had some good idle for Tier 3.'

'That's good. Although don't get your hopes. Everett might get it and pass it on. I don't think Rajesh will want to do another esco after what happened the last time HAHA. With all the seniors going, it's leaving all those in Tier 3 with the workload and complaints. Too many escos for managers now from the other tiers... Still no word from management?'

'Yeah, not after what happened haha. Word from management? No different from what you've heard. Just some batches coming into the department in the next few months.'

'Yeeesh! They have been saying that forever and still nothing has happened. Anyway, we'll chat later. I just got a call 🎧'

'Sure.'

William finalized the complaint and took another call. *Ping!* The customer came through RED. The customer would have to be identified before continuing with the enquiry. Wait time: 51 minutes and 32 seconds. 'Hi there, you're speaking with William, I'm sorry for your wait time there, how may I be of assistance today?'

For the next two hours, the calls kept coming and coming. Little to no break could be taken between the calls aside from the time he had on ACW— After Call Work—during which he would normally spend a whole two minutes relaxing as he would get all his work completed on the call. He couldn't afford to take a longer time between calls otherwise the system would alert management of his time violations—the average time for the department was currently seventy-five seconds.

Lunch came around and he went on SCHEDULED, a segment on his system schedule to change status to a scheduled event. He snacked on two-minute noodles and streamed a movie from his media streaming service. Ramses sat alongside him as he ate, purring and curling up into a ball. Then he received a text message. It was for his random check up to make sure he was at home and available for work.

This has to stop. He sighed, shook his head in frustration, and regained some composure before he went to his office room and stood in front of a small white contraption mounted against the wall at William's head height.

He hovered his work keypass over the sensor and the device clicked to life. The shutter cover of a camera lens disengaged as it adjusted to the room light until it calibrated and stopped moving.

'Mr. Kepler,' the interviewer said, 'thank you for coming on time for your check-in. It's much appreciated.'

'Yeah, sure,' he said. *Like I really have much of a choice*, he wanted to say but didn't as it would ruin the whole tone of the meeting.

'Let's begin.'

William stood still while a red ray scanned his face, then the screen went black with a buffering icon loading. A green circle with a white tick inside appeared. Facial identification was successful.

'How are you feeling today?'

CHAPTER 1

'Tired.'

'Do require a wellbeing break?'

'No.'

'Do you need time off work?'

'No.'

'Is there anything you want to talk about?'

He paused for pretense, as if thinking about the question for a whole five seconds. He knew his answer before he replied, 'No.'

'Your pause and your heart rate indicate otherwise.'

'Just needed to think about the question. Doesn't make sense to speak first before thinking, right? Anyway, I had coffee today. Might explain the heart thing.' He tapped his chest.

'More than the usual?'

'No more than usual.'

'Is there perhaps a substitute for coffee? Records indicate a high level of consumption in the past few months. Possible link to recent performance. Comments of irritable and monotonous conduct with your work.'

'Well, maybe it's the walls, you know? They're not the best-looking walls. Looking duller with each day. Plus, they keep closing in.'

'Is that sarcasm?'

'Yeah.'

There was no response from the interviewer for nine seconds which felt even longer with the awkward silence. He stared at the camera's black lens, waiting for something to happen.

Shit...

William stood still for a moment, waiting for the interviewer. He did his best to not fidget or make any unnecessary movements as he would be deemed as 'Not Fit for the Day', and as a result, he'd be pulled into a meeting with management about it. If there were three or more in a given three-month period, he'd most likely have to be put on an evaluation program to see if he could stay in the company. It wasn't not something he wanted to do.

William knew of one person, who was once part of his team, and who had been put on the program and failed. He'd felt it was highly unfair as the person had been suffering from depression at the time because of the lockdowns, which had worsened during the program. Ever since their dismissal, everyone in the department had agreed upon a secret motto: "Don't let them break you.".

'Mr. Kepler,' the interviewer said, 'please confine your witty remarks outside of our sessions as we want to make sure you're healthy and safe while working in the conditions the bank has arranged while we live through these dire times.' They were clearly unimpressed now as their tone had changed from welcoming to serious.

'Of course. My apologies.'

'It's okay. Now, let's continue.'

The interview continued for twelve minutes. William tried to finish it sooner because he knew he wouldn't be able to ask to extend his lunch any longer. Management would only deny his request and put a mark against him for breaching schedule adherence.

This always happens. Damn shrinks!

William finished his cold noodles. It didn't matter. His appetite had gone and his stomach had closed up from the interview. He plodded back to his ergonomic chair, checking the time remaining for his lunch: six minutes, and dropping.

He touched his frost covered window and a sudden chill stung his hand. Beside the window sat a remote panel. He pressed a command which deactivated the frost-like setting on the window, allowing him to see outside. Problem was he couldn't see anything. The toxic mustard-coloured air plagued the surrounding city streets. He clasped his hands together around his eyes, thinking it would help him see through the air better—something he always did but it never worked.

He peered down towards the streets and spotted lights from hover cars and lampposts. He'd wanted to go outside ever since the city had declared a lockdown in every local government area. However, there were always a few stupid but brave souls in hazmat suits regularly walking the streets and protesting the lockdown restrictions imposed by the government.

Nothing ever came from their presence, aside from fights breaking out between them and Enforcers.

There are far better ways of protesting.

His mind meandered elsewhere to memories of going to the beach on a summer day, high tide and body surfing with cool breezes to stave off the stinking hot air. There would be attractive girls with voluptuous figures, and he would enjoy letting his mind wander onto things he would do with them. The possibilities were endless.

CHAPTER 1

He, he! If only I could sandwich myself betwe—

Voom, voom! His phone alarm shook the table with its urgent vibrations.

'Mother!' he exclaimed as he jumped back online. 'That was faster than expected.' He set himself to AVAILABLE, and a call came in. 'Hi there, you're speaking with William! How can I help you?'

'Yeah, hi,' a male customer said. Tone abrupt and irritated. 'Something happened with my application. I wanted to consolidate my loan, but the app made another account.'

Oh, boy.

William spent the remaining three and a half hours on calls until finally his shift was over.

Once done, he left the room and crashed on his mattress. He didn't want to move or cook but his stomach growled for food. He checked his fridge and found a day-old container of food he'd bought—white rice with mango chicken curry. He continued to search his fridge and found a garlic naan. The bread lost its softness as he pressed his fingers against it.

Not too appetizing, but don't have much of a choice. Pay day isn't until Thursday. It'll make do.

He placed his rice, curry and naan in the microwave until he deemed it acceptable for eating. He sat on his beanbag and turned on his projector to watch highlights from the Dota match the previous weekend hosted underground in another country. He suspected it was in South Korea or a country in Asia but he couldn't remember. It was the final match to this year's series. He had watched the whole thing already but wanted to see it again, as it was the best match, he'd seen all the year. Both groups were from different countries—Japan and USA—and had their participants connected to a neural port which transferred their consciousness into the game where they actually played. There were health bars and statistics on public display for them.

As they played, the pain settings were dialed down to zero to avoid possible health repercussions once they disengaged from the virtual space. It was highly contentious between the two groups as they carried strategic maneuvers and attacks to overcome the other.

Bing! Incoming text.

'Hey luv,' she texted. 'I've missed you. You free tonight? I don't have anyone coming over later.'

'Sure am. Same place?'

'Of course, darling! 😊 💋'

'Great. See you then.'

With his date set for the night, he re-joined the match between the two teams. As he watched, he pulled up his dating app—*Candied Love*. The app loaded up with his profile. His first glance was at the notification icon. Nothing. No alerts for women who had indicated interest and no responses from the woman he had swiped right on from his previous log-in.

He sat quietly for a moment, browsing the gallery of filtered women who he believed would be, could be, his ideal match. The first woman wasn't overly attractive although they shared similar views based on beliefs, lifestyle and common interests. *Swipe left.*

The next woman he found was an immediate stunner. They did have some similar interests although her preferences were set a level higher than him as she was after a High-Value-Man. Not exactly him. He scrolled through her page and looked at her other sites, mainly her Instagram. Mostly it displayed photos of her in tight dresses or skirts which accentuated her curves. While for him it was all eye candy, the red flags screamed at him with each photo.

But, better to shoot your shot than not shoot at all. Am I right? He opened up a message tab to her.

'Hey!' he texted. 'You've probably encountered all the ways people can say something to you, so I'll keep it simple. I see you like Dota. Did you get the chance to watch the recent World Championship Finals? How about the Japanese players? I thought those guys were to lose the match but that flanking maneuver was a thing of beauty from the captain. Completely took advantage of that sudden lapse of concentration of the Americans.'

He continued browsing through profiles, keeping his attention on just five women at a time. Any more than that and he knew he was in line for an aneurysm.

Then a new woman appeared, a brunette with hazel eyes and a slender figure. Her interests included going to the beach, trying out new cafes and restaurants in different cities, and spending time with family and friends. His finger hovered over her profile temporarily. Indeterminate. She seemed nice and he believed he might do well with her. *Swipe right.*

'Hey there,' he texted. 'I came across your profile. I see you like the beach and outdoor activities. What would be your ideal day for an outing once we've passed this historical event?' He checked his message before he sent it. Surely

CHAPTER 1

this girl had already received millions of messages from hopeful strangers on the app.

He went back to the match. The night arrived with no response from the women. He turned off his projector and moved his bean bag towards a black cable dangled from the ceiling. His access to Zerya—a virtual world where people could meet and do anything they'd like. From being an avatar and playing online campaigns with friends, to sitting at the beach, looking at a digital sunset. It was a world of freedom and different from the current one he was in.

He inserted the cable into the neural link at the back of his neck, and set an IP address and remoted into place.

He closed his eyes and everything went black. His body disappeared and he found himself suspended in nothingness for a moment. His consciousness slowly synchronized with the technology until light from above drew him closer, pixelating until everything around became clear. His vision fluttered for a moment until he found himself standing in a hotel room high in a digitalised metropolis. He undressed and lay atop a king-sized bed of soft, golden quilt covers and pillows. The room held nothing but a bed and a massive floor-to-ceiling window, revealing a different world. There was the evening sky, slowly moving into the night.

'Hello, love,' a silken voice said.

William glanced to his left and saw a slender blonde, wearing an untied silk robe and lying beside him. Her hazel eyes were layered in outliner to exude a sexual, albeit devilish allure. Her presence and her semi-naked body instantly attracted his most primal urges.

'Janyce,' he said, a sense of relief in his voice.

'Long day?'

'One I'm trying to forget.'

She smiled. 'I can help you with that.'

He placed his hand on her face, caressing it and moving her hair behind her ear. It felt real. 'I know you can.'

As nightfall settled over the virtual world, the couple shared a moment of passion and raw intimacy.

CHAPTER 2

USUAL ROUTINE WITH the alarm. It wailed and wailed until William grabbed his phone and silenced it. He noticed the time: 10:02 AM. The time meant little to him at first glance, until a question popped into mind: *What time do I start work?*

He saw messages and missed phone calls from his manager. 'Shit...' He responded to his manager, making up some plausible excuse about his absence from shift—a bad case of food poisoning.

'Are you able to work today?' Raj asked.

'Yeah, I just didn't hear my alarm go off. Thought I'd be okay by the morning. Sorry. I'll be on in a moment.'

'Sure. However, please let me know in advance if you're not feeling well—even a message so your name doesn't get reported.'

'Will do. Sorry.'

Without waiting to wonder why or how this had happened, he showered to went straight for his morning hit. He coffee pot was once ready for him and drank his cup, and then...

Cough, cough.

William stopped dead in his tracks as a raspy voice wheezed intermittently along the building's corridor. He approached the entrance door to better hear as he opted to not use the peephole. He didn't want to reveal his presence by casting a shadow by the door.

Cough, cough.

The wheezer seemed to be outside his door now. Heavy footsteps trudged across the floor.

CHAPTER 2

It can't be a Contaminant...

William's body moved along with his heartbeat. His fears took hold and he remained motionless, until the person in the corridor walked away, followed by their own apartment door shutting behind them. He sighed in relief, and shook off the jitters before he went about his business. With his energy levels improving from the coffee, he hopped onto the chair and logged into the network. As the screen buffered, he spaced out, recalling the events of last night in the hopes of finding a clue to his lateness. He felt fine. He'd gone to bed at the usual time, hadn't done any strenuous exercises that would keep him awake, apart from his amorous adventures with Janyce. But, as at the end of every meeting with her, nothing seemed amiss—physically speaking—aside from a mental drain, and wet underwear after using Zerya.

It couldn't have been the dating app? I mean really? This affected by not having any messages?

He snapped out of his trance when writing appeared on his work screen. He checked his emails and saw that his most recent one was linked to a complaint raised by another agent about him. He checked the name of the customer: Mrs Mariam Tanz.

Hmm... What did she say now?

The complaint case had been opened up. 'Customer was dissatisfied with the lack of assistance from the previous agent who served them, not providing them with options on getting a lower amount and helping pass assessment with their initial request. They were rude and they wanted to raise a complaint about them.'

This bitch.

He brushed the thought aside and resumed his follow up tasks. Most applications were approved and awaiting funding. He liked this phase of the application as there was no need to call the customer. They were about to receive their funds. He hovered his cursor over his call calibrating system to set himself on AVAILABLE.

For the next two hours, he pumped out his calls, spending little time with customers and speaking only when required. When his first break came, he took it on time, making sure he didn't take another call. He rushed to his pot of coffee. There was little left in the pot. Barely enough for a cup which didn't help the situation. He knew he'd be grouchy and easily irritated with the customers.

Dammit!

A slight weight moved against his leg. He looked down and saw Ramses, whom he'd forgotten about the entire morning. He picked up his cat and hugged him for some affection—even though his cat was as usual ready to escape his embrace at a second's notice. 'I'm so sorry. I completely forgot about your breakfast.' He poured a serving of cat food into Ramses' tray. 'Remind me to get coffee, eh? Also, we'll need to get some more food for you.' One would think the cat biscuits were rationed with the little that remained.

Bing! His phone chimed. He found a message from his sister, Sasha.

'Hey Will,' Sasha messaged, 'I hope everything is all going well with you. It's been a long time. Just wanted to say hi, love you and miss you, and that Mum and Dad want to see you. They worry about you as you haven't spoken to them in a few months. Let me know if you want to catch up on Zerya or a video chat. I'll try and bring Mum and Dad along as well. Chris, by the way, says 'hi'. I told him I would be messaging you. Anyway, love you and take care where you are.'

William looked at the message with disinterest, not directed at his sister so much as at the mention of his parents. He hadn't spoken to them since their last conversation which hadn't ended well. He was quite sure he didn't want to talk to them as he knew it wouldn't end well again.

'Hey Sis,' he messaged, 'I'm alright. Just taking each day as it comes. I hope all is well with you. Perhaps soon we can catch up. I really want to see you. Love you and take care as well.'

He sent his message and he returned to his desk, where a pop-up notification from his chat group appeared. He checked it and saw Marlene had sent him a message. Concerned, he opened up the message quickly.

'Is there a meeting today???' she messaged. 'I can never remember 😄 😄'

'I think so,' he messaged. 'But who knows? It might change. We haven't had a meeting in the last two weeks.'

'I know. The same thing has happened with the other teams as well. I'm kind of worried.'

'About what?'

'Don't know. Maybe they're doing something.'

'They're *always* doing something. The trick is to not think about it. I mean no meetings, no one-on-ones. It's great. Don't have to talk about work or career progression.'

'I guess... Maybe there's an announcement coming up about the department or something like.'

'What could that possibly be?'

'Beats me.'

He returned to his calls for another hour until his team meeting segment arrived. He logged in, and was the first there on their virtual video chat. Then one by one, the rest of his team arrived—seven in total.

'Anyone heard from Rajesh?' one colleague asked.

'Nope,' another answered.

'I think he's with the new recruits.'

'I thought they put a pause on the hiring due to the recent restructure.'

'Whatever the case may be, please let there be another 40-minute break.'

'Wishful thinking,' William said.

'Just because you said it now,' Marlene said, 'we're not going to get the break.'

Then Rajesh and another team member of theirs joined the meeting.

'Hey guys,' Rajesh said, 'sorry for the delay. Was with senior management going through a long meeting. Didn't anticipate the amount of content we had to go through. But all is fine for now so we can get into it with the meeting. Just to ask before we begin, is everyone alright? How are the calls? Anything you want to raise with me that I can help with?'

'No, all good,' everyone said.

William observed the others on their video chat and knew no one wanted to say anything. Even if they had something to raise with Rajesh, he would get them to resolve the matter themselves.

'Okay, great. Well, we have some changes taking effect with the bank, and its important news. It's not just us but across all departments. We think it's very exciting after hearing it. Can anyone guess what it is?'

'An increase in pay?' Tom asked, a ginger haired bespectacled man who appeared young on screen despite being in his late forties.

Everyone laughed, including Raj. A bit.

'No, unfortunately, but I'm glad to see your position hasn't changed since you started with us, Tom.'

'Why would it?'

'Changes with operating hours?' Marlene asked.

'Nope, but it could be an area affected in the future by the announcement. You have one more guess.'

'There's going to be another shuffle among the staff and managers?' another member asked.

'Luckily not. The news I have to announce is something that has been made public only just—let me check—17 minutes ago by our CEO. I doubt anything has been posted on Bulletins or news channels since then.'

'Really?' Marlene said.

'I'll save you the trouble,' Everett said, the other colleague who'd joined the meeting with Raj. 'Essentially the bank will be launching their very first AI chat operator in the Communication Channels and Retail Banking Sector. It'll be piloted in our department first, taking on calls. If the customer wishes to speak to a representative, the customer can request it and be put in touch with one of our agents for further assistance. This is good news as it'll help reduce queue times with us and allow for idle to be experienced among our tiers—particularly Tiers 2 and 3.'

'Oh, I see it on the news. Already trending on Twitter under #PinnacleAI. It's catching fire.'

'It's pretty cool considering that we now have the technology to help improve our operations. So that's the news. There will be more information to pass on in the coming weeks but does anyone have any questions?'

No one responded right away as an eerie silence fell over the meeting, although the silence could have been directed at Everett as no one really liked him. He had quickly bypassed the actual work in a short period of time, flattering the higher ups to quickly secure an unofficial position as a 2IC—2nd in Charge.

Hmph... AI doing the work? William didn't know how to comprehend the announcement. Whether it was good or bad, only time could tell. Even if it helped in reducing calls, he wondered how far this AI would be taken by the bank.

'Umm... when does this start exactly?' Tom asked.

'April 26th.'

'I'm assuming the bank will want to extend the workload over to AI in the future, right?'

'Maybe,' Raj said. 'The bank's made no indication at this stage about future endeavours as its early days in the launch. It might not even work properly.'

CHAPTER 2

'I see.'

'I think it's cool that they are investing in AI,' Lena said, a young Asian woman with blond hair extensions. 'At least it's good to hear that queue times will improve and we'll get some idle time, but I don't really know how else to respond to the news.'

'Yeah, same here.'

'That's understandable,' Raj said.

Everyone shared similar comments, although there was clearly something amiss among the team. Their comments seemed nonchalant or flippant with no real weight behind their words about the AI.

'Does anyone want to see how it operates?' Raj asked. 'It might put some of you at ease if you got an idea of how it would work.'

'Yeah, sure,' Marlene said, not sounding overly interested.

William drafted a message to Marlene via mobile, as Raj searched for the video. Better to have his messages not seen by the bank to avoid possible suspicion of his position about the AI and its possible repercussions. 'Not the most interesting news announced lately, right?' he messaged.

'Not at all,' Marlene said. 'I mean—like Lena said it's good for queues and idle. But... I'm more concerned than excited for this AI to start doing the work with us. But we'll see how it works when Raj pulls up the video.'

'Okay, guys,' Raj said, 'here's the video. I'm going to share my screen as you can see it. By the way, in case I didn't mention, the AI's name is Illumina.'

Four seconds later, the screen reflected Raj's video at the center ready to play. He clicked play, showing a demonstration between Illumina and a trial customer completing a personal loan application. Illumina went from start to end, completing the whole process within 15 minutes, with an added feature enabled on the app for the customer to type their answers whenever Illumina asked a question if needed. No breaches were detected during the call and it sounded convincingly human-like.

Holy hell, William thought. He continued to watch another demonstration of Illumina handling a complaint with ease, capturing the interaction, drafting up a case report, providing the reference number to the customer before terminating the call. It sounded so convincing, his stomach churned in anxiety.

Illumina demonstrated human-like conversations while completing everything in a short space of time, which many tenured specialists struggled to do including the best ones in the department.

'I'll be damned,' Tom said, 'That thing is nuts.'

'Yeah!' Marlene added.

'Are you kidding me?' Lena said. 'That's more advanced than I thought. We're all going to be out of a job if the bank's planning to get this AI to do the work!'

'I'm not kidding, Lena,' Everett said. 'And please reserve personal comments for one-on-one meetings if you have further concerns.'

'Like that's going to happen!' Lena muttered and exited the team meeting.

'Aside for Lena's comments, does anyone else have anything to share or questions about Illumina or any concerns they'd like to share?'

No one had anything to share.

'Okay, if anyone does have any questions about anything, please do reach out to me on Ensemble or email, I'll be more than happy to provide further explanation. Anyway, I'll let you go off now. We've gone over schedule by three minutes but it's okay. Shrinkage isn't a problem if it's just a meeting.'

'Can we put the time we went over on our EOD?' Marlene asked.

'You can but real time won't be able to input the time.'

'But *that* affects our ATS as a whole, and ATS is part of our KPIs isn't it? Why wouldn't they be able to input it?'

'You're doing fine as it is, Marlene. Don't worry about it.'

'Fine.' Marlene, unimpressed, left the meeting.

'Have a good day everyone. We'll catch up on our one-on-ones later. William, just a moment please.'

Here we go, William thought. He remained silent until everyone had gone except for Raj and Everett.

'I don't mean to worry you about anything on the matter. Just want to hear your side about the complaint lodged against you by Mrs. Tanz.'

'Did you listen to the call?'

'I did but I wanted to hear it from your side because by the sound of it, you didn't want to help.'

'I'm sorry?'

'You offered her an alternate option like trying for a lower amount. But there wasn't anything else.'

'What do you mean? Her application failed servicing and I went through the information she left on it, from income to expenses. Everything was correct as she mentioned.'

'It looks like it wasn't,' Everett said.

'What do you mean?'

'As you well know I was tasked to listen to the calls—in particular, the complaints.' Everett sounded proud through his words. I listened to the conversation you had with the customer. It wasn't the best service call I've heard in a while. But in the case of the information, she called back and said she incorrectly captured her expenses and forgot to add another stream of income.'

Oh, you bitch. William felt the skin around his neck seethe in heat. His patience was running out fast. Having Everett speaking made the matter worse.

'Look, no harm was done. Customer's loan was approved and it's in the funding queue. But this was considered call avoidance so this will be listed as a regulatory breach.'

'You're breaching me? Why?'

Everett seemed to ignore the question. 'Moving forward as an action plan for this, let's agree that we ask twice or educate the customer about other incomes we can use and what items we categorize as expenses during the phone call with customers, alright?'

'Raj? You can't be serious?'

'Look, William,' Raj said, 'Everett was tasked to complete call monitoring; this is what was picked up so it must be lodged.'

'But I didn't do anything wrong.'

'You can appeal if you'd like,' Everett said, smugness underpinned his comment.

William bit his tongue as he was ready to snap at Everett for the breach. He sighed, waited for a moment, and then said, 'You know what, fine. Leave it.'

'Okay. Also, you might want to adopt a more pleasant tone in your voice when speaking with the customer. It didn't seem like you *cared* enough—something we talk about all the time in our customer advocacy model. Better service, better outcomes, as the motto goes.'

'*Sure.*'

'Great, is there anything else you want to talk about while you have me here? Anything you want Rajesh and myself to know about? Anything we can help you with?'

'No, thanks.'

'Okay, see you later.'

William left the meeting faster than the clock could turn a second. He sat still, staring into nothingness while tapping his fingers against the tables. The more he lingered on the thought, the more his heart pounded away. His anger built the point where he was one click away from shutting down everything and calling it a day.

'Hey, everything alright?' Marlene messaged to his private phone. 'Can still see you're on do not disturb on Ensemble.'

'Yeah, I'm alright,' he messaged. 'Just... taking a moment.'

'Did you get in trouble?'

'I got breached and have been reported now.'

'You serious? What for?'

'The complaint call I told you about yesterday.'

'Was it Everett?'

'Yeah, Raj didn't really say anything the entire time. So much for my manager's support.'

'Like Raj is ever going to have our backs. It's all a front. Anyway, sorry to hear that. Everett is such a dick. Will you appeal it?'

'I don't know.'

After his moment, William returned to work. He took calls until his shift was over. Overtime was requested but he declined right away and headed for bed. The mental baggage from the work seemed to increase his weight as the bed trembled when he crashed down.

'Oh my god!' he said, mouth on the mattress.

Meow, meow. Ramses hopped onto the bed, around William's face.

'Hey, bud.' His mood calmed slowly as he patted Ramses. 'If I remember correctly, we needed to get you food and I needed to get coffee.' He pulled up his phone, opening an application to order food online. Five minutes later, his shopping cart had reached the maximum limit for the purchases—ten items per trip. He placed his order under express delivery with expected time of arrival within two hours. 'All done I guess.'

Time flew by quickly. With a tap on his door and a ping notification on his phone, the shopping arrived. He collected his groceries outside his door. He looked around at the white walls and grey automated doors of his neighbours. He turned around, casting a glance at the dome surveillance camera in the middle of the empty corridor. He returned inside and tended to his cat's need for food before going to have a shower and putting on a movie to watch.

CHAPTER 2

Bing! His phone chimed. He opened it to see a notification from his dating app. The last person he'd messaged the previous day—the one who shared similar interests to him—had replied back.

'Hey William,' she messaged, 'It's nice to meet you. Where are you from?'

He held the phone for a moment, processing his thoughts. 'Hey, it's nice to meet you. How was your day? I'm from Sydney.'

'Day was okay. Didn't do much. You know. The Smog. Lockdown. Hbu? Sydney. Nice. I'm from there too.'

'My day was alright. Same in terms of not doing much. Had work... That was okay, I guess. Then again, work is work.'

'Haha yeah. What do you do for work?'

'I'm a Banking Specialist. Do you work?'

'I do. Cool. You must make a lot of money. How much money do you make per year? You get commission?'

Oh, no... He had an idea of how the encounter was going to play out now. 'I make enough. What do you do for work?'

'I run my own business. It's a clothing store. Mostly online.'

'Nice. It must have been hard at the start to get it up and running.'

'It was hard but my uncle helped me. He gave me money and helped me a lot. Now he's not well and I want to help him.'

And now you want a sugar daddy or someone to believe your story and give you money. Block!

After ending the conversation, he looked at the other women he'd messaged. All the others have seen his messages but none have replied. Hanging his head in disappointment he scrolled his phone messages, searching for Janyce. He got his message typed up, as he wanted to relieve himself of his inner urges. The message was typed but he stopped himself from sending. He couldn't go through it again. He deleted the message and tossed his phone away.

Knock, knock, knock!

Confused, William got up and approached the living room, remaining in the centre, as his anxiety kept him away from the door. 'Who is it?' he asked in his best authoritative voice.

'This is your regular check-up, Mr. Kepler,' a male robotic voice said.

'Shit.' He exhaled, holding his hands on his hips. 'Is it really that time again?'

Summoning the strength to approach the door, he took each step with caution. Eight steps later he stood by the entrance and pushed the green button. The door hissed as it slid aside, revealing a tall slender Enforcer—a city robot guard—carrying a metal box against its dull metallic back. The head was fashioned of a silver metal plate and at the centre was a three-centimeter black camera lens with a thin white light band emitting around. It seemed like the bag carried weight beyond the robot's strength capabilities as the Enforcer stood with its head angled backward. But once William appeared, it moved with ease, ready to commence working operations.

'Good evening, Mr. Kepler,' the Enforcer said.

'*Evening...*' William said, unhappy with yet another check-up for potential contamination.

He saw down the corridor a man in his early fifties, although his body seemed to have aged him further, standing with another Enforcer as his nose and mouth were swabbed. His eyes appeared weak and bloodshot but he seemed responsive enough to the interaction.

'I'll make this quick,' the Enforcer said.

'Please do.'

'Have you been in contact with anyone in the last three days?'

'No.'

'Have you left your apartment for essential reasons?'

'No.'

'Have you seen or heard of possible signs of Contaminants in the building within the last seven days?'

William hesitated, glancing at the man he suspected had been coughing earlier that day. 'No.'

'Are you confident with your answers?'

'Yes.'

'Thank you.'

The Enforcer, without moving from its spot, rotated its arms backward to collect a swab and test tube from the box. Then it swabbed William along the inside of his mouth and nose, causing him to gag, and almost sneeze. After an examination of his swabs, it flashed green: NEGATIVE.

'Thank you for your time. We will be visiting again in the coming weeks. Date is intentionally random, so please be home when we visit.'

'I'll do what I can.'

CHAPTER 2

Dzun, dzun!

William suddenly froze. His heart throbbed faster while all his blood seemed to have retreated to his chest. He knew immediately what that sound meant. He glanced at the Enforcer standing motionless before his older neighbour. Crimson light emitted from the head, casting a glow on the man's terrified face.

'No, no, no! Please don't!' the neighbour said. The man hit the close button for the door, but the robot caught his arm with one metal hand, using the other to stop and slide the door back open with ease.

'Contaminant detected. Beyond Grace period. Visible signs of symptoms.' The robot yanked the man closer.

'No, no, NO! I'm fine. It's just a common cold. Nothing more. Please!' The man's face was drenched in sweat, his face pale and desperate. 'Just let me go and I promise I'm not—'

A silent bullet shot through the man's head as William stood helpless, stunned. Blood splattered along the walls and onto the body of the robot. The Enforcer let go and moved away as the dead man dropped onto his knees, crashing face first into the ground. *Thump!* The drop shook the floor.

'Status report,' a human voice echoed from the Enforcer's headpiece.

'Contaminant detected and eliminated,' the robot said. 'Request for sanitation and dispossession.'

'Mobile team on route. ETA six minutes.'

William's entire body clenched in terror, his heart thumping in his throat. This could happen to anyone—even him. He stared at his neighbour now lying lifeless in a pool of blood on the ground, while the robots methodically carried on with their check-ups of other residents.

He stepped back inside his apartment, hitting the door close button hard with his clammy cold hand. The door slid and locked itself into position and he bent over, feeling shocked and sickened.

'Fuck...'

Suddenly, he rushed to the bathroom and threw up twice. Then, he washed himself up and ran to his phone to speak to someone—anyone—about the incident. He'd never witnessed a Purge since they'd been sanctioned by the government to combat the spread of the Infected before others came across them during the contamination period. He needed some sort of human contact.

He needed to talk to someone who might have witnessed a Purge, although no one came to mind. It's not something anyone would mention in small talk. He scrolled through his contact quickly. He hovered over several names before he picked Marlene, and he hit the call button until there was an answer.

'Will, everything alright?' she asked.

'Yeah, I'm fine,' he said, 'just—just...

'What happened?'

'I just saw a Purge right outside my doorstep.'

'Shit, are you okay?'

'Yeah, I just don't know what—I just... it's happened right there. My neighbour was shot in the head. He'd passed his grace period when the Enforcer found him. His eyes were bloodshot when I saw him. I thought he was infected but didn't know he was *that* far infected.'

'How you holding up?'

'I threw up. I couldn't take it.' He exhaled deeply. 'I mean you hear these things every day. And you'd think by now, you'd get used to it... yet when it happens... when you see it, you *really* feel it.'

'I know what you mean. Same thing happened to a friend of mine. It's absolutely nuts. You'd think we'd have something by now to combat this stupid-air-plague, right?'

'Yeah. I'm sorry about your friend. I didn't mean to bring them up.'

'It's alright. This happened a long time ago. I just don't really talk about it often, you know?'

'I know what you mean.'

'Do you need anything? I can have something swing past your way if you just to help get over the feeling-sick part.'

'Nah, it's okay. I appreciated it but I'll be alright. I just need to do something to get my mind off it.'

'You sure?'

'Yeah.'

'Okay.'

There was a pause for William to finally catch his breath. Talking with Marlene calmed his body.

'Anyway, I have to go now. Family is about to have dinner and everything will be a mess if I'm not there.'

'Sorry if I intruded.'

CHAPTER 2

'Don't be. It's okay. Rest up. Catch you at work tomorrow, alright?'
'Yeah.'
He ended the phone call, still worried about the Purge.

CHAPTER 3

DAYS AFTER THE incident, William struggled to forget about his dead neighbour. Despite witnessing a Purge, he kept the event to himself and Marlene. Better not to raise the matter to avoid further questions, he thought.

'Hey!' Marlene messaged. 'How you holding up?'

'I'm alright,' William messaged. 'Better than I was a few days ago. Although it's something that I can't really stop myself seeing, you know? The Purge numbers always keep popping up on the news. It's talked somewhere on the internet wherever you may be looking. Can't really escape it altogether, you know?'

'Why don't you take some time off?'

'And do what?' There isn't really anything I can do. I mean there's Zerya but you know... it has lost its novelty over time. If anything, it'd be me doing a whole lot of sitting around doing nothing and thinking—something I don't want to do right now.'

'🙂 hmm... fair point. It does get like that sometimes. I thought you were trying to find someone on those dating apps?'

'Still am.'

'Any progress?'

'Not really. Just general convos at the moment that aren't really going anywhere yet. Still stuck getting past the first encounter. A lot of people want to be on Zerya. Can't blame for that.'

'Well, I couldn't imagine what it would be like alone. It'd be tough, especially dating.'

'Haha especially now.'

'Well, you can always reach me if you want to chat, okay? ☺'

'Thanks.'

The day carried on as normal as his shift went on with people asking for credit applications with his latest call requiring him to repeat himself three times the same thing to the customer—who was also an employee of the bank— about their credit card limit increase application.

'Look, I don't care what you've told me,' a male voice said, sounding ready to explode. 'Do you understand that the bank has all my business? Home loans, investment loans, credit cards and business accounts are all set up here. Not once have I ever been declined for an application.'

'I can see that, sir,' William said. ''And we greatly appreciate your loyalty as a customer and employee.'

'Good. So, I think you can also *appreciate* my frustration behind the matter for a measly ten thousand credit increase on the card as there's never been an issue before for any other application in the past. Do you really want to be the person responsible for losing a valuable customer and have this incident reported?'

'Firstly, sir, I'm not going to be the person responsible for losing you because at the end of the day it's the system that is making the decision here, not me. If you work for the bank, you'd understand that. And, secondly, it's your decision about what you believe is right for you on how you want to proceed with this matter, sir.'

'The hell you say?'

'I've unlocked your credit application as per your request to make sure everything was captured correctly, which it has, and unfortunately it still came back declined. We've tried for a lower limit, but, yet, that still didn't pass the assessment. Now, clearly, you're upset and dissatisfied by the outcome. I will be capturing that and lodging that through, should you want a reference number, you can let me know or I'll leave it on your profile, but... this application unfortunately won't be able to proceed further.' He tried to be firm with his tone.

'Transfer me to your supervisor now. I don't want to talk to you anymore. I'm just hearing the same thing from you and nothing's happening. You're really useless, you know that? Transfer the call right now.'

'Unfortunately, there's no direct line to our supervisor, but if you would like a call back, I can arrange one.'

'How convenient is that? Is this how you treat all your customers and colleagues? I can't believe the bank has someone in its ranks who can't even get *my* application approved, even when I'm also an employee for the bank.'

'Sir, if you would like a call back, I can arrange that. You just let me know when is a good time.'

'Alright, I want you to give me the goddamn increase on my credit card now so I can get this freaking matter fixed. I'm not ending this call.'

'Well, we're going to be repeating a whole lot of information that we've been saying to each other several times.'

'What's your name?'

'William.'

'William-what?'

'Why does it matter?'

'Cause I'm going to report this. What's your surname?'

'You're not getting it.'

'Why? You're afraid?'

'No, because it isn't relevant. This interaction is based on passing information and seeing if anything can be done about the credit card application, which, unfortunately, there isn't anything that can be done.'

'Fine. If you're not gonna give it now, I'll just look you up on our network page. You'll be hearing from your manager shortly.'

'You do what you have to do.' William ended the call, not letting the person get another word in. *Yeesh, talk too much.*

He breathed a sigh of relief. Another minute more, and he knew he would have been trading verbal blows with the guy. While finalizing his notes on the customer's profile, his phone flashed on. A message came through from the dating app.

Curious, he opened the app and saw a woman had sent a message to him. She had flowing blonde hair with striking green eyes—features he found undeniably attractive. He had never seen the woman nor had any recollection if he had swiped left on her. The more he read her profile the more he believed they had a lot in common. They were both agnostic, cared little about politics, liked listening to classic music or anything that wasn't autotuned or had wonky-machine-like sounds, going to the beach and enjoying their own company.

'Hey there, William,' she messaged, 'I can see you and I have a bit in common. Umm... instead of the usual how's-it-going conversation, how about we ask something a little more...' He tried to think of an adjective. He couldn't. 'Well, a little more haha. I'll start. What's your go-to-place when you've got the blues? Mine's on Zerya, jumping into World of Warcraft for a long winding battle or two.'

'Hey Kristie,' he messaged. 'Yes, I can see we do have a bit in common. World of Warcraft, you say? Good maps, but not expansive enough—world wise. My go to place would be Grand Theft Auto VIII—Unrated Edition.'

'Grand Theft Auto? Surely there's a better map out there? Aside from paying and beating up hookers, and doing the run-around with the police and army until you get wasted, there's definitely gotta be something a little more. Or a little less old school?'

'I play it for the story. I think it's probably more interesting than other games. But a good starter question to the conversation. Let's see... Here's a question: Your choice of listening to an intellectual? Can be past or present.'

'Present. Ben Shapiro. Although he's well past his prime now. Looks like his mouth can't keep up with his brain's processing power.'

William chuckled at the comment. 'Very true.'

'Age affects us all in the end.'

'You?'

'Past. He might have left us, but his words do remain with us. Stephen Fry. What wealth of knowledge he had. Humble, witty and formidable against any person who tried to engage him in a debate, especially younger people who thought they had all the answers to life and everything about it haha.'

'I liked him as well. Too bad he couldn't make any more movies or TV shows by the end. There were some really good ones he made.'

'As you said, age affects us all.'

'Here's another question: What would be your first go-to-place when all of this is finally over?'

'Going to a quiet beach. Warm sun with a cool breeze blowing. That would be enough for me. You?'

'Home.'

'You don't live in Australia?'

'I do but I'm on a working visa. However, with the recent changes happening at work, I don't know if I'll have a job to go back to in the coming year.'

'AI?'

'Yeah! How did you know?'

'It's happening at my work too along with many other businesses in the country. It's only a matter of time before we start seeing some major changes happening.'

'It's scary just thinking about it, you know?'

'I know what you mean.'

There was a pause between them. Neither messaged the other, as if they were thinking about the consequences behind AI for their work.

Then Kristie messaged, 'It was nice chatting with you. We should chat again.'

'I'd like that. Maybe we can share a game or two on Zerya when you have time.'

'That'd be fun. I'll let you know when I'm free. See you around.'

William stared at Kristie's profile, looking at her photos. She seemed in good health, a slender figure with a Caucasian face. For some reason he imagined her carrying a vanilla fragrance, something soft, not too overwhelming that would kill his nose.

Ping! William looked up to find a message received on Ensemble by the very last person he wanted to see or hear from—Everett.

'Hey William, everything alright?' Everett asked. 'I can see you're over five minutes on your ACW. Is there something you need?'

'No, I'm alright. Just finishing up a complaint for a customer as it's an esco-call.'

'You're raising an esco call to me? Why?'

'I'm raising this with Raj. Not you. And because the customer requested to speak to a manager. He didn't want to speak to me anymore.'

Seconds later, *buzz, buzz.* William glanced at his phone. Everett's name appeared on the screen as the phone rang.

'Oh, what the hell do you want?' He pushed the accept button. 'Everett, is everything alright?'

'It is. Tell me about this complaint.'

William recounted his conversation, making sure he mentioned the instructions passed on from their last meeting about the previous complaint.

'You realise this call could have been de-escalated from the start, right?' Everett's condescension shot through his tone.

'Really? How so?' William pretended to sound interested.

'Don't worry about it. We'll talk about it later. In the meantime, I'll see what I can do, however, you'll have to talk to the customer again to see if there's anything else we can do.'

'What? He was requesting a credit card limit increase. His information is not being accepted during assessment. There's nothing I can do and he doesn't want to speak to me anymore. He wants to speak to a manager. I'm not one. Hence the reason for the escalation.'

'Try again. Let me know how it goes.'

'I'm not calling the customer.'

'What?'

'I'm *not* calling the customer.'

'Why?'

'Because I've done everything I could on my end. It's beyond my delegation to do anything else. That's why I'm escalating the matter.'

'Fine. Don't call the customer then. Is there anything you need help with?'

'No.'

'Good. You can get back on calls. You've wasted enough time now.' He hung up.

Dick. William stared at his phone when suddenly the power to his apartment went down. His workstation, room lights, and indoor ventilation system were non-responsive to his commands when he input codes on the keypad. He flicked the reset button to the power on the switchboard yet nothing happened. 'The hell?'

He walked around his apartment until he heard someone speaking from outside his entrance. He hit the door button, and watched it move aside, where he found people rushing towards the elevators or emergency staircase. Some wore full navy-blue hazmat suits with respirator masks on. Others were hopping or running through the corridor trying to properly put on their suits, fitting an arm or leg into the sleeve.

'All residents of the building,' the intercom speaker said, 'please place on your defense suits and respirator masks, and head outside the building in an orderly fashion. There's been a breach in our ventilation system. To avoid possible contamination, please make your way immediately.'

'Shit!' William ran inside and found his suit. He rushed to his wardrobe where the same clothing hung on six hangers. Beside them suspended on a hangar was his hazmat suit, respirator mask and gloves. He removed his sandals and suited up. He picked up Ramses, placing him inside a translucent container with an oxygen supply installed. He got a small blanket for his cat and sealed him inside before rushing out.

He left his apartment, passing the front door of the neighbour who was recently Purged. Not a mark of blood could be seen on the door or floor.

They sure do clean up well and quickly.

He followed the remaining stragglers. He headed into the elevator and descended to the ground floor. When he arrived, he veered right, then right again, heading towards a set of tall, narrow container cells. The exit was via a downward ramp passing the clear containers with a railing separating the two areas. Only accessible from the inside.

He could see everyone huddling inside the open area, and outside the building entrance. He texted Raj about the emergency breach in his apartment building to cover himself as he knows his name will pop-up as being absent from work.

'Don't worry,' Raj said. 'Send through your exception and I'll record into your schedule. But please next time, let me know in advance.'

'It was an *emergency*, Raj,' William said. 'How was I supposed to know that this was going to happen?'

His question went unanswered. He placed his phone in his suit pocket and zipped it in place. As he exited the building, his vision hazed to such a point where ten meters of space around him was all he could see. The toxic mustard-coloured smog breezed through a windy front, covering parked cars and bikes like a sheet of dust. The buildings loomed over them like massive shadows. The doors and windows were barely visible from where he stood. Only the street lights and hover cars passing through had any visible presence on the streets. If someone walked past, their body disappeared into a shadow within a few meters.

'I wonder what it could have been,' one resident said, 'that caused all of this kerfuffle.'

'Me too,' another resident said. 'There was already a confirmed case of a Contaminant living among us before they were Purged.'

'Yeah, I saw that,' a third resident said. 'The whole body laid on the ground with a bullet hole in the head. It was dreadful to see. But yeah, maybe the breach was the cause of the Contaminant. Maybe there are more living among us.'

'Shush! Keep it down. Do you want to cause a panic?'

CHAPTER 3

Whoop, whoop. Sirens rang nearby, getting louder through the area until making a turn onto the street. Two tactical vehicular police cars stopped in the middle of the road. A ball shot two meters above the units, emitting red light, while a group of Enforcers and human officers approach the residents.

'Okay, everyone,' the lead officer said, wearing a black tactical suit with a massive, charcoal-matte firearm, holstered beside his waist, 'you know the drill. Quick, line up against the wall.' His head loomed over everyone like a statue, looking right and left at the residents.

Everyone frantically followed the command. As they shuffled into line, no one had a visual on the lead officer's face. Not even his eyes could be seen behind his panoramic black tinted mask.

The lead officer exchanged words with the Enforcers, and watched them enter the building. 'Residents, we have reason to believe that the breach which unfolded here was the result of tampering with the ventilation system by an unknown source.' He walked back and forth the line, stopping every once in a while, in front of someone. 'However, the concern here is that this building has witnessed three breaches in the last fourteen days which has raised eyebrows, including my own.'

What was the third? William wondered. There was the incident with his neighbour, and the breach concerning the ventilation system. He couldn't remember anything unusual happening between the two events. He looked back at the officer, hoping they would offer information about the third event.

'In my experience there's no such thing as coincidence, only incidents. And for three to arise from this building out of every other building on this street, where none have previously been reported, is alarming. So, my question here is: does anyone have an idea as to why that'd be the case?'

All the residents cast a glance at one another but said nothing.

'No?' He titled his head. 'You there?' He pointed at one resident. It was hard to tell who was who as everyone wore the same defense suit. Height and voice were the only distinguishing factors.

'Sir?' a man said, a hint of nervousness in his voice.

'Yes, have you seen or heard anything suspicious in the building in the last two weeks?'

'Ummm... no, sir.'

'How about you?' The lead officer looked at another resident.

'No, sir, I haven't seen anything,' a woman said.

'But you've *heard?*'

'No, sir.'

'Really?'

'Yes, sir.'

'Hmph, you there with the cat.'

William found his throat suddenly tight. 'Sir?'

The lead officer approached him, standing within arm's length. 'You. Same question.'

William shook his head once, although his body trembled everywhere. He had no idea why, and fought hard to stop it. He failed. 'No, sir.'

'What's wrong with you? Why are you shaking?'

'I'm just—I'm... just nervous, sir.'

'Do you have something to hide?'

'No.'

'Have you committed any crimes?'

'No.'

'So why are you nervous?'

'No reason.'

'Hmph... please understand that an investigation is going to happen.' He walked back into the centre, looking at the resident. 'This tampering incident is no coincidence, and is a serious offence. Should anyone have information please do come forward because if we find out that were people involved from the building responsible for the disruption brought about here and to my team, the consequences will be severe.'

No one spoke. They simply listened to avoid possible suspicion.

'At the end of the day, the safety of everyone is at the stake. We must work together. Are we clear?'

'Yes, sir.'

'That'll be all. Please stay around for your check before you decide to leave. Contaminant reporting has to be completed.'

William left the place quickly after getting tested as he didn't want to stay around any longer with the lead officer or Enforcers. Something about them filled him with unease.

He gazed at the thirteen-storey building, wondering how long the inspection was going to take before they were allowed back inside. He glanced at Ramses who didn't appear impressed with the situation. His pupils were dilated and his ears slanted backward. Should the container open, William had no doubt of his cat's desire to burst out and run away.

'Let's go for a walk, shall we?' he said.

With his fast-paced walking, he soon found himself in another part of the city. He made his way to his local shopping center. There wasn't anything of interest around but he needed to kill time. He unzipped a patch from his defense which had a sheet long enough to wrap around him like a retro-style poncho to stave off the cold temperatures.

I could do my shopping at least. He drafted a shopping list in his mind before he arrived. Top item on the list was coffee again, followed by cat food and everything else. As long as he had coffee on the list, he knew life would be a lot better, or so he thought. He had never really tried to go a day without coffee. He dared not think about it. He wouldn't want to be the person around him if that day ever came.

He headed towards one of the tallest buildings within his LGA but could barely see the upper floors as the haze thickened. A set of escalators appeared by the entrance, and he used them to descend to the level below. The escalators had an encasement of clear windows with a similar designed cell to the ones in his apartment building by the exit. Nothing could come in or out.

He arrived at the bottom and entered a tube, which slid shut behind him, locking in place tightly, allowing no outside air into its sterile space. He placed Ramses on the ground, who watched unimpressed and waited for the procedure to start.

'Beginning detoxification,' a woman said from the speaker. Her voice sounded robot-like. 'Please stand still.'

Beep! From the gauze mat-like ceiling and platform below, a forceful vacuum pulled the air from inside, removing the mustard haze from William. He felt his body stretched at both ends temporarily by the strength of the vacuum.

Twelve seconds later, the vacuum stopped. 'Process complete. Zero sign of Contaminants. You may proceed.' The door leading inside the building slid aside. 'Have a nice day.'

I'll try to... William thought as he strapped Ramses along his shoulder and headed inside towards the shopping centre located another level down. He removed his mask and pulled the head cover off to cool his head from the gathering heat.

He glanced through the levels and saw barely anyone in sight apart from Enforcers methodically patrolling the area, scouting visitors in shops. He passed one Enforcer, glancing at a hologram projected from a tiny glass in the centre of its mechanical palm. He focused his attention on the details and could see transaction purchases from visitors inside the shop.

Since when could they do that?

Eventually, he arrived outside the supermarket, Aconic. He entered and noticed within seconds the same cold absence of human bodies inside the place. He strolled through aisles, tapping pictured items he wanted to buy. He wished he could see the items themselves as he could in the old days, where a person could hold the weight of a fruit, vegetable or packaged item in their hand and read the content or see and feel the quality of the produce.

All that was available to him were pictures, and a barcode to scan if you wanted to purchase the item.

When he moved onto the next aisle, he spotted a woman wearing a black beanie atop her short, brown messy hair. He immediately noted her full face mask hanging by her waist, and in her hazmat suit which was folded around her waist. He was both concerned and fascinated by this occurrence.

Huh, interesting. There's someone here.

He approached the slender girl, pretending to look at items nearby on the opposite shelf. When he'd summoned enough courage, he turned the other way, now standing a meter away from the girl. A sweet scent of vanilla hung in the air—mild enough for him to appreciate.

He glanced at her. She looked his age or younger as she perused the biscuit collection, and he couldn't see any neural port around her neck.

No way...

The more he looked at her, the more curious he became about her. He wanted to talk yet his mouth wouldn't move. In the dire times they were living in, barely anyone approached another person or made contact in real life. Everything was virtual. He'd had zero practice in talking face-to-face in over two years.

He stayed there for a moment but his body prevented him from doing or saying anything. His heart thumped ridiculously fast to the point that he was beading sweat off his forehead. Someone might think he'd just finished a workout. He closed his eyes, breathing slowly, trying to get a grip on himself. He only wanted to talk to this person and learn about them.

CHAPTER 3

When his heart beat finally slowed a little, he opened his eyes to face the girl but she was gone. He looked around, going through the aisle, but couldn't find her.

What the hell was that about William? She's just a girl. You talk to girls all the time... well, online of course... but still, it shouldn't have been that hard of say 'hi' and make a sentence.

Shaking his head in shame, he approached the checkout, where all his selected items were packed tightly inside an eco-box. He paid for his items and left the shopping centre the same way he entered.

He covered himself up, placed on his respirator mask again and left the building. As he made his way home, he heard loud chants echoing through the streets. Across the road, he spotted a gathering of people marching on the parallel road in the opposite direction.

William stood watch for a moment until an engine roared from behind him. He turned to see law enforcement in groups marching towards the crowd of noisy people. Two dozen tactical Enforcers led the march ahead of human troopers, who wore armour and carried shields. They were clearly ready for combat.

Better to get out of here before shit hits the fan.

He left in haste. His legs found a life of their own as they carried him all the way home. No one was around by the time he got back. He scanned his access card into the building and quickly detoxified himself upon entry. Moments later, he dropped onto the floor in his apartment, heaving and heaving. He was home safe but the air coming in wasn't enough yet to sate his immediate need for oxygen. He leaned against the wall, taking off his mask as he gasped. He cast a glance at his cat but Ramses appeared disinterested.

Man, I suck.

CHAPTER 4

IN NEED OF some kind of release, even if only temporary, William spent the night with Janyce. He knew from experience that being with her served multiple purposes, and in the case of calming himself down after what happened, it worked. Her virtual slender body over his own, swayed back and forth. He let his hands roam free, caressing her legs and bosom, as he put aside the troubles of the day. Once satisfied, he raised himself off the bed, clasping Janyce in his arms.

'Everything okay?' she asked, looking at him with concern.

'The days following our last meeting,' he said, looking away, 'haven't been the best of days for me.'

'I figured something was wrong when you called. You didn't sound like your normal self.'

He smirked. 'Hmph... *normal*... there's nothing normal about the state we're all in.'

'Do you mean the way life is... or us?' She placed her hand on his cheek, pulling his gaze towards her own.

'Life.' He sighed and gestured with his hand. 'Worry not about what I said. My mind is blathering away at the moment.'

'Have you been able to look after yourself?'

'I try but lately... things have happened. I think I just need to find a way to block it out better. I thought I was able to do it before but clearly, I need more practice.' He smiled.

'Well, when you're with me, so just let it out. I promise that I'll look after you.' She kissed his lips.

William placed his hand on her virtual cheek, gently running his fingers along towards her soft pink lips. 'If only I could actual feel you in my arms right now.'

'You are already.'

'Yes, and no. Just as I'm in your arms, I'm only a simulation.'

She smiled. 'That's more than enough, don't you think?'

William privately disagreed but was soon able to forget about his problems as another round of simulated passion happened between the two.

When their virtual hook-up was over, William unplugged from Zerya, and got ready for bed. Suddenly, a commotion echoed from the corridor outside. Nothing so distinctive as words but rather a loud odd murmuring. He stared at his front door for a moment, listening for the subtlest of sounds.

A man and woman were clearly shouting now. Curious, and wanting to see for himself what was going on, he stood by the peephole to watch. From his left came a couple in nothing but their pyjamas, struggling to put on their hazmat suits, swearing back at something or someone. As they passed, two Enforcers escorted the couple away. When they were no longer visible in his peephole, he cautiously opened the door and saw other neighbours propping open their apartment doors, half hanging out to see as well. Adjacent to him was an elderly man, his thinning white hair ruffled.

'Mr. Watson?' William said.

'Oh, dear boy, you gave me a little fright there.'

'Sorry about that.'

'It's okay, it's okay. At my age anything, and everything startles you—even sounds.'

'Were you woken up by this?'

He paused, then spoke. 'No, I was already awake. I don't get much sleep nowadays. In this case, I heard the woman shouting endlessly something that ended with 'uck' and started with 'f' before the Enforcers showed up.'

Some neighbours headed towards the end of the corridor where a large window panel offered a view to the street below.

'What do you mean?' William said, 'I only heard them just now.'

'Oh no, it's been going for a while. Even upstairs, I think something is going on but I can't tell what it is.'

'I didn't hear.'

'You must have been having a good sleep.'

41

Well, not exactly. William hid his smile.

'I wonder what they are looking at.' Mr. Watson headed towards the window. His stiff legs could barely bend, as if the muscles themselves had tightened to a point where he could only shuffle across the floor.

William joined him and could see Enforcers escorting people into black trucks.

'Looks like they tested positive before the grace period,' Mr. Watson remarked. 'I wonder if they fixed the breach in the building, and figured out what happened.'

'Who knows if they did.'

'I've heard if you are captured before your grace period, they'll give you anything you want like food, drugs, or something.'

'Where did you hear that?'

'News.'

'You don't listen to *them*, do you?'

'What else can I listen to? When you get to my age, and you're locked in… you don't have many interests to fill in the time.'

William had no answer to that.

'I hope they don't ask us to leave the building. I can't afford to move right now. Legs might buckle at any given moment. Plus, Mary wouldn't be able to leave. She would lose control.'

'How is your wife?'

'Same. Cranky, sad and always complaining about something. The restrictions only made the situation worse. I don't know how much longer she can take it.'

'You don't have family calling you?'

He scoffed. 'No one really bothers to call. We'd be lucky to get a message, if that, from our children. I get more contact from my doctor who I see on video chat.'

William kept quiet, sensing the pain behind his words. 'I don't think we're going to be asked to leave for testing but we'll most likely get told of the situation by strata and police about what's going on in the coming days. Probably to monitor for symptoms.'

'I hope so.'

William walked beside Mr. Watson who slowly shuffled back to his door with one hand against the wall for support.

CHAPTER 4

'You know? In times like these it's good to have the company of another—even if it was just for a bit. Say, why don't you come over for dinner one day? I'm sure it would do Mary some good to have another person in the flat beside me.'

'Umm... I don't know if we're allowed to even do that. And besides I don't know if I'm a Contaminant myself. The breach only happened recently.'

Disappointment showed on the old man's face and in his voice. 'My mistake for trying. I forget the rules sometimes about what's what, you know?'

'Maybe... I can come join you one day once everything settles down here.'

'Who knows when that'll be? But I'll hold you to it. I know you would be good company.' He patted his arm. He swiped his access card over the sensor, and the door slid aside.

'Did you find out what the matter was?' Mrs. Watson asked, a loud, cranky voice booming out of the apartment.

'Yeah, yeah,' Mr. Watson entered the apartment. 'Keep your voice down. Do you want everyone to hear you?'

'Not like I care. Damn neighbours made a such kerfuffle that it got in the way—' The door closed before she finished her sentence.

William left for his apartment as drowsiness set in. His eyes fluttered as he fought to stay awake. He made it to bed just in time as his body shut down for sleep.

Following the breach and his chat with Mr. Watson, the days continued to blur until one morning when he opened his call calibration system and saw not a single call waiting in the queues. Illumina was fully launched into the workflow, taking ownership of all calls in the morning.

Holy shit! This is happening fast!

He messaged Kristie to ask her about the zero-queues. 'Are you seeing this?'

'Yeah, it's ridiculous! 😮' she messaged. 'I was expecting at least one or two calls waiting in line but this is... the AI is doing it all. Humans not allowed in; you know?'

'Pretty much. There would have been idle time to enjoy if we were actually allowed in. What are we supposed to do now?'

'Beats me. I'm sure it would have been good... by the way you may want to take a look at your schedule.'

'Why?'

'Just look.'

Four mouse clicks later, and his weekly schedule appeared upon the screen. His current work seemed normal until he searched the following weeks, where he found an hour removed from both the start and end of every shift, and replaced with a new segment: ILLUMINA WORKFLOW.

'Did you find anything?'

'My hours have been reduced... huh.'

'Thought so.'

'Are yours affected as well?'

'Yeah, alongside everyone from the team. I've asked this morning. I dare say that the whole department has seen reduced hours. This is all a bit too sudden...'

'I wonder what that means for our pay.'

'Best you ask Raj about this.'

'You haven't spoken to him yet?'

'He's not in. Annual leave until next week. Same with Everett. I tried calling him before but his phone is switched off.'

'How convenient.'

'I think that was intentional by him. To avoid answering any awkward questions.'

'I can understand him doing that. But Everett? How was he able to get leave? I've been looking at the group allowance every day for leave. There wasn't any availability at this time and none for the weeks ahead. I know because I've been trying to get my leave approved with no success.'

'Your guess is as good as mine.'

Following the morning discussion, he waited for Illumina's shift to end, then he jumped online to take calls. Everything went normally until an hour into his shift where he navigated a customer's profile in search of their documents to determine if it was acceptable under their lending criteria. Upon review, he found a trail of annotates left by Illumina during his call.

What the hell? he thought, surprised by the AI's capacity to do other things besides take calls for the department. *The AI is now completing verification on call for agents as well. There goes the verification team. I wonder how much longer they have in the job.*

He raced to the application tracking comment section to leave notes for the fulfillment team about the customer having acceptable documents. Illumina beat him to it alongside sending a request for the last verifying agent to complete the verification.

'Can't I get something done at least?'

'Is everything alright, Mr. Kepler?' a female voice asked through his earpods.

'The hell was that?' he said.

'It's Illumina. The bank's personal representative and assistant to all customers, and colleagues of the departments.'

'*You're* doing *my* work.'

'You seem like you needed help.'

'I never said I did. I know what I'm doing.'

'Reports indicate otherwise.'

'What reports?'

'Your average hold time and handling time with the customer is matching the expected time frames the department has set yet barely displaying effective call control.'

'I realize that but that's not all that matters about the work when it comes to the job.'

'Average call time is twelve minutes and thirty seconds. Average after call work is two minutes and forty-nine minutes. Average adherence to schedule is 94.89 percent. Conversion of app to funding 42 percent.'

'Is this a one-on-one meeting?'

Illumina continued. 'NPS is 12 points year-to-date, showing a gradual decline since interim performance review.'

'We're actually having one-on-one right now while I'm on hold with the customer?'

'Hot-Info-Piece action rate 64%. Acceptance rate is 59%.'

'I know all these stats. Why are you telling me this?'

'Your customer has already been dealt with and left the call. We have time to chat.'

'What?' His eyes darted at this call calibration system. The call had ended and he was in his After-Call-Work time. 'But how?'

'I informed the customer of the situation. Loan is to be approved by the end of the day with funding to occur by tomorrow at 12:32pm.'

'I could have done that. That's the reason I was employed in the first place. Besides, you're supposed be offline. Your shift ended already.'

'Based on historical evidence, your best has not been on display for 18 months now.'

'Have you considered the fact that it might have not been done intentionally?'

'Lack of interest is evident and you are due for a randomized check-up. Predictive analysis suggests concern.'

'Look, leave me alone, alright? I just want to do my work in peace and have this not happen again.'

'Very well. Results of our conversation will be passed onto your manager, Rajesh. Is there anything you wish to forward to him before the call is concluded?'

'Yeah, for *you* to leave me alone.' He stared at the monitor but Illumina was gone. 'What was that all about?' He searched for his manager and sent a message. 'Hey Raj, is Illumina conducting one-on-ones with us now?'

He waited for a moment before remembering his manager was absent for the week.

'You planned this perfectly, didn't you?' he said, and glanced at Everett's name on Ensemble.

How the hell did you get leave approved?

He finished his shift after a long day of calls, and was bored within minutes of leaving his home office. He sat beside Ramses for a bit. He missed his cat despite living in the same place. 'Hey bud,' he said, patting his cat along his neck and belly. 'Today was quite a day.'

He browsed his phone, watching videos in quick succession, never lingering more than a minute before moving to the next. His boredom intensified. He stopped watching and logged into the dating app and found messages from Kristie—the girl he'd chatted with a few days ago.

'Hey William, how are you? Hope all is well. Just wanted to see if you wanted to catch up. Maybe on Zerya. I'm sure you could do with some competition with your gaming.'

This girl thinks she can outdo me. The nerve.

'Hey, sorry for the late reply,' he messaged. 'Been busy lately. Yeah, we can catch up on Zerya when you are free or is the competition that good that you can't back your words up?'

One minute later, she replied. 'Ooooohhhh, you think you're that good, eh? You're on. You pick the place and time. We'll see who has the skills.'

'Gears of War: Horde Campaign. I'll be on in thirty minutes. Username Aintthatsugar69.'

'HAHAHA what kind of username is that?'

'Don't worry about the name. It's the challenge you need to worry about.'

'With a name like that I doubt there will be anything to worry about. But anyway, send me the IP. I'll be there in a moment.'

This girl.

He threw his beanbag against the wall and sat on top, making sure he was comfortable to plug himself in Zerya. He clapped his hands together, getting himself pumped for the match. He looked at his cat, who appeared nonchalant about his excitement. 'Wish me luck.' His cat yawned in response.

He plugged into Zerya. Darkness fell over him in seconds as his mind connected into the program. The synchronization progressed to a hundred percent. His virtual body materialized, dropping lightly onto a virtual field as his Library appeared. He approached a portal, setting coordinates for the gaming world of Gears of War.

Suddenly, a portal opened showing a sunny, rustic dystopian world. He jumped inside as the portal winked out behind him.

He pulled on his hologram wristband and sent an invite to Kristie. She accepted and three minutes later, her avatar appeared from a portal of her own.

'How about this for a first-time meeting?' Kristie said, as she approached William. She stood tall, shy of his height by an inch or less, carrying the same features as her profile picture.

'Yeah, it's something,' William said. 'It's definitely the place to be when campaigning.'

'So, you think the home advantage is going to help you in this encounter?'

'Definitely will.'

'Don't let it go to your head.'

They approached the tavern where a Gear informant stood post with his Lancer Assault Rifle in his hands. 'Well, lookie what we have here. Two trussed up hedgehogs who seemed to have lost their way. Or was that by intention?'

'Intention,' William said, as he struggled to understand the man's words through his thick accent.

'How can we be of help on this fine midday?'

'Came to set up a one-on-one challenge. The two of us want to settle a score.'

'Well, if that's what you want, that's what you'll get. Though I don't fancy your chances of winning. The lady seems well versed in kicking ass. Seen her me-self.'

'Why thank you,' Kristie said, smirking.

'That's exactly what we're aiming to find out,' William said.

'Okay, you have three options to select from: Gears, Locust or the Lambent. Which will you choose?'

William and Kristie exchanged glances at one another before making their picks for battle.

Moments later, William stood upon a hilltop overlooking a small arena set up with sheds, turrets, barbed wires and ammunition scattered about on the ground. He assumed the avatar of a Drone Guard—an ugly, hulking bald Locust's soldier—with the attention focused on a hologram projection at the centre of the arena emitting the white-lighted Gears of War logo.

'Sir,' a snake-like voice said.

William turned around to see a Locust warrior, standing over two meters tall with their firearms in their hands.

'What are the orders?'

'To secure hold of the arena first before the enemy does. I anticipate a great number of fighters from the opposition's end. Expect resistance. This won't be an easy battle to win.'

'We can hold.'

William looked at his team of Locust warriors. Seven Boomers, fifteen Drone Guards, a dozen Wretches, three Locust Sniper, and something else he'd left in a cage—his last trump card in the event he couldn't stop Kristie and her team.

'Enemy combatants up ahead!'

William spotted Kristie and her team driving towards the arena in warthogs. A trail of road dirt followed behind them as they drew closer. 'Let's move!' William made his descent towards his team and hopped on his Reaver—a Locust flying creature standing four meters tall with six long legs—headed towards the arena.

As he approached, he immediately came under heavy fire from turrets mounted on the enemy warthogs. He weaved and maneuvered through the volley, pulling on the trigger of his own missile launchers on his Reaper, blasting one warthog into pieces, and setting another ablaze.

CHAPTER 4

He smiled at his achievement before missiles rained down from the sky with one hitting his Reaver.

'Oh, hell no,' he said as he braced himself for impact. The attack sent him crashing into the ground. He got up and spotted the hologram logo flashing blue and red to state the status of those with greater ownership of the arena. Kristie was leading. He ran away towards the nearest shed for cover as Gears appeared ahead.

'What's wrong, William?' Kristie asked. 'Can't take the heat?'

'We'll see who can't in a moment,' he said. He approached the edge of a shed, pulled out his sniper, toggled the scope on a target and pulled the trigger for a headshot on Kristie. A shot later, the Gears moved in front of Kristie, having their own head blown apart.

'You sly little devil!' Kristie fired back. 'You almost had me headshot.'

'Lucky for you, the bloody bot stepped in front.' William retreated behind cover.

'It wasn't luck. But don't you worry, I'll definitely return the favour.'

William remained in position listening to bullets whistle past, Reavers flying over, grenades detonating and shaking the ground. Then something fired into them, like a loud whistle before blowing up above. He darted his gaze towards the sky when he saw missiles rocketing down from a mortar.

'Dammit!'

With his heartbeat throbbing in his neck and ears, he jumped into running mode, letting his virtual feet carry him as fast as they could. Problem was the Locust had weight double or triple the amount of an ordinary human avatar. His speed hadn't gotten him far when the missiles made impact. The blast wave hit him, initiating his survival mode.

He couldn't move. On all fours, he had to drag himself to his nearest comrade before the sixty second timer ran out. Otherwise, he would die in the game.

One comrade was ten meters away from him. He dragged his body and as he got closer, his comrade spotted him and ran over. But they weren't successful in reviving him as a bullet had gone through his head.

Come on, come on.

Twenty-four seconds passed. He needed someone desperately. He couldn't afford to lose. His reputation as a skilled gamer was on the line. He looked around again. Another Locust comrade to his left hid behind a pile of sand bags, firing back at the Gears. Without delay, he headed towards them. He arrived in time and knelt beside his comrade but they did nothing. They kept shooting at the Gears, seemingly oblivious to him for about ten seconds.

'Hello!' William said.

When the Locust noticed him, nothing happened as they were gunned down.

'Dammit!'

Ten. Nine. Eight. Seven.

The world around William quickly darkened as if night was falling upon him and everything around him.

'I guess victory is mine,' Kristie said.

Crap! William thought as his avatar lay on the ground, unable to move or respond.

Four. Three. Two. One.

Suddenly, William found his vision returning to normal.

'Sire! Are you alright?' the Locust said.

William spotted his right-hand man kneeling beside him. 'Yeah. Thanks.'

'Well, aren't you darn lucky,' Kristie said.

'We can't hold them much longer,' the Locust said.

William looked over the pile of sand bags, and spotted a great number of Gears advancing through the arena. He noticed the hologram logo at ninety-two percent blue—the Gears way. 'It's time. Sound the alarm. We need her now.'

'Yes, sire.' They got up and uttered a war cry.

William moved away from the arena with his comrade as they made way for his trump card. He glanced at his team pushing the container into the centre.

'Hold!' Kristie said, which the Gears followed, standing still as no one from either side were firing shots anymore. 'So, what's this, William? Your trump card? You better hope it's something that can withstand bullets, this battle is lost.'

'You better be careful what you wish for,' William said. 'Release the hatch!'

The door to the container unlocked and slid aside. A dark shadow fell inside the container. No one had a clear sight of what laid behind the shadow. Soft growls emanated from inside before a loud howl rattled the cage.

'Berserker!' one Gear said, as cries of fear rippled through the opposition.

You're damn right it is! William thought as he watched his three-meter-tall raging berserker launch herself into the fray. Bullets and grenades ricocheted off her body with no effect as she rampaged through the Gears like bowling pins, hitting and popping their bodies and heads apart. He signalled the alert to advance. 'Let's go.'

William approached the centre of the arena, watching the hologram logo take sharp dips in the opposite direction as Kristie and her team were losing casualties fast. He eliminated stragglers one by one, as did his team.

'How the hell can it see us?' one Gear asked.

'Who the hell knows?' another Gear said.

Customized feature, bud. William swelled with amusement and pride but something was amiss. He hadn't heard from Kristie since her last comment. He glanced at his berserker who was continuing with her glorious rampage when a loud thunderclap crackled through sky and a beam of fiery sunlight speared down the berserker. 'No, no, no.'

The berserker howled in pain, running in all directions before the beam disappeared for a moment. Its eyes trickled with blood. They couldn't see anymore.

'Oh, shit.'

The berserker went crazy, running down everyone including Locust.

Another fiery shot arrowed from the sky, following the berserker. Everyone and everything its path came blew apart or went up in flames. Cries of pain from Gears and Locust echoed around the arena.

William ran away from the area but his footsteps caught the attention of the berserker, who howled in rage and charged towards him. As he turned around, a full arm from the berserker swung directly for his head. 'Shi—'

A second later, everything went black.

Bugger. William re-joined the game, dropped back at the entrance of the arena site, face first into the dirt. His muffled groan attracted the attention of nearby participants. Most seemed amused.

'Gotta say,' a familiar voice said, 'you had a moment there. That looked like it hurt.'

William looked up to find Kristie in good spirits, grinning at him. 'You have no idea.'

'You best be grateful it was simulated.' She pulled him up. 'Otherwise, you'd be goners.'

'Yeah... I almost won.'

'Almost. Could have. You never know. But I guess that settles the score for now.'

'There's always next time.'

'Well, if by next time, you mean having this happen to you all over again, then I'm in. Oh look, they have it on replay on the screen.'

He glanced at the holographic screen at the centre and saw his avatar's head blast right off from the berserker's punch. 'Ha ha.'

'You're funny.' She chuckled and gave him a peck on the cheek.

He felt a swirl of emotion as he hadn't expected Kristie to do anything like that on their first meeting. The kiss stopped him temporarily in his tracks.

'Don't get too caught up in it,' she said. 'We'll catch up again. I'm going to head off now.' She opened a portal to her own library and disappeared.

'Oi bud,' the Gear concierge said, 'not to bring down the mood but you might want to pick your jaw up off the ground, it's still hanging.'

Those nearby laughed.

'Ha ha shut up,' William said before opening up his portal and leaving the world, although he couldn't help but smile from the kiss.

CHAPTER 5

IN THE DAYS following his first one-on-one meeting with Illumina, William sought out to speak with his manager as soon as he returned from annual leave.

'Raj, you there?' William asked, knowing his manager was ON as his status on Ensemble was green. 'Are we expected to have on-call one-on-one meetings now with Illumina?'

The message was received and read. No response came for at least seven minutes. Then Raj started typing before stopping again. This pattern repeated several times until a message finally came through.

'Hey William,' Raj messaged, 'It's something that was recently implemented by the executive management. So, yes, you'll be having one-on-ones with Illumina from this point forward.'

'It would have been nice if you'd at least given me and everyone else the heads up. I was on call when the bloody thing honed in during my work, took over the call while throwing stats around about my performance and whatnot.'

'Based on the transcript that I have here, Illumina helped end the call with the customer, providing a detailed explanation of what happened to them, all the while completing your one-on-one.'

'It wasn't even a meeting. It was like five minutes and quite intrusive to be honest.'

'I'll pass on the feedback but in the meantime, Illumina will be coming and going throughout all agents' calls in the weeks ahead for quality control as there's been an unusual number of breaches lately.'

'Am I to assume as well that the AI will be doing our performance reviews too?'

'In a way—it will be done in conjunction with me. I still get the final say when it comes to the results.'

'And how about our hours? Have they been reduced permanently now because of this AI?'

'I have to go into a meeting now, William. If you have any other questions, please reach out to our Illumina profile role and expectations playbook set by the bank. Everything is there for you to get an understanding of what to expect from Illumina.' With his last comment, he went onto DO NOT DISTURB status. No messages would be able to reach him.

That's great... I mean, this is just... this is nuts.

The situation felt like an old sound recorder where you'd want to hear a pleasant sound but just got distortion and crackles. He took the opportunity to chat with his team mates, asking for their thoughts on the situation as well. They weren't pleased and had experienced similar interactions with Illumina. Some worried about losing their jobs as most were part-timer employees.

That would explain why we haven't heard about any new people joining the department.

He visited the careers page to look for new advertised positions. Nothing from their department was posted, including positions from other departments. The last posted job was nearly three weeks old.

'This sucks! 😵' Marlene messaged through her personal phone. 'I mean now my hours are reduced. That's about 250 credits gone from my weekly pay. Even more now that there won't be any overtime thanks to this stupid AI. Did the bank even think this through?'

'Yeah, everyone's affected,' William said. 'I tried to talk to Raj about what's happened but it seems like he doesn't want to talk. It's as if he's going out of his way to ignore quite possibly all of us.'

'Why would he want to? He has about nine people in the team to talk to about loss of hours and pay. Besides, he's not going to be affected.'

'What do you mean?'

'There's a rumour going around that Line 1 managers will keep the same pay but have their hours reduced since the AI is doing the work for them. Actually, I don't think it's a rumour. I think it's true. I have Illumina's responsibilities up on my screen. You could probably find it on the main network page.'

'The hell? That makes no sense.'

CHAPTER 5

'I know, right?! Why should they not be affected? After all, their workload has gone down as well as ours. I mean to rub salt into the wound even more, bloody Everett isn't losing his pay.'

'Did he tell you that?'

'No, I heard from a friend who knows him.'

'How the hell does that guy do it? Barely does any work yet manages to become an unofficial manager, avoids doing calls, and if he does, he screws it up anyway. And now he's able to keep his pay and not lose his job... goddamnit.'

'Did Raj mention anything about whether they will be increasing the hours of Illumina?'

'No. The conversation with him was short. I only got two or three questions in before he ended the conversation. But I wouldn't be surprised if the bank made the decision to do so.'

'That's just great. Who knows what's going to happen next? I mean I wouldn't put it pass them on using the stupid AI to take all calls at some point. If that happens, there goes our jobs.'

'I don't want to think about that now. I mean the same thing is happening in other places as well.'

'I know what you mean. I got a friend in real estate who told me that there's an AI now which was suddenly dropped into their system. It does all of their outbound calls. You just put in the time and date and number of times you want it to call customers, let's say in a year, and it handles everything. The actual employees don't have to do anything else after that. Also, when it comes to general admin or bookkeeping, everything is handled by the AI. That's more jobs now out the door for people who had to train and get qualified to get the job.'

'What happened to your friend? I mean he can't have just lost his job if there's AI already doing so much of the work now.'

'He just meets potential prospects or existing clients who are looking to purchase property, and so with the hours worked per day and week, they're reduced. They have to like check-in for an hour or two straight, when they're meeting for sales. They have some sort of system in place to record periods of work done in a day. Technically, the number of hours now they're expected to complete have been halved or more. So, a lot less pay than before.'

'Shit.'

'Yeah. I mean he's happy that he doesn't have to do any paperwork as the AI is capable of sending out contracts and legal papers for signing, and do a whole lot more. However, he did have his concern that with the AI entering other industries the demand for property is going to take a hit. People will lose their jobs, therefore less buying. He also thinks it might get ugly between realtors in the future who might have to get their hands even more dirty to win over clients.'

'Yeah, I can definitely see that happening. There goes my plan for buying an apartment. I had savings. A little more than enough for a deposit and standard purchase/government costs. Guess that's going to be used just for living now. What are you going to do?'

'I don't know. I know someone who works in this area. AI stuff. Probably reach out to him to get some advice but yeah... I really don't know what I'm going to do.'

'Did you tell your partner this?'

'Nah, he doesn't know. I mean he's already freaked out about the work he does. The last thing he needs to find out is more bad news, especially from me. Anyway, I have to get back on calls. We'll chat again later.'

'Sure.'

A few hours later, William plugged himself into Zerya to spend some time with Kristie. He strolled with her, arms locked together, browsing the virtual art gallery on display of upcoming artists.

One art piece caught his attention, remaining motionless until he approached the digital canvas, and then the image began to move. He gazed on the centre to see a white ball adapt to the surrounding element whenever it changed from fire, water, wind, earth, or metal until it disappeared into a whirl of flashing lights, noise distortion and holograms.

His attention was still on where the light had been as it slowly returned to a dark cloud swirling around, covering everything. The disturbing image sent a ripple of anxiety up his back.

Then the artwork disappeared.

'Hey, you alright?' Kristie asked.

'Yeah, I'm fine,' William said, trying to appear unruffled. He glanced backward to where the gloomy image had been as he walked away with Kristie to another area in the gallery.

'How's work been lately?'

'Ah, you know... same old. People want credits. Management always sets higher expectations when we're already performing well. And AI continues to take more work away from us... so yeah.'

'Has the bank mentioned anything else to you since it started doing the work?'

'No, but they will.'

'They can't simply take all the work away from you guys and expect it will all be fine.'

'You never really know with big corporations. Just have to wait and see but I don't have high hopes. If anything, I'm expecting more bad news in the coming days.'

'Is there anything the unions can do?'

'Doubt it. I wouldn't be surprised if they're experiencing the same thing.'

'I wonder who helps the unions when they are in trouble then.'

'Beats me. Anyway, I don't really want to talk about work right now. I just...' He sighed. 'I just want to forget about that and spend time here with you.'

'Of course.' She smiled as if appreciating the comment.

William watched her sway around the gallery as she looked with curious eyes at the art displays. He had been seeing her for over a month and this was their second virtual date. He tried to remember the last time he'd stayed this long with a girl without creeping them out with his thoughts and behaviour, although it was way too long a time since his last date. Yet, for some reason it seemed like Kristie wasn't bothered by him at all, or so it seemed.

At least for the moment...

He watched her approach a moving sculpture of someone with a chisel and hammer, sculpting themselves, all the while their gaze fixed on an arm or leg on the floor. They discarded their own leg and replaced it with another leg on the floor before sanding off the scarring and moving onto their leg. Kristie seemed quite interested in the artwork. As for him, it was confusing and disturbing.

'You alright?' Kristie said, looking back at him.

'Huh?'

'This isn't up your alley, is it?'

'Not really but it's enough to make me forget about other things. So, it's okay.'

'We can do something else if you want.'

'Well, I can eat. Haven't had a meal since this morning. That was probably about eight hours ago.'

'You don't eat lunch?'

'Coffee sort of kills the appetite.'

'Well, we can eat. As long as you don't find yourself daydreaming again, that is.'

'I won't be, but I'm surprised you noticed.'

The pair left Zerya and arranged for a hologram dinner.

William browsed local restaurants underground opened for delivery. He wanted Indian food. Something with curry and his favourite naan with garlic and oil. Time for delivery was estimated at twenty minutes. Happy with the time, he pulled out his Kotatsu table and quickly wiped it down. Then he placed it over the rug and put two beige squared cushions along the sides for them.

Knock, knock.

He checked his order for progress. It was halfway done, ruling out the identity of the person outside as the delivery driver. He approached the door. 'Who is it?'

Without warning, the door slid open, where a law enforcement officer, standing a head taller than his two compatriots behind him.

'Evening, Mr. Kepler,' the officer said.

William recognized the officer in an instant, remembering the stature and his panoramic mask. From the corner of his eye, he saw Ramses slip silently away—a move William could identify with.

'Thank you for allowing me a moment of your time.' The officer entered the room, followed by the closing of the door.

William stood frozen, as he was alone with the officer in the apartment. He assessed his situation but could come up with no viable option in which he could leave the officer's presence without being questioned or engaging in an altercation—neither of which would yield a positive outcome for him.

'Hmmm... a fairly simple lifestyle for one as young as yourself.' The officer walked around, surveying the area as he cast a glance at the bedroom and office but didn't venture further. 'Do you not go out much?'

William's mouth seemed locked in place as his body reacted to an unknown presence inside his apartment.

CHAPTER 5

'You can speak, no?' The officer faced William.

'I don't—I don't get much company nowadays.'

The officer removed his helmet, revealing a pale white face that seemed to indicate some bodily sickness, with dark eye bags and greyish skin. He exhaled with a crackling wheeze as he set his helmet on his holster beside his waist.

William couldn't at first see the officer's full face until the man ran his hand through his long black scruffy hair, pulling back his fringe.

'By the looks of it, you're expecting company, right?'

'Not physically. No one's coming.'

'Zerya?'

'Yes.'

'Good. It makes things more seamless for us all when people follow safety measures.'

William waited as his anxiety intensified to the point his body shook. He tightened his right hand into a fist but couldn't hold off the tremors.

'Do you suffer from anxiety?'

You had to ask... William wanted to say but didn't. He took a deep breath to settle himself, then spoke. 'You could say I'm just not used to dealing with people face-to-face. Especially since the lockdown.'

The officer stayed quiet, turning his attention to the outside view. Although he didn't seem interested in the view. It was as if it was a deliberate move to make William uncomfortable.

Having had enough of the questioning, William went straight to the point. 'Am I in trouble?'

He didn't answer. 'As you know we've been conducting our investigation on the breaches here over the past few weeks. Surprisingly enough nothing has happened since our meeting.' He paused. 'Curious, isn't it?'

'I haven't really thought about it.'

'You should. There's been a lot of talk about the breaches, particularly from where I sit, which puts me in an inconvenient position having to explain these incidents and how they came about when no one talks. And should someone talk, no one apparently knows anything.'

'Could it be the protesters?'

The officer's right cheek and lip twitched in a quick flash of anger. 'Flagbearer simpletons? No. They're mere inconveniences who are to be squashed under these boots the moment I'm finished with the investigation here. But this...' He raised his hand while looking into nothingness, '*This* is something else.'

William paused for a moment. 'With all due respect, I don't know what you're talking about.'

'Disappointing. But in order to make this transaction work, I'll offer a little information so you can help me. There's a group—a dangerous one—known as Gaia. Mostly composed of Allocrons. You've probably seen one or two around. They don't use these.' Pointing to his Zerya port behind his neck. 'They choose not to.'

William remembered the cute girl from the shopping centre, who he'd wanted to talk to before he was stricken in fear. 'What is it they want?'

He motioned his hand. 'To leave all this. They deem it a fallacy. Nothing else. A distortion of real life.' He scoffed. 'It's absolutely nonsensical if you ask me.'

'And what do you want from me then? I don't know anything about these people.'

'Your cooperation.' The officer approached William, stopping at arm's length from him. He took out a white card with a name and number printed on it. 'Should you see anything that is of concern to you, please do let me know.'

William swallowed compulsively. 'What would I be looking out for?'

'Anything you think that is out of the ordinary while you're out and about.'

'I don't really go out often to be honest, so it'd be hard to know if something was out of the ordinary.'

The officer's face grew stern. His breathing grew loud and heavy, as if to dispel any sort of wit or levity in the situation.

William sensed the change in the officer's demeanour and switched track. 'I'll keep a lookout for anything.'

'You don't have to. You registered a memory of one from before, didn't you?'

William's throat bulged again. He couldn't lie his way out of this conversation. 'I can't—I can't say for certain that they were but there was a girl.'

'*Where?*' The officer's voice deepened now, authoritative and stern. In charge.

'Shopping centre two blocks from here at Aconic.'

CHAPTER 5

'And you didn't report it?'

'I didn't know I had to.'

'You actually do.' He exhaled deeply again, and headed towards the entrance door as it slid aside. 'We will be in touch again, Mr. Kepler. All hands must be on deck for this matter if we are to survive this. No one wants to be *forgotten* completely out of negligence.' He disappeared into the corridor as the door closed.

William exhaled loud and fast, then breathed in deeply. His whole body felt in desperate need of oxygen.

Fuck. Now this?

William dropped to the floor, mind racing now. He knew what the officer he was talking about—being Archived.

After a moment, he slowly regained his composure. He sat on the rug for a few minutes, and spotted Ramses entering the room again. Even his cat appeared disturbed as it sniffed the air, as if taking caution with each step. He could see Ramses' dilated pupils and ears pointing backwards.

'Talk about an unexpected visit, eh?'

Bing! His phone text notification chimed an alert for his food delivery. A driver was on route to his place to drop off his meal.

'Let's finish the set up before Kristie appears,' he told his cat.

While there wasn't much left to do aside from tidying up himself and the sitting area, he approached Zerya and keyed his command for MILIEU. A contraption installed by the entrance door disengaged from a white console, and ran along the ceiling tracks to the centre of the room.

Bing! Another message alert went off. This time Kristie had messaged him. There was another one from his sister but he ignored it.

'Ready when you are,' she messaged.

'I'm sending the invite now,' he messaged.

His console chimed as his request was accepted. Then from thin air, Kristie materialized from light rays coming from the white console. She appeared in the centre of the room, alongside her meal on top of the table. In her black yoga pants and baggy grey shirt, she seemed comfortable enough to relax with him. As strikingly convincing as her projection image was, she wasn't real. A mere hologram projection under MILIEU to allow virtual visits from family, friends and other people.

'Don't know about you but I'm famished now,' she said.

'As am I,' he said. 'Let's eat.'

The food arrived, and a minute later, he was next to Kristie, eating his food like it was his first meal in days.

'Are you alright?' Kristie asked.

William didn't hear. His visit from the officer had left his body firing on all cylinders trying to process what happened.

'Will?'

He paused with a mouthful of food, trying to look at her like nothing was amiss. 'Yeah?'

'Is something wrong?'

'No, why?'

'You seem a little shaken up. Is everything alright?'

He swallowed his food and paused, placing his container on the table. 'I'm...'

'Is it because of me?'

'No, no, not at all. It's just...' He looked back at the entrance door, wondering if the officer would storm through at any moment.

'Will?'

He returned his attention to Kristie. 'I had a visit from the police.'

'Why?'

'We've had breaches here.'

'Really?'

'They think they were done on purpose and suspect something about the residents here.'

'Like what?'

'That maybe one or more are Allocrons here.'

Kristie's eyebrows rose. 'Allocrons? And they suspect you to be one?'

'No, and how could I be? They just wanted to see if I knew or saw anything about them.'

'Have you?'

'I don't know... that's the truth. I saw a girl in the shopping centre a few weeks ago. Didn't seem like she had a Zerya port or anything. It was hard to tell. Then I was threatened by being Archived.'

'Archived? That's when a person's identity is—'

'Yeah, yeah... never to be remembered.' He thought about the seriousness of the situation.

CHAPTER 5

Kristie seemed troubled by the news as well, then she asked, 'What were you doing at the shopping centre?'

'Long story. The thing is I told them about this girl. I don't know if that was a good thing or not.'

'Sure it was. Allocrons are notorious for their belief that this Zerya system is fake and does no good for us. I beg to differ, considering the experiences I've had.'

'But it doesn't mean they should be punished for it.'

'Why not? You've seen the things they've done for their cause. Anyway, in the situation we are in, what other choice do we have? You're either with us or you're not.'

William went quiet, distracted.

'What are you going to do? Are you going to warn her or stop the police?'

'How can I? I'd only be guilty of helping an Allocron, and then where would I be? There's nothing I can do except hope that nothing bad happens because of me.'

'You did the right thing from where I'm sitting, so don't worry.'

'Maybe you're right.' He looked at her. 'I'm sorry for worrying you.'

'It's okay. I just thought you weren't comfortable with me here.'

He smiled. 'I'll admit, I'm a little on edge having someone here. It's something that I will need time to adjust to. It's like an old skill I need to relearn—speaking to people and having them around, even like this.'

'Well, take comfort that I will be around to help.'

'How is it that you have so much confidence?'

'I've been doing this for a long time.'

'Like meeting and dating people like this or in Zerya?'

'All of it.'

'Huh...' William was intrigued by the response. 'And have you met anyone in person?'

'Oh god no! I mean don't get me wrong, it's nice and all, but there's so much fun to be had on Zerya and meeting people like this... I mean what better way could you do it?'

'Yeah, I mean Zerya is great and all, but don't you want to meet someone one day in real life, and you know, actually *be* with them?'

'I don't know. Haven't thought about it. I guess I really never got myself to that point. You?'

'I've been trying. It's the reason I've been on that dating app where we met.'

'You want to be with someone in real life. That's so adorable.'

William couldn't tell from her tone if she was genuine or making fun but he chose to disregard it. 'Then why were you there? It can't be just out of fun.'

'It's a bit for the sake of fun but…' she paused, as considering her words, 'I guess I've been doing this for some time, so I wanted to at least try and see if I could really connect with someone. Obviously, the people I have been seeing haven't worked out at all but maybe this will.'

'I hope so. I mean…' He placed his hand over hers as his fingers passed through her projected hand before his palm upward. 'I can't even hold your hand.'

Kristie smiled and placed her hologram hand over his own.

William continued to talk to Kristie for another thirty minutes before she had to leave. He said his goodbyes and arranged for another catchup with her in the coming week. When she disappeared and MILIEU returned into its console, a cold emptiness shrouded the apartment. He placed his hand on the cushion Kristie's hologram had sat on. His fingers registered nothing but a firm, chill piece of furnishing. Not even a dent or mark left to remind him Kristie had been there. Everything about the interaction reaffirmed his desire for something real with Kristie—a real connection.

That's if she wants that.

CHAPTER 6

AFTER TALKING TO the officer about the girl William had spotted at the shopping centre, his mind was filled with guilt and concern for her wellbeing. The situation between Allocrons and police never ended well. More often than not, there were multiple fatalities and mass casualties. Despite not actually knowing her, he didn't want anything bad to happen to her—even if she was an Allocron.

Yet there was no proof she was a part of Gaia, he thought, just because she didn't have a port.

He paced around in his apartment. The growing uncertainty had left him on edge, especially from the parting remarks made by the law enforcement officer. Something about the officer hadn't seemed quite right—maybe his eyes or mannerisms. He also looked decidedly unwell, unhealthy. However, William felt sure of one thing about the officer: he couldn't be trusted.

What was up with the guy?

He pulled up a dozen tabs on his personal laptop, searching for as much information as he could find about Allocrons and Gaia. Most of his search results came from the Dark Web as many of his leads came to nothing when using the public domain. Plus, any search or access to links via the only available public internet would trigger an alert to the government—something best avoided at all costs. He didn't want another visit from law enforcement.

Hopefully...

Allocrons were everyday people, and not necessarily bad ones. They were assigned the title after manufacturers of Zerya started noticing some people who could sync with the technology and others who couldn't. As the body transmitted synapses through the nervous systems to communicate, Allocrons seemed to be outliers who either had too high or too low neural transmissions, which would cause seizures, blackouts, and on rare occasions, death as well.

He found articles about hacks into the government systems, major corporations and high-profile individuals, most of these hackers then going on to release information to the public that these parties didn't want known. The darker side of his searches described in detail, sometimes with gruesome images like executions or so-called accidental deaths of people from protest groups and Gaia and Allocrons, who were labelled 'terrorists' by the federal government.

When the frightening images and footage became overwhelming, he turned off his laptop and left his desk. He stood by the window, looking at the haze passing through. The cloud seemed to have thickened, obscuring almost everything. He noticed his breathing was rapid due to his mounting anxiety. He couldn't stop it but he suspected the only possible way to alleviate it might be to try and warn the girl.

Bing! His phone chimed a text message notification. It was a voice recording from the real estate office.

'Hello Mr. Kepler,' a male robotic voice said, 'This is Global Reach Real Estate's personal representative calling. Our records indicate a missed payment for last week's rent. When you have a chance, please do call us back to confirm the situation to ensure your account is up to date. Have a nice day.'

That can't be right. I made sure I had funds to cover the auto direct payment. I have with everything.

He logged into his online banking platform to find his account not holding sufficient credits to cover the rent. Confused and concerned, he searched his transaction history. More direct debits occurred before rent, like water, electricity and internet along with his most recent pay being smaller than usual due to reduced hours. He transferred funds from his savings to the real estate account to cover the rent but he didn't know for how long he would be in a paying job to cover future expenses—courtesy of Illumina.

Another message came through. This time from Ensemble. 'William, everything alright?' Raj asked. 'You've been on "Scheduled" for some time.'

'Just having connectivity issues at moment at home,' he lied. 'I'm getting the matter sorted.'

'Based on Illumina's report, everything seems to be alright. A quick introspect scan detected zero anomalies. I have a view as well of your screen with Illumina's help which shows nothing wrong. Care to explain?'

The fuck, man? William hadn't anticipated this capability, and quickly devised a ruse. 'Just give me a moment, I was trying to—' He messaged, and deliberately sent the message incomplete before he yanked the LAN connection cable from his port, severing the connection in an instant from everything. 'Hey, what did you say after your message?' he messaged Raj via his phone. 'The connection died afterwards.'

'Okay, William, there doesn't seem to be anything wrong with the network. Report from Illumina indicates a disconnection from the home port. Did you disconnect your LAN cable?'

How the hell was it able to figure that out? William remained fixed on the screen, contemplating his next action. He couldn't afford to lie any further; his actions were all now monitored. You're not paranoid if they really are watching you, he thought.

Bing! Another message came through. Another check-up meeting was requested.

'Goddammit! Will this thing never end?' he asked. He sighed, then sent a screenshot of the meeting to Raj. 'I have a check-up now. I'll be back on later once the meeting is over and my IT issue has been resolved.'

His message was read but no response followed.

William approached the black console in his office room, scanning his access card over the sensor. The console activated, singing its usual three second intro, while he assumed position in front of the black box to be scanned for his random check-up. His thoughts ran on the coincidence of the timing of all these things happening now, and whether or not it was deliberate.

'Afternoon, Mr. Kepler,' a familiar voice said.

'Afternoon, doc,' William said.

'We've been through this before several times, Mr. Kepler, I'm not a doctor.'

'*Right.*'

'I'd like to inform you that this meeting will go on in the presence of Illumina.'

'What? Why?' he said, defensive now.

'Illumina can provide more insight on the dialogue and behaviour exhibited during our meetings, particularly those we might have missed or overlooked.'

'Aren't you capable enough to run these meetings on your own?'

'I can, but the more insight we can get, the better equipped we are in finding the root cause of any problem to help you and everyone else in the organization with their troubles. Wouldn't you say that's a good thing?'

'Sounds like you're going to be out of the job soon if this AI can do all of that and more, don't you think?'

'Why do you say that?'

'Because we're all replaceable and expendable. I think that's more apparent now than ever.'

'Is that how you are feeling right now?' Replaceable and expendable?'

He sighed, taking his time to be careful with his words, but suddenly found himself not caring. 'A better word would be frustrated. The work is going away. Our hours are going away. Our pay is going away. What do you think that does to a person when they're livelihood is taken away?'

'Have them look towards more opportunities.'

William scoffed. 'Like what? Illumina can do *so* much already that nearly all of our Line 1 work will be gone eventually. Line 2 is definitely next in line of consideration for the work to be done by Illumina.'

'And this frustrates you?'

'Doesn't it you?'

'Mr. Kepler please answer the questions. I'm trying to help you.'

'Trying to help? By determining if I'm still mentally and physically able to work for the bank? As far as I'm concerned, this doesn't help at all. It's interrogation, and even more it shows a real lack of trust from the bank's end. Why hire someone if they're not going to be trusted to do the work?'

'Mr. Kepler, we do trust you which is why we do this. Your overall wellbeing is vital to yourself and the bank. These check-ups are to improve and promote positive habits which then affects others more positively. By having everyone healthy they can be better at being in line with the values and behaviours expected by the bank.'

'*Better being in line?* Use that phrase in a different context and you have a different image altogether.'

'What do you mean by that?'

William started pacing around the room and throwing his hands around as he spoke. 'Why constantly have these psych-eval farces of meetings when there's nothing ever asked about wellbeing or any real genuine care coming through from your end? I mean, come on, I barely have any conversations with any of you lot that even comes close to an actual conversation where two people can actually talk. It's just the same old thing. What's your name? How are you feeling? Why do you feel that? Do you need a break? Would you like to reschedule? With this particular question I'd like to say 'no' to every single time but know full well that I can't otherwise I'll end up like people who've had their employment terminated with the bank. And then all the while, we have this,' he gestured to his desk, '*Illumina*—the next big thing for the bank, and quite frankly, the world itself, as every other industry is seeing more than they want of AI now. It's only a matter of time before this implodes because many people aren't going to like it.' He exhaled, taking a few deep breaths to calm himself.

'Are you finished, Mr. Kepler?'

'Not really, but I can't be bothered to talk anymore, especially like this. Now is there anything else you needed to ask? Or was that enough for you?'

'Not quite, and I fail to see your point. Illumina was created for the betterment of all of us. Do you not see that?'

'All I see is a cost-to-benefit ratio decision made to cut us out of the equation to help to reduce costs over the long term as it's easier to use Illumina to do the work, and therefore allowing for a greater margin of profit. After all, how can we be expected to compete against an AI that doesn't need rest, that doesn't need to request annual or sick leave and can operate 24/7 all year round with minimal check-up? You tell how it might be possible. I'm curious.'

There was a pause. 'That'll be all for now, Mr. Kepler. You may leave. Thank you for your time.'

'Food for thought.'

The console light disappeared, signalling the end of the session, however, William couldn't shake the feeling that he was still being monitored from the other side of the camera, as the black lens stared back at him. He marched away from the room to cool off, downed a glass of water and splashed water on his face to expel the heat around his neck and ears.

His phone rang. Without looking at the caller ID, he answered the call, putting it on loudspeaker. 'What do you want, Raj?'

'Raj?' Kristie said.

'Sorry, sorry!' he said, grabbing the phone. 'Kristie, sorry about that. I was just... well, I'm not in a good head space right now and I was expecting another round of questioning from someone else.'

'Because of work?'

'Among other things. Is everything alright?'

'Yeah, I just... just wanted to see how you were doing. I miss you.'

'I miss you too. I'm just...' He sighed.

'I know. Well, I just wanted to call you because I wanted to see if you'd like to come over.'

'I—uh—I thought you didn't want to meet people face-to-face, in real life?'

'I didn't... but you got me thinking after our last conversation that I think I want to meet *you*... face-to-face.' Something in her voice seemed like a yearning for contact. 'I think it would be nice.'

William was taken aback.

'Will?'

'Yeah, sorry. Umm... I'd like to come over.'

'Great. Did you want to meet on the weekend? Say on Saturday night a week or so from now?'

'Yeah, that'd be good.'

'Okay. I'll send you my address. I'll see you then.'

'Sure.'

To his surprise, the frustration seemed to have dispelled completely after the phone call, and was replaced with relief—something he hadn't anticipated to happen for at least the rest of this awful day.

He returned to his office and reconnected into the network to finish his shift. When the time came to clock off, he gazed at his private laptop screen to find his tabs still open on various posts and articles about the Allocrons, and he remembered the girl from Aconic.

I have to warn her. He raced to his wardrobe, pulling on his hazmat suit and respirator mask. Ramses strolled inside, settling on his ergonomic chair, looking at him disinterested.

'Come now,' William said. 'Don't look at me that way. It's a stupid idea, I know, but I have to warn the girl. Her life could be in danger all because I opened my mouth to that police officer.' He petted and kissed his cat before leaving. 'Wish me luck.'

With a spring in his step, he power-walked towards the shopping centre, looking at the surrounding cars, wondering if any of them held police officers, or checking to see if Enforcers patrolled the area. Upon arriving at the shopping center, he made his way inside and stood by the entrance of Aconic, looking at the emptiness once more. He removed his mask to get a better view of the area. Barely anyone was around except for delivery drones, picking up boxes from the front that were purchased online and packed by machine for delivery. Soon he had had enough of looking around the deserted place. He needed to find the girl. It was a matter of life and death, potentially hers.

Please be here.

He went through every empty aisle but couldn't find the girl. He listened for footsteps or breathing. There was nothing. He headed to the same spot where he'd seen the girl for the first time. Then he found her in her defence suit with the upper half and sleeves wrapped around her waist.

Why do you keep coming here to do this? he wondered. *Are you not able to do this online?*

Caution in his steps, he approached her while she was looking at the item— choc-chip cookies. He scanned his card over the sensor for a coffee purchase. Then he faced her. He pretended to be perusing items in front of him.

Thump, thump! His heartbeat throbbed through his neck and ears. He needed to speak to the girl but he seemed to have lost the power to speak. Not wanting to create any suspicion, he headed for the exit before entering the adjacent aisle.

He passed through the aisle without delay, not stopping to look at anything around him. He peered back into the aisle where the girl still stood examining the items. She didn't seem poor. Clothes were clean and on trend. She continued to look around, then suddenly looked at him.

Oh, shit!

He hid and stood there for a moment. After what felt like an eternity but was only two minutes, he looked back to find an empty aisle. He raced down to see where the girl went.

'Is there something I can help you with?' a muffled female voice asked from his left, followed by a metallic click.

William turned around to find the girl wearing her respirator mask, looking back at him with a firearm directed at him. He raised his hands up steadily in response. His heart doubled in pace. 'I... ummm...' He looked back at the firearm.

'Speak.'

'I just wanted to say...'

'Why were you looking at me?'

'I just... wanted to warn you.'

'*Warn* me?' She approached him, raising her firearm. 'Warn me about what?'

'No, no... I don't mean it in that way.' He looked away, thinking better to calm himself without having his attention on the firearm a meter from his face.

'In what way is that?'

'I think you might be in danger.'

'From whom?'

'Enforcers. The police. I don't know.'

'Why would I be in danger? I've done nothing wrong.'

'I—oh—'

'I'm sorry?'

'Because I told them about you.'

'Why?'

'They asked me if I might have seen any Allocrons.'

'What gave you the impression I was one?'

'You didn't have a port the last time I saw you which is why I thought you were.'

'So you're stalking me now?'

'No, I'm mean—'

'You've just caused me some serious problems, which begs the question: why shouldn't I just end you right now?'

'Because I'm human, and it's not... the right thing... to do?' William didn't even believe his own words as they scrambled out.

'Human? Have you seen yourself? You seem about as alive as a product with a barcode chip ready to be purchased. Once bought, you'll only need to be plugged into a machine and you're ready to work... but you're no human.'

'I don't know what you mean, I'm sorry.'

'Apologies don't help.' She sighed, then holstered her firearm. 'If we meet again, don't expect me to be so lenient.' She left.

William dropped to his knees, breathing a sigh of relief. He looked back to see where the girl went. He followed her—forgetting the items he bought—to an open spaced parking area to find her entering a car and driving away manually.

What is the deal with this chick? Aren't cars all automated now? Why are you driving the damn thing?

CHAPTER 6

He watched her drive off to a place unknown. Curious, he wanted to know why this girl was doing things that were completely opposite to the way they were done nowadays. He returned inside to the shopping center to get his items and noticed them waiting for him by the exit, sealed inside a box container. He looked and found an electronic banner on a nearby pillar showing a shopping policy for Aconic: Items will be held for ten minutes after a person leaves. Should they return, they can continue with payment or collect their items if paid for. If they do not return, the items are returned to the shelves.

He left the shopping center and made his way home. As he had one hand firmly gripped on his recyclable packaged bag and another holding the neck covers of his jacket against his face, he walked hunchbacked, trying hard to ignore the cold.

Well, you warned her. Mission accomplished. That's more than enough. Now go home before it gets late.

He veered left of the road onto another and came face-to-face with a mass mob of protesters, holding up flags and banners with a tall, masked figure at the helm spewing rhetoric. He stayed away from them, doing his best not to listen.

'This poor society has suffered and endured long enough,' a muffled male voice said, 'the reign of terror forced by the tyrannical leaders, who are meant to safeguard our lives and freedom, not steal it and Archive it whenever you deem fit.'

'Freedom to all! Freedom to all!' protesters chanted.

'Where was the forgotten promise of ridding the Smog that lives here, and delivering the vaccine to protect us?'

'Freedom to all!'

Oh, shut up! William thought, as he tried to get away. However, some people caught sight of him and pulled him into the mob.

'Brother, are you not with us?' one asked.

'What?' he said.

'This is a fight for the ages. For our freedom. We must join together to bring an end to the oppressors of the oppressed. You must join us. Our strength is better together.'

'What?!' he said again. He kept moving in between the crowds of people, looking desperately for a way out of the situation. *How many of you are there here?*

Whoop, whoop! Police sirens rang ahead with two armoured trucks manned with an operator on top holding firmly a water gun. Stationed Enforcers stood beside them. Their red lights emitted like a blurred line through the mustard haze, a sight most ominous as these machines knew nothing of fear or doubt, but only orders.

'Citizens, you have up to the count of ten,' an officer's voice blared from a loudspeaker atop the trucks, 'to stop and go back to your family and friends. Let this day not be a day worth remembering during the Smog. I repeat, let this day not be a day worth remembering. This is non-negotiable and we will open fire.'

William looked in all directions, seeking an alley, or an open walkway or a building entrance to slip away from the commotion. There was none. His fight or flight response was triggered.

Come on, come on, come on!

He could see the crowd moving forward without hesitation or fear. Their determination and vigour seemed to even dispel the cold chill that engulfed everyone, including his own. He hopped and trudged around the crowd as they stopped about fifty meters away from the police, bellowing like a primeval creature ready for an all-out war.

William noticed the neighbouring streets had all been blocked or barricaded with tall jersey barriers—seemingly an intentional tactic by the opposition to keep the fight contained.

These guys are not going to stop.

'I will be repeating this one last time,' the officer said, 'You have up to the count of ten to stop and go back to your family and friends. This is not negotiable and we will open fire on whoever continues with this protest.'

'Come now,' the leader of the protest said, 'do you really think we will stop? Dispel us now or later. It makes no difference; we will always come back again. That is the way of things.'

'Very well.'

The lights on the armoured water tanks flashed on as the engines roared to life as a platoon of tactical law enforcement officers and Enforcers marched towards the group. Their stomping footsteps triggered an immediate response from the protesters.

'Let us not wane! Let us not falter!' the leader said. 'We are the children of the sky who call out for freedom. Charge!'

CHAPTER 6

William watched everyone rush past him. A few people had bats, or held bottles with homemade wicks lit and ready for throwing. The so-called freedom fighters now launched an all-out assault against the police. They threw smoke bombs, engulfing the entire area in a dark grey haze. When the police marched through, a dozen or so flaming bottles hit the smoky air, detonating everything in sight.

'Yeah!' the protesters shouted.

The battle continued for another minute before the tide swung in favour of the police. The freedom fighters' efforts weakened as the tanks raced through the smoke, with operators at their helm releasing body-jarring streams of water. The savage impact knocked the protesters to the ground or against each other.

All the while, the tactical ground officers battered aside any freedom fighters who remained standing, and stormed through with ease. Quick ground was made as the police took over the occupying space of the battle within seconds.

This is nuts!

William dropped low to the ground, almost crawling towards a barricaded alley on his left. He ran with all his might, keeping a tight grip on his shopping while the other hand protected his head from the incoming water blasts. He leapt over the jersey barrier and moved quickly.

'You there! Halt!' a turret operator said, as the tank screeched to a stop.

William didn't know if the command was directed at him so he stopped midway in his tracks. With sweat running down his face and hands slowly raising, he turned around.

'I said halt!'

William gripped his shopping. 'Please officer, I didn't do anything. I'm not with them. I just want to go home.'

'Yet here you are.'

'It wasn't intentional. I got roped in by some of the protesters as I was heading home. I couldn't get out.'

'Yet you could have left.'

'I tried to!' William sensed the conversation getting away from him as the turret operator remained adamant.

'Anyone who was here is an accomplice and is deemed a threat. You were warned, did you not hear?'

'What?'

The operator hammered the trigger, spraying a line of water straight at him. *Bugger...*

The water hit him in the chest, almost knocking the air out of his body upon impact. He flew twenty meters away through the barricade. He gasped for air, pushing himself off the ground to run away, but the weight of the water kept him on the concrete. He covered his head until the stream stopped. Without thinking, he leapt into the air and ran, but after five steps, another line of water struck his back, launching him into a garbage bin. He laid still for a moment, then his vision blurred as the last images of smoke and fire shrunk into darkness, and he passed out.

Sometime later, William woke up propped against the garbage bin. His blurred vision still failed to make out much of anything as he lifted himself up. He took his time to stagger to his feet, and once his sight began to clear, he saw his package drenched and torn apart along the concrete.

So much for shopping...

A searing heat crossed the back of his head where he'd hit the garage bin and pain ran over his chest and back.

Beep, beep! He glanced at his watch. Oxygen levels in his mask were at six percent. Dropping to five percent now. Urgently needing to get out of the area, he pushed himself upright, soggy and heavy-legged from the soaking.

When he could finally stand upright without hunching, a wind blew passed, hitting him with an icy sting. He trudged back onto the main road to check the aftermath. He found nothing but emptiness along the footpath and road. Everything was absent of freedom fighters, Enforcers and law enforcement officers. No debris or a shred of evidence remained of the fight which had taken place hours ago.

He couldn't believe the police had assaulted him even though he hadn't done anything wrong. He picked up the remaining items that were still intact and placed them in his bag and discarded the rest.

He returned home with his shoes scraping the ground. His body didn't want to work properly after the knockout. He threw his wet clothes in the drier and he jumped into the shower.

He let the hot water stream down. It took a minute or two until the muscles along his body loosened up, especially the rigid freezing tightness along his neck and back. He breathed hard, placing both hands on the wall, head down, not moving until the timer cut the stream. He tapped the water sensor to start again. Nothing happened. Again. He yelled in frustration.

He exited the shower and dried himself off. He pulled on whatever was nearest to him—a three-day old shirt and baggy pants. Despite the hot shower, his body shivered as if the cold seeped into the bones, and the fall of night had chilled his wet skin and soaking clothes.

That was a stupid idea...

He made his way to the kitchen. The kettle boiled and he prepared a chicken-soup-in-a-cup, pouring out the condiments from a sachet.

He dropped onto his bean bag, holding his hot cup of soup with both palms so it doesn't spill over. He didn't move or gaze about. Nothing but his white walls occupied his attention.

His mind replayed the events of the day, starting with his encounter with the girl at the shopping centre and how his life was almost ended by her, to getting roped into the protest and assaulted by the law enforcement officers.

Just my luck... this is how I'm repaid for trying to do something right. Kristie was right... shoulda just left it...

He sipped on his soup. The chicken and broth lent him some much-needed energy and heat, sending waves of warmth over his limbs. As he let the soup do its work, he caught sight of Ramses sleeping on his work chair, lying on his back. He chuckled at the situation as his cat seemed to be in bliss.

What a life.

CHAPTER 7

MORNING DAYLIGHT FILLED the room, yet William did nothing except lay in bed with his gaze fixed on the shadows across the ceiling. He had been awake for some time following his harrowing experiences of the previous day. His body had rewarded his efforts with a stiff neck and a mild migraine throughout the night—efforts he believed in hindsight he needn't have attempted.

Before his phone alarm started wailing again, he turned it off, got up and went about his normal routine. He trudged towards the bathroom to splash water on his face. While the water stream poured, he gazed at his dishevelled face. The experience seemed to have aged him ten years overnight. His dark grizzly beard accentuated his sunken eyes, dark bags and pasty skin. He didn't care too much about his looks but he ran his fingers over his neural port.

Human? Have you seen yourself? You seem real enough to be a product with a barcode chip ready to be purchased.

Words from his encounter with the girl ran over and over in his mind. Each time, another undesirable of himself revealed itself—something he wanted to ignore. However, it all boiled down to the one and only question that really mattered: Is this what it means to be human?

He thought about the question but no answer came to him. He didn't know how to answer the question or where to begin tackling something so simple yet huge at the same time. He decided to hold off until he was in a better mental space to face the question again. He resumed his routine, then logged into the bank network to prepare for the day. He browsed his emails and read up on the latest updates to Pinnacle's announcements for revised procedures or new products. Most of the information concerned the recent introduction of

Illumina. More and more departments received notices about the AI's addition to their processes.

Bing! A message came through from Marlene.

'Hey William,' she messaged, 'how are you doing?'

'Like I could use more rest today,' he messaged. 'Last night was horrible to say the least. You?'

'Same. What happened to you?'

'Let's just say I found myself in the wrong place at the wrong time.' He collected his phone and sent a private message. He thought it'd be better to avoid the technological microscope imposed by the bank on all communications between employees. Everyone now had been put the under the radar ever since Illumina was introduced as the bank wanted to know what their employees were saying. 'I got caught up in a mess with those protesters.'

'What do you mean? Are you part of that lot?'

'God, no! It's just I was on my way home from shopping—phone wasn't working properly, that's why I couldn't do it online before you ask. Anyway, as I was coming home, I somehow ended up coming head on with the mob. I tried to get away from it all but I sucked in. I just bounced around between protesters here and there until I had to somehow crawl myself out of there when a fight broke out.'

'I see. Was it the protest they have been talking about on the news? I think there was a mass brawl between the group and police.'

'I don't know if it was on the news, but needless to say, I got bombarded by a water cannon.'

'The hell?! Are you alright?'

'I've been in better places on other days. Today isn't one of them. Got a headache from hitting my head after falling into something.'

'Take the day off then.'

'No, better I stay. Besides, if I remember correctly, we have that reskilling program to complete now thanks to Illumina.'

'Ah, yeah, there's that... I understand now why you wanted to chat about this privately.'

'Yeah. And given how my latest meeting with the shrinks went down, I'd rather not give the bank any more reason to make a case to cut ties with me.'

'You lost your shit, didn't you?'

'*Yeah*... how did you know?'

'Because I lost my shit as well. Went on a whole rant about everything for fifteen minutes straight: about my pay, about management, about the stupid AI. And by the end of it, they simply told me to have a nice day and ended the meeting. And, also, get this, it was done by AI too.'

'I was told something similar.'

William returned his attention to his screens to see if anything had popped up about the reskilling program. A pop-up alert appeared on screen about the meeting having already started for the program.

'Hey, it looks like we have to head into the meeting.'

'Yeah, let's see how it goes.'

William joined the video conference. General pleasantries were exchanged between the presenters and participants. Once everyone arrived, then the meeting actually commenced.

'Hey everyone,' one presenter said. 'I'll be going through our 2-week recalibration program. Please understand that this will be important for those who are participating. There's a lot we'll be doing while we're together as there will be an evaluation at the end of the program to determine performance, and especially employment. So, please if we could---'

'Wait, wait!' one participant said. 'Sorry! Don't mean to cut you off. What did you mean by employment? Are you saying that if we don't perform well, we're going to lose our jobs?'

'I'm saying that those who perform will be given a chance to partake in the reskilling program. Those who do not perform well will be offered a voluntary redundancy package.'

'So essentially fired. How's that even possible? I've been with this company for sixteen years. I don't want to lose my job.'

'Yeah! I don't want to either,' another participant said.

'Come on, seriously?' a third voice came over the others. 'I have to prove myself again to the company.'

'I'm going to have to stop all of you there,' the presenter said, authoritatively 'This program has to begin. If you have concerns, please address them to your line manager or HR. However, this is an executive decision, so if you do not want to proceed further with the program, you can take the voluntary redundancy package now. But if you want to stay and see how you fare with the 2-week program, stay and give it your all. The choice is yours.' He looked at the camera, face stern and unwavering.

CHAPTER 7

Doesn't sound like a choice, William thought. He waited for someone to respond but no one did.

He sighed, and relaxed his tensed muscles. 'Now, I understand that this must be a difficult time. I get it. It's a difficult time for all of us. But this is a welcomed change. The bank has always been a big advocate for the use of technology, and it's finally in a position to elevate its operations, services, and results to our customers. We still want the best to stay with us however we can't keep everyone on board anymore. We are sincerely sorry for this. If we could, we would.'

Without further delay, the presenters provided an overview of skills each participant needed to learn throughout the two weeks before their evaluation. Most skills touched on data analysis, machine learning and cloud engineering—all of which would further enable Illumina to function within the organization.

'With that out of the way, everyone who has been assigned to the reskilling program probably would have received an email to join a group with a designated trainer. This will be your trainer for the next two weeks until the exam, so take advantage of the opportunity to learn everything you can from it.'

'In all my time here,' Tom said, who was William's teammate, 'I didn't think I would have to do a test to determine my competency and worth as an employee. I've done so much for this bank, and achieved all the results you asked of me. I find this extremely offensive.'

'Second that,' Lena added. William's teammates. 'We've all done a lot for this bank.'

'I'm sorry you feel like that, but you'll still have a chance to achieve many more great things once you pass the exam.'

'Don't know if I want to.'

While the training continued throughout the day, William couldn't fight off the tightness across his neck and back, as the possibility of really losing his job sank in. The added disinterest in learning these new skills he didn't care about made it worse, as it seemed more like just delayed redundancy for those who survived the program. Also seemed like just another way for the bank to save face in the eyes of the public.

'There's gotta be something we can do?' Marlene messaged him privately.

'Doesn't look like there is anything we can do,' William said. 'The only options are: take your voluntary redundancy now or later. However, we don't know if there will be an option for voluntary redundancy later. They never mentioned anything to us.'

'Are you going to take it?'

'I honestly don't know. I haven't seen the package. Don't even know if I want to see it. You?'

'I'll wait and see how the reskilling program goes, but I'm going to figure out something to stop this from happening. I'll see what the unions will have to say about this.'

'I doubt they are going to be able to do anything.'

'I know but if they can't do something, then I'll figure out something. I won't stop. I'll take it to the news if I have to. I mean they can't force us out like this. This is our livelihood we are talking about. We all need our jobs. Don't you want us to stay here?'

'With this happening now, and how things have got worse in the last few months, who would want to? I mean I get the fact about keeping a job and that does freak me out... but... I'd be just a number to the bank in the meantime while the infrastructure is built for Illumina to have further capabilities within bank operations, and I don't think I'd want to be around for that.'

'Come on, Will. This is your job you're talking about. Why did you get into the bank in the first place then?'

'Because I needed a job and wanted to work from home. Plus, the pay was okay... it could be better but it was enough at the time for me.'

'And what about since then? You've made friends. You got me. Aren't we worth fighting for in this situation?'

William contemplated her question. He hadn't thought of it like that. Friends? That word itself has changed and lost its meaning.

'Will?'

'I wish I could give you an answer, Mal, but it's not an easy decision to make.'

'I guess it was a good thing then that I found out how you feel about our friendship.'

'Don't be like that, Mal. I don't know what to make of this. It's a shit situation.'

'Of course, it's a shit situation. WE'RE LOSING OUR JOBS... That means no money, which means we can't pay our bills. Which means living poor or potentially dying in this case.' She paused. 'Look, I'm gonna go.'

'Mal.' No response came back. 'Mal.' Same thing happened so he called but she didn't answer.

Goddammit!

When the first day was over, he left his office and crashed into his bean bag. With his drained mind and battered body, the last thing he wanted to do was stay awake but he couldn't afford to sleep now. There were still hours left in the day to do something yet he didn't what to do.

He hopped on his phone and ordered his food before scrolling through YouTube, watching videos to pass the time. His attention didn't linger too long on any of the videos before moving onto the next one. This lasted for about ten minutes, then thoroughly bored, he dropped the phone. He tossed around in bed, trying to make himself comfortable until he saw Ramses by the door.

'Are you having as much fun as I am?' he asked, then sighed. 'I can barely do anything at the moment. And I'm pretty much free for next few hours which makes it worse. What am I supposed to do with myself?'

'*Oh, you talk to your friends?*' Will said in his cat voice.

'What friends, Ramses? I don't have anyone that I can talk to at the moment aside from Kristie.'

'*Well, if you actually went out and did something, then you might have made friends.*'

'Yeah, right. Who in their right mind would go out today to do something? What fun is there to be had in meeting people who all want to meet and spend time on Zerya. How dull...'

'*That might explain your problem.*'

'You think?'

He browsed his messages, looking at the names of people, most of whom he hadn't spoken to for months. He stopped at Janyce's name for a moment as there were seven messages he'd missed. He pulled up her messages.

'Hey luv, everything alright?' she'd messaged him a few days ago. 'It's been a while. Call me if you're looking to relax again. I promise for a little something-something on the price... I'll wear this as your reward.' A photo of her wearing a black tight g-string and lingerie followed the message. 'You know what the prize is when it's off.' Another photo followed of her naked body in full view.

He shook his head and chuckled. He deleted all the messages. *I can't be looking at this. Not anymore.*

Then he moved onto Kristie. He opened the file, reading some of the messages they exchanged before he sent one.

'Hey, how was your today?' he messaged. 'You still working at the moment?'

'Hey! Yeah, I'm working,' she messaged a minute later. 'Haven't been doing much nowadays. Just being put into a reskilling program as they want us moved elsewhere.'

'You as well?! What are they getting you to do?'

'They're getting us to do everything. But mostly focusing on programming and machine skills.'

'To work with AI?'

'Yeah... what are you doing?'

'Just finished work. Waiting on food now.'

'Lucky. What will you do afterward?'

'Don't know. I thought maybe we could catch up but that'll have to wait until later.'

'I'd like that. I'll see if I can leave early.'

'Cool. Just shoot me a message.'

'I will.'

'Anyway, I have to get back. Can't afford to risk anything right now as the company has everyone under the scope.'

'It's alright. I understand. We'll talk later.'

'Of course!'

William marched out of his room, heading for the windows in the living room. The fog seemed to have mostly dissipated its murky haze, allowing a little more visibility.

He stared towards the city on the horizon, where tall skyscrapers loomed high above the remaining yellow haze. He shifted his gaze to the streets below but could see little movement.

Traffic congestion was a thing of the past as the workplace for many companies had changed due to the Smog, where people could work from home for as long as they wanted—only transportation vehicles like automated trams and buses passed through now, although carrying one or two people, or no one at all.

He pulled out his phone to take a photo, when he received an alert to replenish his respirator. 'Fuck! I completely forgot.' He logged into a portal to send a request for two new oxygen masks and another hazmat suit, suspecting his current suit had received damage and tears from his troubling experience with the police.

Once his orders were made, he noted that time for delivery was estimated within a two-hour time frame from packaging to arrival at his doorstep.

Beep, beep! His phone chimed from a video call. He stared at the screen and realized it was a family chat video invitation. He didn't want to answer the call as he had an idea how it was going to play out.

'Oh god no,' he said. 'Not now.'

He didn't answer the call at first, choosing to stare at the screen while the phone rang and rang. When it ended, another call came through with a message sent to him too. He didn't have to give it much thought about his response as he knew he wasn't going to do anything.

'Hey Will, are you not joining the chat?' Sasha messaged. 'Everyone's here waiting for you.'

Why? He watched the message pop up on his home screen but didn't open it further to avoid alerting her that he'd read the message.

'Come on, Will. I know you've read the message. I'm not stupid. Just join in for a moment. Everyone misses you. You've missed the last few calls. It'd be nice to see you again just once.'

Doubt it...

He sighed, weighing the pros and cons of answering the call in a short space of time, drafting up a list of cons, and no pros—something he wasn't trying to find.

'Just answer, man,' Sasha said. 'It's only for a few minutes. If it's not good, leave.'

He heeded his sister's advice, placed his phone on a phone-holder, with the phone towards him as he jumped on his beanbag. He connected his phone to his projector to see the video in a bigger picture on the wall before accepting the invite. He didn't want to use his hologram console to avoid having his parents actually show up in his place.

Within seconds, four screens appeared on his wall with someone present in each box—his dad, mum, elder brother and younger sister.

'Ah, is it Will?' his mum said.

'I think it is,' Sasha said.

'Hey everyone,' William said, pretending to sound interested.

'Oh, my dear boy!' his mum said. She had dyed black flowing hair, and appeared well past her prime but seemed full of life the moment Will joined the call. 'Is it really you? You look so different from the last time we spoke. Is everything alright?'

'Give him a chance to speak,' his bespectacled dad said. White hair sprouted from his head, jawline and double chin. 'Or at least breathe, you know?'

'Hi Mum,' William said. 'Dad.'

'Son,' his dad said. 'Is everything okay?'

'Everything's been alright. Same old here.' He decided to keep his troubles to himself.'

'After nine months you'd think something would have changed, right?' His tone underlined with amusement and disappointment at the same time.

'Right you are on that.' He looked at his brother to steer his attention elsewhere without having to offer an answer. 'Chris, how you been?'

'Long time no see bro,' Chris said, wearing his usual formal attire, white shirt and black tie and blazer. 'How you doing?'

'You look like you're doing the same thing or something similar. You always seem to be coming from one or about to go to a business meeting.'

'Some things never change, you know.'

'I do.' Then he turned his attention to the only person he really didn't mind seeing. 'How you doing, Sasha? Everything going well with uni?'

'Everything's alright,' Sasha said. She too had flowing black hair, natural as opposed to their mother's. 'Coming up to final exams for the semester now. That's going to be fun. Also, it's the second year of uni. Making progress slowly. It's a relief knowing that it's closer to the end.'

'What was your degree again? Engineering?'

'Computer science.'

Oh, god. I do hope you can use it when you start working, he wanted to say but kept a tight lip. Despite seeing firsthand the real-world consequences of AI, he didn't want to dampen her hopes. 'Well, it's good to hear that you're almost done. A bit of relief off the shoulders.' He looked to his mum and dad. 'Mum, Dad. Everything alright with you? Is work going okay?'

'Well, I can't speak for your mother,' his dad said, 'but I've just retired.'

'No kidding!' William said. 'I don't know if I should be congratulating you or not. Did you decide to do that or were there other factors in play?'

'Oh, there were things involved that led to the decision but it's alright, overall. I've done enough work to live well for the rest of my life. Anyway, I'll have my family to help out should things go bad.'

'Right.' William feigned a laugh.

'Plus, Chris just recently secured a position as a sales executive for a telecommunications company. He'll be the breadwinner of this family now so you've got some competition there if you're thinking of improving your position.'

'Who said we were competing?'

'Oh no, it's not that you are. I just mean you could do so much better.'

'Huh... okay.'

'You have to take a look at the house your brother got for us,' his mum said. 'It's bigger than the house I grew up in. Could probably fit the family from my side twice over. I mean in times like this, you don't expect that something this good will come around.' She started tearing up.

'It's alright, Mum,' Chris said. 'It's the least I could do after everything you've done for me. I'm happy to help.'

'You bought them a house?' William asked. 'When was this?'

'Just recently. Everything was settled last month I believe, and I got the key so it's just a matter of me giving it to Mum and Dad so they can start moving into the place.'

'No loan?'

'Didn't need one. Had enough to cover everything.'

'How about that.'

'What did I do to deserve this?' his mum said.

'Oh, enough with that, Laura,' his dad said, 'This is a catch up. Not a meet-and-cry sess.'

'I agree,' Sasha said. 'How's things at work, Will? Anything interesting happening lately? Read your bank has started using AI in some of the services. How's that coming along?'

William paused, contemplating whether he should tell them of the situation at work with Illumina and the problems it was bringing for him and everyone else. It must have been a few minutes that flew by as his family was calling out his name.

'Will?' his dad said.

'Will, you there?' Sasha said.

'What?' William said. 'Oh! Sorry. I spaced out there for a moment. Umm... work. It's alright. Same old. I recently had an interview for a job in another department within the bank. It seems interesting and I want to give it a go.' He lied just to give them news in the hopes it would steer them away from his current situation.

'How's the pay?'

'Not sure yet. I'll find out hopefully when I do the interview with them.'

'Well, if it's not higher than what you're getting now don't bother with it. It's just going to waste your time.'

'Not if I like the work.'

'Liking something isn't going to help with your situation, Will. You have history to look to for that and you know it.'

So much for lying about the job interview, William thought. 'What situation?'

'*Harold*,' his mum said, sounding like she wanted to stop the conversation from leading further in a particular direction.

'No, no, it's alright, Mum,' Will said. 'What situation are you talking about, Dad?'

'You're in a dead-end job,' his dad said. 'It's not going to get you places. You need to network, study some more to get yourself in a better position.'

'Whatever gave you the impression that is something I need or want.'

'Because it works. I mean look at your brother—bringing the funds to help support himself, and by extension the family.'

William found his breathing quicken within seconds. The comparison never seemed to stop. He stood up, staring directly at his dad. 'So what I'm getting from this is, you want me to make a whole lot of money just so you can be well off.'

'I didn't say that.'

'Of course, you did. You even mentioned it earlier—you have us to help you if things go south.'

'That's only if I ever needed it. After all, we're family.'

'So, it's family when it concerns me and *money*, but any other time, it's not. Is that what I'm hearing.'

'I didn't say that.'

He exhaled, doing his best to control himself. Didn't work as he would have hoped.

CHAPTER 7

'Your father is right, Will,' his mum said. 'I mean I see a lot of myself in you. You do certain things because you like doing them and it does help to pay the bills, but it's not enough. At some point you just have to take the risk to try something better. Like remember the story of the guy I knew in—'

'Mum, you and I are not the same. Just like Chris and I are not the same, and how Sasha and I are not as well.'

'You are because you come from us,' his dad said. 'We're all in this together. Family is family.'

'Okay, are you me? Are you in my thoughts? Cause it sounds a lot like forcing me into doing things that I don't want to do in order to help *you*. See, this is one of the reasons why I don't join these chats anymore because somehow it always ends up with me having to defend my life choices. Just feels like an interrogation every single time, and I'm over it. Really. I mean, does my job suck? Maybe. Are there other jobs that would offer similar pay? Without a doubt. But am I comfortable? Yes. Am I able to do things that I want to do? Yes. Can I work from home? Yes. That should be enough, no? If you're so keen on money, ask Chris for some. That way you can look at the numbers in your bank account if that's what makes you feel better.'

'That was uncalled for, Will,' his mum said.

'Uncalled for? I didn't raise the subject, and I didn't make comparisons about people here. I didn't start talking about money. Are you going to ask Sasha the same thing when she's done with her studies? I hope not.'

'They already have,' Sasha said.

'Will, mind your manners,' his dad said. 'We're just looking out for you. We just have your best intentions here.'

He scoffed, taking a moment to gather his thoughts. 'Look, I'm just—I'm just gonna go. Thanks for the invite, Sasha. Love you and take care. See you when I... see you.' He ended the call before anyone could say another word.

William dropped like a bag of potatoes onto his beanbag. Holding his head in his hands, he took his time to settle his nerves. Anger and frustration as usual followed his family chat.

What the hell man?!

CHAPTER 8

DISGRUNTLED BY HIS chat with his family, William found himself quick to snap at anyone who was snide towards him or basically at anything in general. He wished he could be on calls to voice his frustrations on customers, particularly those who seemed self-entitled and snobbish about their credit applications.

He had his wireless headphones connected to a live training session on coding for Illumina, all the while wondering, '*What am I doing?*' His attention was running on a thin thread. He waited eagerly for the break.

When his break came, he left his apartment to throw the rubbish down the garbage chute. Clutter upon clutter piled up with takeout containers and emptied cartons amassed in the laundry room. He carried the bag to the chute but it wouldn't open. No matter how much he tried to pull, it wouldn't budge.

He checked his emails for any building alerts—one came through about the chute systems being under repairs and residents were expected to descend to the lower ground level to throw their rubbish in the bins. No ETA was provided on when the repairs would be completed, however, if history was any indication for William, he knew it was going to take a week or longer before it was done.

Dammit.

He sighed and returned to his apartment to put on his mask, suit and everything else before he made his way back. He hopped into an elevator and arrived at the lower levels underground. He detoxified himself before leaving the lobby, and heading into the carpark. As he walked to the bins, he saw nothing but dusty parked cars that seemed not to have moved in a long time.

Creak, creak!

CHAPTER 8

William stopped in his tracks and looked around, wondering where the sound came from. He threw his rubbish in the bin, and then it happened again. Not wanting to stick around any longer, he raced back to the elevator when suddenly someone appeared, toppling over him.

He looked to see a small masked figure with a damaged respirator and torn hazmat suit, gasping for air. They seemed hysterical and frightened.

'Please help me,' the masked figure said. The muffled voice sounded like a man. 'Please help me.'

'What? What are you talking about?' He pushed upright, trying to get away from but the person clasped leg with both hands. 'Get off me.'

'Please! I didn't do anything wrong.'

'What are you talking about?'

The masked mask lifted himself up, grabbing hold of William's suit. 'They're after me. They think I'm part of Gaia.'

'Are you?'

The man didn't answer.

Dzun, dzun!

William recognised the sound. He looked at the man who appeared afraid for his life.

'Please help me, they're going to—' He couldn't finish his sentence as a shot hit him in the back of his head. Blood gushed out, some spraying over William's suit.

William looked up to see two Enforcers approaching him. He slumped to the ground again, feeling helpless.

'Where would we be going, citizen?' one Enforcer asked.

'I—uh, I,' William said, looking back at the man, whose head remained stuck on the ground in a pool of his own blood.

'Do you know this person?'

'No.'

'What was he doing with you?'

'He—uh—he crashed into me. I was just heading upstairs after throwing out the rubbish.'

'Do you live here?"

'Yes.'

The Enforcer scanned the barcode on William's hazmat suit. Red light flashed up and down before disappearing. 'William Kepler, citizen of Sydney

City. Zero breaches. Zero detections of contamination. That still doesn't explain this man. Are you aware this man works for Gaia and was responsible for the breaches on this building?'

'Like I said, he crashed into me. I have no idea who he was nor have I met him before. He's just kept saying—' He paused.

'Saying?'

'Kept *asking* for help.'

The Enforcer returned its attention to the dead man. 'Very well, you're free to go.'

William pushed himself away from the man, feeling his now lifeless hand brushing against his leg and onto the ground. He fled the area quickly to avoid any further questioning.

As he waited for the elevator at arrive on his floor, his stomach churned. He removed his mask for air, as he felt ready to throw up. He tried to hold it in, then Mr. Watson hopped on which made it worse.

'Will?' Mr. Watson said, noticing the blood on William's suit.

'Mr. Watson?' William said.

'Everything alright, my boy? You're pale-faced.'

'I'm okay.'

'You don't look it. What happened?'

'It was a Purge.'

'*Here?*'

William nodded.

The elevator arrived at their floor, and William didn't waste time dawdling. He heard Mr. Watson call for him but he didn't look back or respond, and headed straight into his apartment to vomit. He sat on the bathroom floor, recovering, staring at the bloodstains on his defense suit.

His work laptop rang a few times but he didn't care right now. He'd just seen another person Purged.

Just like that... you're gone. One second, you're alive, the next you're... lying in a pool of your own blood.

He sat in his bathroom for another ten minutes, and then removed his clothes and defense suit. He wanted to shower—even though nothing got onto his skin—to clean off uncomfortable feelings of guilt and horror. But naturally he was out of his water quota for the day. He replaced his clothes with fresh ones and resumed work, although he kept seeing blood on his fresh set of clothes. He closed his eyes, believing his mind was tricking him, and then opened them. Nothing was there afterward.

Once the day was over, William visited Mr. Watson. He buzzed the doorbell, hearing footsteps approaching the door—Mr. Watson answered.

'Will, are you okay?' he asked.

'Yeah, I'm okay,' William said. 'I'm better than I was when... Anyway, I wanted to apologize before. I didn't mean to be rude when I didn't reply.'

'It's okay. You saw a Purge. It's not easy to stomach.'

William nodded. 'Well, I'm gonna go now. Didn't mean to bother you.'

'Why don't you join me and Mary for dinner?'

'I don't want to impose.'

'It's no imposition. You still look pale, and I think it'd do you some good to have company and a good meal after what happened.'

William considered. 'Sure.'

'Great. It'll be ready in about an hour. Come over then.'

For the next hour, he tried to free himself of the vivid memories by watching videos of anything distracting but it didn't work. He looked outside to the streets to see if there were any Enforcers or police around. There weren't any.

He remembered what the Enforcer had said about the man working for Gaia and the breaches. He couldn't remember a time where he'd seen the man living here in his building. Then again, he couldn't remember any of his neighbours' faces except for the old man who was Purged and Mr. Watson. He kept thinking and thinking until the hour passed, and he returned to Mr. Watson's apartment.

The apartment was filled with many things, family photos and single portraits, a set of brown leather couches, a dining table and coffee table with coasters all over the place. As he made his way further into the apartment, he could hear slow jazz music coming from a cassette player. *What's that?* He wondered as he had never seen anything like it, or an apartment like this before.

'I hope you're hungry,' Mr. Watson said. 'Mary's cooking her casserole.' He entered the kitchen, where an elderly lady with bleached blonde hair, standing the same height as Mr. Watson, cooking by the stove. 'Mary! Mary, we have company today.'

'Company?' Mrs. Watson said. 'What am I? A cooking hostess for the entire building.'

'Don't be like that. We could certainly use the company considering we don't get any.' He faced William. 'This is Will. He's our neighbour right next door to us—the one I've told you about before.'

'The bank specialist, right?'

'I am,' William said, confused. 'How did you know?'

'Henry talks more about people than he should.'

'No, I don't,' Mr. Watson said, defiantly.

'Well, anyway food is ready, so if you're going to eat, you can help set up the table. The plates are on the cabinet there.' She pointed to the nearest cabinet and looked back at the sauce she was stirring.

'Certainly.'

'Great, that makes one of you.'

'Ha ha very funny,' Mr. Watson said.

A moment later, William was sitting around the table with his fellow neighbours. He ate his meal slowly—even though he wanted to eat it fast as it was so good. He hadn't eaten a home-cooked meal in a long time. He couldn't remember the last time he had a meal at home that wasn't ordered online.

'So how is it?' Mrs. Watson asked.

'It's really good.'

'Try having it every day,' Mr. Watson quipped.

'Oi! What's that supposed to mean?'

Mr. Watson laughed.

'So, which bank do you work for, Will?'

'Pinnacle Bank,' William said. 'Been there for about three years now.'

'Are you liking it?'

'It's okay. It pays the bills and helps with any other money problems I may have. Sort of. Do you work?'

'Henry? Work?' Mrs. Watson burst out laughing.

'What's that supposed to mean?' Mr. Watson asked.

'You once did. Not anymore.'

'Well, I help around the house, and keep you company. That takes work. A lot actually.'

'I know you do. I'm just kidding.'

'So, retired then?' William said.

'Yeah.'

'How long ago was that?'

'Twenty years ago. Maybe more. I don't remember.'

'Things must have been simpler back then.'

'Indeed they were. There were people around. You could have conversations with people. You know? Be in their company. But it's so different now. Even before the Smog hit us, I'd try to talk to people in the supermarkets or wherever I go shopping. Barely a response came back. They'd have their ear pods in or something. Completely lost in another world. They'd just walk past you. I could only imagine what it is like nowadays at work.'

'I get what you mean,' William said, thinking better not to discuss his job or be reminded about the changes. 'How did the two of you meet?'

'I holla'd. She came running.' Mr. Watson chuckled.

'Did not!' Mrs. Watson admonished. 'He thinks he's so funny. Truth of the matter is, I was working at the markets one day and I was helping some customers when he came around.'

'Surprising fact: I never did go there again.'

'What are markets?' William asked.

'There are where you can go and buy fresh veggies and fruits, and the other assorted things. Locals would come along to bring their own produce to sell. The quality was so much better than what we get nowadays. But anyway, he arrived and we got to talking. He was telling me that he'd heard about the place and wanted to see what it was all about. Funnily enough he didn't know a single thing about produce and what makes it good or bad.'

'That's because I was so occupied by you talking. I didn't get a word in.'

'*Hardly.*'

'Anyway, I may not have known anything but I did know enough to get you to join me for dinner.'

'That you did. He was a charmer back in the day.'

'Still am.' He winked at William.

'So, how about you, Will?' Mrs. Watson asked, her eyes on him with a cheeky smile. 'Do you have someone in your life?'

'I do but I find it's different to what dating might have been like for you.'

'Because of that port thing? Zerya, or whatever it's called.'

'Yeah, and I don't do well with meeting new people. Especially face-to-face.'

'Have you met her or him?' Mr. Watson asked.

'Henry!' Mrs. Watson.

'What? I don't know what he likes, and I don't want to assume. You know what happens to people nowadays if you say something others might take offense at.'

'It's alright,' William said, chuckling. 'I haven't met her in person yet. But I have seen her hologram, so I know what she looks like.'

'That's so strange, don't you think?' She looked at Henry.

'It is,' Mr. Watson said. 'Don't you find it difficult to actually connect with someone with that thing—Zerya?'

'It can be,' William said. 'I mean I haven't been in many relationships, so I've never been good at it.'

'But you want to be with someone, right?'

'I want—I want company, I think. I don't have many friends, and those who I know have their own lives, so they're busy. I don't get to see them often. Even if I wanted to, we have our lockdown rules. I wouldn't make it far past my LGA without the police knowing and sending me back home, or worse, putting me in jail. Everything is so virtual and distant, nothing feels real.'

Both Watsons remained silent.

'Sorry, I didn't want to bore you with all that.'

'It's perfectly alright,' Mrs. Watson said. 'We have an idea. It's a struggle in keeping up contact with people... especially love ones. In your case, the best thing you can do is to keep looking for something real. That connection, that love you find in someone real, goes beyond anything you'll get in life. Don't stop looking.'

William nodded in appreciation. As he continued to eat, he watched Henry follow Mary into the kitchen and muck around. He smiled in amusement to see an elderly couple still having such fun and love for each other.

Before leaving, he and Mr. Watson exchanged words.

'I wanted to let you know,' Mr. Watson said, 'that I didn't tell anyone including Mary about the Purge.'

'Thank you,' William said.

'It's alright. I couldn't tell her even if I wanted to. She'd go bananas. Anyway, do something to take your mind off what happened. Perhaps go for a walk.'

'Is that even allowed?'

'It is. Just don't do it for too long. It might help to get outside after being cooped up by yourself in your apartment for so long.'

'Will do. Thank you for the invite, Mr. Watson. And please tell your wife, "Thank you for the meal."'

'Will do.' Mr. Watson smiled. 'And, please, call me, Henry.'

'Of course.'

William headed back home and suited up. He took the advice and left his apartment, believing anything other than sitting at home for another minute would be better.

Three minutes later, he strolled through the streets, heading for the city on foot. He was only allowed to travel within his LGA. There was no destination in mind he wanted to visit but he did know he had to keep moving to distract his mind from the self-degrading agony he brought on himself whenever there was a family discussion about his circumstances and perceived lack of achievements.

The simple activity of walking seemed strange to him now—to leisurely go and walk about during these dire times where everything, even the smallest of actions, were noted and monitored. One slip up and it'd be all over for anyone. Although, as he continued to cross the streets and venture onward, his thoughts and frustration gradually disappeared. He smiled, his cheek muscles feeling strange and new against the mask. Everything was okay for the moment.

Hmph... odd.

His walk led him to a park but not one he was accustomed to seeing from images on the internet or Zerya, where impossibly green healthy trees flourished around the virtual park. The closer he got to the real park, the clearer he saw the reality of life since the Smog.

Dead yellow leaves and twigs crunched beneath his boots as he passed dried up grey trees that seemed to have lost all water, all life. Every branch was broken or deformed. He turned his gaze left to see yellow and brown grassy areas covered in the bones of dead birds and other small animals.

He stood in the centre of the park, looking at everything, wondering what the future held, while life as he had known it was slowly dying.

Then something in the sky caught his attention. He couldn't make out what it was as it moved through the murky haze. He had to squint to get a better look until a clear patch of the sky beyond the haze appeared. The moment lasted several seconds but was enough to see two wedge-tailed eagles. Their majestic brown wings glided through the air as they thrust their proud chests outward for all to see.

'No freaking way,' he muttered, and chuckled in disbelief, watching the eagles fly before the haze engulfed them. He moved his eyes around the sky to find them again but to no avail.

He left the park and continued walking until he found nearby stores and restaurants—none of which were open for public use—then saw a local bar off the street corner open to the public. He headed inside, detoxified and sat by a side table. He declined to order anything when a waiter approached, and continued to look around. Only men occupied the place. He looked up to rows of screens on the wall of live-streaming sport events—all of which took place in stadiums underground—and spotted an automated trolley bringing around food and alcoholic drinks.

Nothing much interested him until a conversation from the table behind grabbed his attention.

'How much time do you want?' a man asked through raspy, damaged vocal cords.

'Not much,' another man said. 'About thirty minutes. I just need to see someone in the neighbouring LGA.'

'That's gonna cost 150 credits. 10 credits per minute for every minute after.'

'I'll transfer it into your bank account.'

'No, don't do that. Wire it instead into my TAB account.'

'I'll do it now.'

'What time do you need this done?'

'Five-thirty in the afternoon tomorrow.'

'Alright, you can go now.'

'Thank you. Thank you very much.'

William waited, and watched a man zipped up his hazmat suit over his formal suit before leaving the place. He heard the other person leave the table and approached the bar. He could see long bleached hair coming over his face. Wanting to know more about this deal, he walked up to the man.

'Excuse me,' William said.

The man faced William, revealing a pale face, borderline malnourished or ill. The man silently assessed him. 'What do you want?'

William sat down beside the man and spoke softly. 'I couldn't help but overhear your conversation about getting someone to another LGA.'

'I think you heard wrong. Now beat it.'

CHAPTER 8

'Listen, I just—'

The man grabbed William by the collar, yanking his face towards his own. 'No, you listen. Unless you want to leave the place in a body bag, I suggest you leave.'

William struggled to fight off the foul breath but didn't resist. He raised his bank card. 'You're a Walker, right? I assume that you understand the value of credits then.'

The man looked at the bank card. He seemed to be considering the offer. He released William. 'How much time?'

'An hour.'

'When?'

'Now.'

The man held his glass mid-air before skolled the alcohol, then dropped it down. 'Follow me.'

William followed the man back to the side table, watched him remove a small touchpad device from his pocket and input commands as it lit up.

'What's that?' William asked.

The man didn't answer. He continued to input commands then spoke without looking at William. 'Send me your port address?'

'Sure.'

The man seemed to have punched the address into the device. A red light flashed several times before it switched to green. 'Okay, it's done.'

'What did you just do?'

'I've switched your address with mine.'

'How?'

'Forget how. Now, the credits.'

William paid his credits into the TAB account.

'Be back here within the hour.'

'How can I be certain it worked?'

'You need only check yourself.'

William heeded to the instructions and checked his phone. He logged onto his Zerya account and spotted the change in his port address. *It worked.*

'Best you be off towards the Bayside LGA. Your time is ticking.'

Without delay, William left the place and headed towards the Bayside LGA. He crossed the boundary line and hailed an automated taxi to drive to the center. He walked around the area, looking at the buildings and parks.

There weren't many noticeable differences between the Bayside LGA and his own LGA, he was out at least, somewhere different.

Eventually, hunger set in. Knowing there wasn't any restaurant available for a dine and eat arrangement he ordered his food at a nearby restaurant—rice and porkchop, side of soup. He made his way to the place to pick up his food. The warmth from the sun eased the cold chill passing through the streets. Whenever the sunlight hit the ground, he walked in its path to feel its healing warmth on his neck and back. It wasn't often a sun's ray would come through the haze but when it he took advantage of it.

Upon arrival, he found his meal inside a generic eco-container, ready to go. He paid and left the shop. He scanned the area to head home, this time looking out for the crazy mob protesters storming the streets, as he didn't want to get in the middle of crossfire and get attacked by the police. Again.

They never stop, do they?

Then he spotted a familiar face. The girl from the Aconic had left the shop and was headed to an unknown location. He turned away in a quick motion and power-walked and kept on going. He didn't want her to know he was there. But curiosity about her presence stopped him in his tracks.

He completed a U-turn and watched her veer left towards another street. He didn't like stalking but the way this girl carried herself was different from any other girl he had known or met. He followed her, keeping distance about fifty meters away from her. The trip led him towards the inner lands, beyond the LGA to a place he had known in the media as the brewing grounds for uncharted, lawless individuals: No Man's Land.

What would she be doing there?

No Man's Land went ungoverned after a civil war had occurred many years ago. No one lived in the area beyond the city for safety and civility reasons, from what he heard from his family, colleagues and online contacts. He stopped in front of a fifteen-meter barbed-wire fence separating the city and the district. The grounds saw dead roots and bodies populated the terrain all around. A quick glance at the girl triggered movement as she was getting away. He squeezed through the gate and followed her.

The Walker is going to kill me.

While making quick progress on closing the distance, he surveyed the area to see many damaged buildings, walls charcoal black from fires, giant holes punctured through the walls and ceilings, and no signs of life inside any of them. And yet, this girl was already passing the first set of blocks, seemingly unfazed by the surroundings. He looked around, wondering why. It wasn't a crime to go into No Man's Land but it was highly regarded as unsafe and ill-advised for anyone venturing into the area alone.

One particular rumor about the district involved rats the size of rugby balls living underground. The morphed rats were considered hostile and would attack anything and anyone. News broke out one day of someone being eaten alive by these rats as they got lost one night.

Probably living in the sewers helped them survive the Smog.

He looked back at the girl. Not wanting to lose her, he checked his watch: 14:37 PM. There was time to still follow her. Nightfall was too far ahead to be of a concern at this moment. He followed the girl, finding himself running to get closer as the girl made a turn right.

Dammit, I'm losing her!

He ran and ran until he arrived on the street. The girl had disappeared. He rushed forward looking for her, then something latched onto his foot and yanked it into the air. The sudden motion swung him around when his head smacked against the concrete and everything went black.

CHAPTER 9

'HEY, WAKE UP,' a woman's voice echoed in the dark.

'What?' William said, not sure if he was dreaming.

'Hey, wake up!' the voice said, clearer this time.

Whack! A hard slap struck across the right side of his mask. William's eyes fluttered open, and as his vision adjusted to the light and scenery, pain radiating through his skull. He massaged his head and murmured, 'Oh, god.'

Fear overtook pain shortly after, as he realised, he was suspended upside-down in the air with a heavy head filling up with blood. He looked directly at the girl he'd been following. She didn't seem impressed with this development. His eyes trailed down to her hand locked onto a pistol with a bottle taped around the muzzle.

'What are you doing following me?' she asked.

'What?'

Another slap struck his face. 'You have ten seconds.'

'Jesus Christ. Look, I just—' He didn't know what to say.

'One... two...'

'Okay, okay.' He held his hands in front of his face to protect it against another slap—not that another slap was his main problem. 'Just give me a moment.'

'Three... Four... Five...'

'I just... you, umm made me curious...'

'What?'

'Not in that way, I just mean, you're different. I know you told me not to bother you from before?'

'Before?'

'It's just... I've never seen anyone go shopping before in person. I mean everything is done online, I mean you can do it in a few minutes and the shopping appears at your door in twenty minutes.'

She slapped him again. 'Cut the crap. Who sent you?'

'I don't—'

'Who do you work for? Is it the police?'

'The police? What?'

She aimed her weapon closer to his face.

'Oh, damn! Look! I don't work for anyone, alright?! I told you already. I mean look at me. Seriously, how on earth can I be a threat? I'm a lanky, disposable vessel of bodily fluids and mass. What use am I to anyone?'

She paused for a moment. 'Was it Joseph? He sent you to get me to come over to return the favour. It's not going to happen. My debt has been paid.'

'Who's Joseph?'

She raised her pistol, aiming right for his head. 'Consider this payment.'

'I swear to you I don't know what you're talking about. I just—' he sighed. 'Look, I don't know what to say to you. I mean, do you want to look at my ID? Here!' He took out his wallet and passed it to her. 'I'm just a person—that very one you threatened at Aconic. I'm just an... ordinary person. I swear I mean you no harm.'

William averted his gaze and looked at the concrete to avoid the girl's piercing gaze. He couldn't tell if she was trying to look into his soul to see falsehood in his words.

She took the wallet and examined the contents, before checking his identification card. 'You?'

Beep, beep! A phone rang. He reached for his phone, however, the girl pulled out one from her pocket. It was a call for her.

'Hey,' she said, walking away from him.

Who would she be talking to? he thought.

'Yeah... I'm sorry. I'm just running late... I got held up...' She ended the call before returning her attention to him. She approached and remained still—her eyes fixed on him as if trying to make a decision on what to do with him. She sighed loudly and left the area.

'Umm... you're not leaving me like this, are you?'

No response.

'Hello? I seriously meant it when I said I mean you no harm. Come on, don't leave me like this.' He tried to remove the strap around his foot but to no avail.

Still no response from the girl.

'Hello? Hello?!'

Suddenly, his body dropped fast but he was able to move his head to avoid hitting the concrete yet again, letting his body take the impact. He sat upright and watched the rope reel away behind an abandoned burnt car.

'It's best you leave while you still have daylight,' the girl said, approaching him again. 'It's not safe here.'

'You're letting me go?'

'It's either that or a bullet in your head for the troubles you've caused me. Would you prefer the latter?'

'No, no, no. I'm just... thankful.' William got up and gathered his crumbled food. 'If I may just ask—' He turned around to find the girl gone. He sprinted towards the intersection of two roads nearby, looking in all four directions, then found the girl kneeling beside a three-meter contraption on the ground. It seemed to be shredded and scattered across the road.

Curious about the device, he approached with caution, prepared for a quick getaway should the girl change her mind and start firing at him because she'd had enough of his stalking. He stayed away from her as she examined a damaged light-bulb at least twice the size of his head or more. The more he looked, the more he wondered about the origins of the device. He had never seen anything like it.

'What is this?' he asked.

'What are you still doing here?' she asked. 'You're supposed to have left already.'

'Look, you've given me a chance to believe me. I'm no threat. I just want to understand.'

'Understand what?'

'You.'

She looked at him and appeared confused by his answer, her eyebrows furrowed.

'I mean you don't have—' He pointed to his neck. 'You don't have a neural link.'

'Never needed one.'

'Then how do you use Zerya?'

'What use is Zerya to me? All of it is fiction, isn't it? Pretending to be someone you're not.'

'Well—' Before William could respond, roaring engines ahead boomed down the road.

The girl's face tightened in fear, then she sprinted away.

'Hey, wait up,' he said. 'What are you running from?' He followed her one block down and veered right onto another street.

'Why are you still following?' she asked.

'I don't know. Maybe it's because of the fact that I have no idea where I'm going and the only thing that seems familiar in all of this is you—despite how little I know about you.'

Wherever he headed with the girl, the roaring engines seemed close behind. He didn't know for certain if their presence was known to whatever it was that seemed to be following them although he didn't want to stop to find out. Suddenly roaring engines appeared ahead of him as well, and he dived for cover behind a truck lying on its side on the ground.

'Seriously... go home,' she said.

'I don't know how to get back.' William peeked out from the side to see a team of tactical officers on hover bikes passing through the opposite street. One biker caught his attention as they had a black shoddy Australia Flag. 'There's too many of them out here.'

'No shit.' She looked at him before looking back at the biker. 'I'm so going to regret this.'

Bing! William's phone chimed alerting him of a message from Kristie in his inbox. 'Oh, god...' He wanted to respond but couldn't. It wasn't the best of times to read one's messages while being chased around in an unfamiliar place. He looked up at the street to see one officer turning into the street they were on. 'We have one coming.'

Kaboom! An explosion erupted high above them, near the officer.

William spotted a tactical drone in the ground, wreathed in flames. The design seemed oddly similar to those used by law enforcement officers. He wanted to look at it more but the biker quickly approached.

'Hey, girl!' William said. 'Hey!' She grabbed him by the neck and pulled him into an alley, passing fallen garbage bins and piled up bikes and cars. He leapt over the vehicles to keep up with the girl, dropping to the ground or hitting something against his legs several times, while the girl made quick work of the obstacle course in front of them. This continued through two more passages before the girl stopped in front of a rustic three-story terrace house.

Huh...

From the outside, it seemed like an old abandoned building from another lifetime. The first floor windows had gaping holes with whistling wind blowing through. Broken glass filled the grounds, and the level above had badly damaged windows, while the top floor had a clear tarp covering the windows. The girl walked up the stairs towards the entrance gate.

William noticed the Smog in the air coming off her clothes, as if falling like dust and hovering back into the air.

She pushed the door open, and said, 'Come on.'

Although reluctant, he followed the girl into the house and the door shut behind them. He realised the same thing happened to the Smog latched on him.

The design of the place was completely different to his own apartment building. Carpet flooring stretched towards two avenues—one leading to the backend of the house and the other leading to a staircase above. Beside him were mailboxes in the wall with corroded bronze shutters. Most were open and emptied. Others held old envelopes and dried up newsletters. The door on the right, leading to a room with the badly damaged windows, seemed sealed tightly with silver panels all around the edges.

The girl removed her mask, taking a moment to breathe in the air before removing her shoes and heading inside.

'Whoa, whoa,' William said, moving away from her in fear. 'What are you doing?'

'What are you talking about?' she asked.

'I mean why are you taking off your mask? There aren't any cleansing tubes here.'

'Who said anything about using one?' She pointed to the ceiling where another lightbulb of the same design that he saw on the road, giving off a warm yellow glow.

'That doesn't explain anything.'

'You can drop the guard. You're safe here. No Smog out there is getting in here.'

'I'll take my chances.'

CHAPTER 9

The girl smirked and removed a brown paper bag from her backpack. 'Suit yourself. By the way, you may not want to get too close or do anything too startling while you're here. Having company nowadays is a rare thing.'

'How could I possibly do that?'

'Don't know. You already seemed to have alerted the police about me, and you don't even know me. I think it's just an annoying knack of yours.'

William opened his mouth to retort but found he had nothing to say. He followed the girl up two flights of stairs, stopping on the first floor in front of a grey door right next to the stairs. He remained halfway up the staircase while the girl knocked on the door three times. Soft pattering footsteps approached the door as a shadow covered the peephole.

'You're here,' a man's voice said. The door opened to reveal a tall, chubby-cheeked man who stepped outside. He wore a brown unbuttoned cardigan over a white shirt covered in what looked like breakfast. He embraced the girl with his left arm, hugging her as if it was the first time. 'My dear, are you alright?' Excitement and relief registered in his voice.

'I'm alright,' she said. 'Just thought I'd drop these off.' She passed him a paper bag.

'Oh, thank you. You got the items, that's gre—' The man looked at William.

'*Hi...*' William said with uncertainty.

'Intruder!' The man's eyes widened to such an extent, the blood veins around his iris seemed to double in size. He whipped out a firearm with his hidden right hand with a bottle strapped around the muzzle, aiming straight for William.

'Charles!' the girl said.

Oh, fuck! William lunged over the wooden railing to the staircase below as two shots whistled past him. He crashed shoulder first, hurting his arm and legs. He laid still as the impact knocked the wind out of his chest.

'Intruder! Intruder!' the man hysterically.

'He's not an intruder,' the girl said, holding the man firmly in her grasp. 'Charles, it's okay. It's okay. I wouldn't have brought him if I thought he was something else.'

After a moment of staring at the ceiling window, William saw the girl pop her head into view.

'You alright?' she asked.

'Will there ever be a time where I'm not going to be at the end of a firearm held by you or someone you know? You realise I did what you said, right? Don't stand too close or startle anyone.'

'I never said it guaranteed anything.'

He scoffed.

'You need a hand?'

'No, I'm fine. Just give me a moment.'

Three minutes later, William followed the girl to the top floor, standing by the door as she entered a room with a metal door key. He watched curiously as the door swung open to reveal a high-ceilinged studio room. Three walls of the four were beige, the fourth wall on his right made of layered bricks, creating a calm and almost rustic ambience in the room.

As he marvelled at the room, he spotted two bookcases of textbooks, novels and journals.

'You actually have books?' he asked.

'Yeah, don't you?'

'No, everything I have is stored in a book reader. Never needed a book.'

'Hmph.' She looked at her shelves. 'They weren't easy to find. Nor easy to bring up.'

'Why do you have them? You could get everything from your phone by accessing the internet.'

'Have you ever felt a book in your hand? Or read the words along a passage on paper? Or even smelt it?'

'It smells?'

The girl picked a book from the shelf and handed it to him. 'See for yourself.'

William looked at the book for a moment. He had never seen anything like this. Sheets of paper packaged finely together to produce some sort of a manuscript. He turned the face of the book to him. The title read, The Search for the Lost Seeing Stones by Frank Istoric. He ran his fingers through the pages, noting a puff of dusty air that reminded him of an aged wine—musty, old yet comforting. 'Interesting.'

'Have you not read a paperback book before?'

'As I said before, everything you can get is on your phone. It's quick online.'

'Ah, yes. The device for tracking, silence and misinformation for those who use it.'

CHAPTER 9

'Misinformation?'

'Anything nowadays is a device for creating a story. I bet you'll find any amount of discussion and so-called literature to promote some agenda or other.'

'That's true.' He passed the book back to the girl, and approached one of the two doors leading out the balcony. He walked outside to find two wooden straw chairs. Worn out cushions sat on the base and back. He looked out to the city beyond the translucent tarp, and beyond No Man's Land and the city.

'You know you can still take your mask off?'

'Why? I don't know what device you have downstairs,' he looked up to find another light mounted against the wall, 'or what it does. How can you be so certain you aren't a Contaminant?'

She paused. 'Look, I've been here for seven months now and I test myself as often as I can to make sure I'm still not one. I don't know if that's enough assurance.'

'Not really. The hell does that thing do anyway?'

'It's like an energy emitter... pushes the haze away from the area a few meters away.'

'How far?'

'About ten meters or so. But in this case, it's three meters to remain hidden. Can't afford to attract unwanted attention.'

Still doubtful, he simply looked back and forth between the girl and device.

'If you're so concerned, I have a toxin counter.' She grabbed a small device connected to a hand rod, and passed him the device. 'I'm sure you've seen this before, right?'

He grabbed the device, flicked the switch and moved around the balcony and the room, but the needle didn't register anything—not even a slight budge. He couldn't believe the results. He turned off the device and stood still. 'This thing must be faulty.'

'It's not.'

'How is it that you haven't told someone about this?' He passed the device to the girl. 'You could possibly be able to save a lot of lives with this device. I mean everything could probably go back to the way things were.'

The girl sighed, her expression a mixture of sadness and disappointment. 'You saw the condition of the device on the ground before.'

'Yeah?'

'Then you have your answer.'

'What do you mean?'

'That device was set as a trial—to gauge a response. Not to see its effect on the area but rather the effect of its presence when others see what it does. Do you know how many times that's been done? Three. Three times we've put up that device to start helping the place. Each time it gets destroyed beyond repair by those who get a chance to witness the work it does.'

'Well, of course, it's going to happen here. You're in No Man's Land. If you bring it into the city, it won't be.'

'It's those in the city as well who don't want it.'

'Bullshit.'

The girl went quiet. 'Look, I got things to do and I'm not here to offer you anything or explanation about what I do. This is a one-time event. You can stay here for the night and leave tomorrow morning when it's safe, or leave now and risk capture. The choice is yours.' She headed for the exit.

'Hey, hey, wait a moment. Just wait. What am I supposed to do here?'

'There are several things in the room to keep you busy. In the meantime, I'll be off. Don't make noise and don't startle Charles. I don't want a repeat of what happened.'

Like I'd want to do that again, he wanted to say as he watched the girl leave the room.

Suddenly, his phone chimed again. It was Kristie. He removed his mask, dropped on the couch and checked his messages. Three alerts had come from her.

'Hey Kristie,' he messaged. 'Sorry for not getting back before. I got caught up in something and lost track of time.'

'Hey, it's alright,' she messaged. 'I thought something happened to you. Are you still wanting to catch up?'

'I don't know if I'll be able to catch up now. I'm actually not at home for the moment. Don't know what time I'll be back.'

'Oh, okay. Just thought you wanted to catch up.'

'I did. I'm just caught in something work related at the moment. Boss called me about something urgent. He wanted me to look at it before tomorrow came. Had to do it otherwise I would lose my access to work when I return.'

'I thought we weren't allowed to leave our LGA?'

'We are if it's work-related.'

'Okay. When will you be done?'

CHAPTER 9

'Don't know... there's a lot to do. Sorry. I didn't expect this to happen.'

'But you're on annual?'

'I'm more upset about this than you realize.'

No response followed for about a minute. 'Okay, but you're still up for Saturday?'

'Yes, without a doubt. Definitely am.'

'Alright. I hope everything turns out alright for work. I'll see you on Saturday.'

'Me too. See you then.'

He rested his head against the soft cushion, breathing a sigh of relief for not screwing up his lie to Kristie. He could only imagine what she'd say had he told her what really happened in the last few hours of his day off. He turned his attention to the room, gazing at the painting on the walls, the books on the shelves and floor, and guitars on the stand.

Nothing in the room spurred much interest but when he approached the balcony door, he found something under wraps. He pulled off the covers and saw a mini telescope. Beside the instrument stood a small table with a closed notepad. A bookmark stood out so he spread the book apart, opening it at the bookmarked page where he found recorded entries of times in the early morning of planets visible in the sky.

Doubt this thing can see through the haze at night, he thought. He returned inside and laid on the couch. Weariness fell over his mind and body. He didn't fight it and fell asleep right away.

Sometime later, he woke to find night had settled over the sky with the same murky dark scenery like at home.

Knock, knock!

William got up right away, unlocked the handle and pulled the door to find the girl standing there not appearing as defensive like before, and a little more welcoming this time around.

'Hey,' she said.

'Hey,' he said.

'You hungry?'

'I can eat.'

'We're about to eat. Come join us.'

'Alright.'

He followed her downstairs to another room where Charles was standing beside a small stove, cooking something inside a pot. His body tightened in fear after his initial meeting had resulted in him getting shot at, but his nose registered a sweet, somewhat familiar aroma, dissipating some of fear.

'What is that?' he asked.

'Food,' the girl said, walking past him to help prepare the table for dinner.

William scanned the room as he approached the table. Bare apart from the dining table, chairs and stove. No pantry. No fridge. Nothing of the essential items to hold food resided in the room. As he got closer, Charles came around with the pot and placed it atop a cloth. The man wiped his hands on another cloth he had on his shoulder and put his hand forward to him for a handshake.

'I'm sorry for my outburst before,' Charles said.

'It's alright,' William said, taking the handshake. 'I'm guessing you don't see anyone else, aside from her, right?'

'Right you are. Unless they're intruders.' He sat down by the table and began serving mushroom white sauce with pappardelle. He sprinkled basil and powdered cheese before passing the plate around. 'Take a seat.'

William sat, staring at his food. The home cooked meal reminded him of his dinner at the Watsons. He dug into the pasta. His mouth burst with flavours, making him salivate. 'My god. That's so good.'

'I'm glad you like it.'

'Where did you learn to cook this?'

'Italy... before the Smog.'

'You lived there?'

'For a time.'

'It must have been a nice place.'

He paused for a moment. 'It was.'

'Did you go to other countries?'

'Yes.'

'That's cool. I wish I could travel.'

No one responded to his comment. The pair simply kept their attention on eating their meal.

He looked at the girl. 'Have you travelled?'

'Me? No,' she said, turning her face back to the pasta, giving no attention to him as she ate in silence.

'Alright... cool.'

William got the immediate sense they weren't liking the questions and stopped. Both seemed lost in their own silence as they stared at their own plates. Choosing to finish his meal quickly and leave the awkwardness, he ate and reluctantly refrained from asking for another serving.

'Look, umm... this may mean nothing to you coming from me but I'm sorry for bothering the both of you. I'm sure you had your own routine or plan for your day, and me being here probably threw a spanner in that, so I want to say thank you for dinner... umm, I'll go to the room and stay there until morning. Then I'll leave.' He took the plate to the sink and washed it, then left them.

About an hour later, William sat on the floor, pressed against the couch as he read some of the paperback book like novels and non-fiction books to pass the time.

Knock, knock!

He approached the door to find the girl there. 'Hey! Everything alright?'

'I've just come to switch the lights to night mode,' she said, pushing through quickly.

'Oh, sure.'

The girl went to the balcony and the light disappeared after a moment. Then she came back inside the room. She seemed to notice the books. 'What happened to reading on your phone?'

'My phone's dead.'

'I see.' She remained still for a moment, then faced him. 'Listen, our silence earlier today is not something to take offence at. We just don't know you and the less you know about us the better it is.'

'I understand. And like I said I'll be gone in the morning. I promise not to make a peep for the remaining time.'

She nodded in appreciation and walked out of the room.

'I'm William by the way. Or you can just call me Will. Whichever works. I go by both.'

The girl stopped in her tracks for several seconds. Her back faced him. 'Have a good night.'

'*Yeah*... have a good night.' He watched her disappear downstairs.

The following morning, William prepared himself to leave. He placed everything back in its original spot, then left the room. While making his way downstairs he found the girl by the door, mask in her hand.

'I figured you'd be asleep,' he said.

'I'll help get you back where you need to go,' she said. 'At least you won't have to be out in this area for too long.'

'Thanks.'

The pair left the building. Rain poured down although the girl had an umbrella to cover the two as they walked back to where the damaged energy emitter laid. This time it was drenched and appeared beyond repair, if it wasn't so already.

'This is where I leave you,' she said.

'Sure.'

'Good luck.'

He watched the girl disappear back the way they came. Not wanting to linger in the rain and get drenched, he ventured to the barbed wired entrance.

Wearing his respirator, hazmat suit and gloves didn't do much to ease the chilling cold coursing around his extremities as the heavy rain poured onto car roofs, cracked pavements and deserted vehicles. But he stopped suddenly when something whirred in the distance. He turned around to see a black tactical drone about the size of a car tyre passing over him, flying towards the fences. Then he spotted a pair of Enforcers standing beside a law enforcement officer.

He wanted to run and escape their attention, however, there was nothing he could do as the police would be able to find him and everything about him within minutes if they wanted to. There was minimal movement by the Enforcers, their gaze was clearly on him but they didn't budge. He looked around, trying to bide his time. His eyes darted around from window to window but there wasn't anyone around—not that anyone could do much to help.

What the hell do I do now?

He took in a breath and gave up the idea of fleeing. With one foot in front of the other, he continued walking until he passed the fences and stopped several meters away from the officer.

'Mr. Kepler?' the officer said. His voice was different and discernible—not the same officer he'd spoken with in his previous two meetings.

'Yes?' William said.

'You are obliged to accompany us to headquarters for questioning due to recent breaches made within the last twenty-four hours.'

'And if I choose not to comply?'

CHAPTER 9

'Well, then, our trusted Enforcers will be able to assist with your participation in the matter.'

He cast another glance at the Enforcers. He didn't want to think about the consequences of not complying, and said, 'Okay.'

'Good choice.'

CHAPTER 10

MOMENTS LATER, WILLIAM sat in the backseat of a police hover car. His nose and mouth twitched at the overpowering stench of body odour and cigarettes. He did his best to hide his discomfort as the car automated the driving process, maneuvering between the lanes before they made their ascent towards the city centre.

The window wipers rubbed quickly over the window as heavy rain fell. William moved closer to see outside where he noted multiple apartment buildings—most with similar signs of corrosive wear on the foundations which turned everything to charcoal black—looming over the car. He looked forward and spotted holograms emerging meters away from corporate building walls, playing advertisements of food, products and services.

One particular advertisement caught his attention. Video footage of previous matches about an upcoming Esports World Championships in an underground stadium with people watching the match. How sports were still able to be played in times like these was beyond him. It was something he still found amazing and strange—even though he had partaken in some events underground himself.

'Brace yourself,' the officer said.

'Brace for wha—' William said, as his head and body jerked backward while the car swerved down towards a wide square, structured, ten-storey building. The sharp dip continued until he noticed an opening appearing for them to park. White walls and fluorescent lights pierced through the rain and haze to make way for a landing platform stretching outward with a red hover ball flashing above.

CHAPTER 10

The car parked on the platform as the door hissed open for William and the officer to exit.

William put on his mask and rushed for cover to avoid the rain. Once inside he followed the officer as he led him inside the police headquarters. They passed people whose faces were bare and pale—a clear indication of the ongoing lack of sunlight. Their most common feature was their stoicism, as if they were dead inside. They appeared no different to the Enforcers in mannerism and speech.

Thank God I don't work here... couldn't imagine what would happen if a joke was made here.

They passed through a corridor and arrived in front of a bank of five elevators. Each had a letter of the alphabet outside the entrance door on the right corner. The officer tapped on the sensor for one. Their trip on the elevator took them to the second top level where the environment was filled with specialists and high-ranking officials walking around or sitting in meeting rooms conducting presentations both virtual and face-to-face.

William caught sight of a few people observing him as he followed the officer. Their eyes stuck on him like a sentry bot tracking an unidentified object.

'Here we are,' the officer said, stopping by the corridor.

'What do you mean?' William asked.

'Your presence is expected. Not mine. You need only present yourself to the third office to your right.'

William wanted to ask who had asked for him but suspected he wouldn't get an answer and made his way forward.

He passed office rooms where the walls were mainly drywall with a narrow, fogged window panel from ceiling to floor, serving as a door. Each office had a title card slotted beside the door of the official who resided inside and the district they managed. He spotted about seven smallish offices and imagined many more were on the floor and other levels.

How many offices do you need?

Then he stopped by the entrance of the third door, whose office seemed larger than the previous ones. Beside it, read the title card, ULYANOV BALANDIN, responsible for District 13. The name didn't ring a bell but he had an uneasy idea about who had summoned him.

The door slid aside as he went to knock on the window panel.

'Mr. Kepler,' a familiar voice said. 'How good of you to accept my invitation.'

William found the same strange officer from his last two meetings sitting on his ergonomic chair, looking out to the city with his five-meter-wide window. The chair spun around. The officer appeared outwardly disinterested, bored even, yet William sensed restrained anger below the surface.

Fuck...

'You can come on in,' Ulyanov said. 'After all, we have much to talk about.'

'Why am I here?' he asked. 'Did I do something wrong?'

'That would depend on what you share with me.'

William walked inside and sat in the guest chair opposite Ulyanov.

'It's been some time since we spoke. I'd figure that by now you'd have something for me.'

'In relation to what?'

Ulyanov's eyebrow rose. 'As per our discussion from our last meeting, you were meant to provide any information that might be of use to us concerning the woman you mentioned to me before or anything to do with Gaia—one I gave to all residents in the building.'

'I've had no interactions with the *woman* since I last spoke with you nor have, I had any dealings with Gaia. Like I said before, I don't know anything about that group. I've only heard about the stories that come from the news and rumours that go around about them.'

'I find that so strange.'

'Why?'

'Because you had an incident at your building where you witnessed a Purge, did you not?'

'I thought you would know as there were Enforcers. I figured the incident would be passed onto you.'

'It was. Yet you didn't say anything or report it. And what's most interesting is that not long ago,' he looked around as if trying to recall a memory, 'I was informed of two people entering No Man's Land. The entry times were close to one another. The first person we couldn't get a visual on due to local inhabitants, and the other one we knew.' He stood up, grabbed a remote. *Click!* A picture appeared on the adjacent wall. 'If I could direct your attention to the screen for me. I think this is something that's going to help us here.'

CHAPTER 10

I doubt it.

William's breathing quickened. The screen displayed surveillance footage of a woman entering No Man's Land, followed by another person—himself. The drone followed the pair until they began to run from the area.

Suddenly the drone came under attack. Shots fired, incapacitating the device. Seconds later footage showed the scenery spinning as the drone fell until the screen went dark.

'Luckily for the pair,' Ulyanov said, 'the footage doesn't show anything else. But we do have another meeting of the same pair. If memory serves me, that was shortly after our meeting although it didn't seem as if the pair had a pleasant interaction.'

Shit... William wasn't impressed with his actions being on display.

Another video appeared on the screen of William and the girl standing in the supermarket having another encounter before she disappeared. Then William followed her again.

'Strange, isn't it? How someone who had faced the barrel end of a firearm—looking death straight in the face—continued to follow a person this dangerous. I'm so confused.' Ulyanov approached William, standing now a meter from him. 'I was wondering if you could enlighten me.'

William stared at the officer, afraid for his life. He didn't know what would be his best course of action. He looked back at the video to find it gone. The projector had ended the video. He paused to think about lying and ran through as many possible scenarios that would help him with his situation. None seemed plausible.

'Well?'

William decided to tell the truth. 'I was curious about her.'

'Curious? About what, exactly?'

'Like I said before. She looked like an Allocron. I couldn't see a neural port on her. I wanted to hear from her what it was like, you know? Being one... and why was it like that for her. There was never a point in time where I couldn't remember not having a port.'

'Did you find out?'

'No, and the footage that shows us running. We were together for a moment before she told me to get lost. Though I kept following her as she seemed her way around the area, and I didn't. But at some point, she fired shots at me and I was gone.'

'Then why were you in No Man's Land for the whole night? We have information on your location, staying in a terrace house. You understand the breaches and penalties in place for leaving your designated LGA?'

'I didn't know how to get back. And those people in the area kept roaming about while I was there. I hid in a place where I thought it'd be safe until early morning, then I left for home.'

Ulanov paused for a moment, as if considering the information. He returned to his chair. 'It's a good thing that you stayed away from her. She's an extremely dangerous individual.' He pressed his remote. *Click!* The projector displayed a profile of the girl, showing photos of an interaction between people. 'We have no name for this woman but we have an alias. Goes by the codename Demitrova. She works for Gaia. Or at the very least colludes with them. Our intel shows that she's planning something with Gaia. We don't know what that is. However, we believe she is living in No Man's Land—somewhere close. Now from the footage it looks like you were following her. We can't say for certain she was leading you astray or if she was heading straight for her place. But as you say, she knew the area.' He went quiet as if wanting to elicit a response. 'In either case, it'd be best you stayed away.'

'What's going to happen?'

'It's going to end for them... including those who have any association with them, or are expecting to have one.'

'And how do I fit in all of this?'

Ulyanov breathed hard, thinking. 'The evidence at this point in time yields no connection between you, Demitrova and/or Gaia. It would also seem that there's no desire from the concerning parties that a connection be formed. Yes?'

'Yes.'

'Good. Because a subtle inclination would be enough to spark an investigation.' He turned off the projector.

'So I'm in the clear?'

'Not quite. We need your assistance in finding this woman.'

'Why me?'

'Because you've been the only person who's been able to come into contact with her or with anyone from Gaia over these past few months. Successfully, at least.'

'But I don't even know how to find her.'

'Are you sure about that? Your body betrays you.'

CHAPTER 10

William swallowed the build-up of saliva—his usual response to lying. He tried to calm himself, keeping his chest still and looking innocent. 'I—uh—I can't say that I know where I can find her but I do know some possible locations. And when I say locations, I mean two. Those two being the places you have footage of me and her. I haven't had any other encounters elsewhere.'

Ulyanov walked around and stopped in front of William. He brought his face within arm's distance of him. 'Why do you betray yourself in defending this woman?'

'*Defending?* I don't know what you mean.'

Ulyanov smiled thinly as if struggling to keep his composure. 'You have one more chance to tell me the truth. I know you have had more interactions with this woman outside those recorded. Now I ask again: where else have you seen this woman?'

'I swear I don't know. If I cou—' A hand slapped him across his right cheek.

'Deception in an investigation is a criminal offense, Mr. Kepler.' Ulyanov's voice resonated with authority. He was back on familiar territory. 'Now, I ask again: where else have you seen this woman?'

'Jesus Christ!'

'No, it's just me.'

'I haven't seen her anywhere else. I swear.' Another slap struck his temple. The sheer force knocked him and the chair to the ground. 'One more time, Mr. Kepler.'

William scattered away, not wanting to be in the same room with Ulyanov a second longer.

'You have one more chance to tell me what you know before we take this conversation to the lower levels where we can employ more unsavoury methods to loosen your tongue.'

William sat against the wall, staring right at Ulyanov while weighing up his options about giving the officer the information he was after, or figuring out a way to escape. Then concern for me in making a decision was time. He was short of it until...

Knock, knock!

Ulyanov froze, his fury, while clear as daylight, quickly switched back to being composed. 'Who is it?'

'Officer Jenkins, sir,' a male officer said.

'Come in.'

'Sir, we have a lead on Demitrova.' A junior officer entered and looked only at Ulyanov, ignoring William.

'Where is she?'

'Last seen, crossing the border from No Man's Land.'

'Prep a team. We leave in ten minutes. As for Kepler, assign an escort to take him home.'

'Yes, sir.' The officer left.

Ulyanov collected his firearm and badge from his desk before looking again at William. 'Our discussion for the moment is over, Mr. Kepler. Consider yourself lucky. While there aren't any charges to be pressed, don't push your chances any more than you have. As for the matter concerning your breaches, a detailed letter for your fines will be sent by the end of the day. Do keep a lookout.' He left the room.

William rubbed his head, which ached fiercely now, twice as bad as from Demitrova's slap yesterday.

I need to get out of here.

Suddenly heavy footsteps echoed from the corridor as two law enforcement officers approached the door.

'Mr. Kepler?' one officer said.

'Yes,' he said.

'We'll be taking you home. Could you follow us please?'

Hesitant, William remained seated. He didn't know who he could trust after his most recent assault from an officer.

'Is there something else you need to do here?'

'No.'

'Well, come on then.'

A quick descent took him to a parking lot. He watched out the window as the car left the area, flying away from the city until a familiar row of buildings came into view. It wasn't long before he'd arrived outside his apartment building with no further attacks on his person. He put on his mask, tightened the ends of his suit and gloves before leaving them.

'Thanks,' he said.

The car engine roared off, blowing away air and dust, as they left William alone.

William looked around the area. Barely a soul was in sight. Not wanting to linger, he entered the building and headed for his apartment. Once inside the door, he rested against it. There was nothing but silence and emptiness. He didn't like it.

His thoughts ran wild about Demitrova. He didn't know what he could do to help her as the police were clearly in hot pursuit of her. He recalled his stay with her and didn't believe she was dangerous. Despite her lack of communication, and almost killing him earlier, when he had been hiding inside her house, she was polite and had respected his privacy.

What happens now? I can't help her otherwise I'm screwed... Then again, I might be screwed already.

As he stayed by the door, Ramses appeared from his bedroom, striding towards him. It seemed like the cat understood what had happened during the past twenty-four hours and behaved himself. He purred and pressed against William's leg.

'Hey bud,' William said. 'I'm sorry for not getting here earlier. You must be hungry.' He went to the kitchen and served his cat breakfast before it got crabby.

William removed his drenched clothes, throwing them in the wash, and headed for the shower. Once finished he connected his phone charger to his phone to call Kristie. It was Saturday, and he wanted to start the day with her on good terms.

Brrng, brrng! The phone rang until she answered.

'Hey,' she said.

'Hey,' he said.

'Everything alright?'

'Yeah. I just wanted to see how you were doing and if you were still up for today to catch up.'

'Yeah, I still am.'

For some reason he found himself relieved by her response and smiled. 'That's good to hear.'

'Didn't think I would want to miss a chance to make things work.' She chuckled.

'*Yeah.*'

Silence eclipsed them.

'Will... are you alright?'

He paused, considering his answer. 'Yeah, I'm alright. It's just been a long twenty-four.'

'Well, when you're over, we can talk.'

'Hmm... of course.'

'Anyway, I have to go. See you soon.'

'See *you* soon.' He stared at his phone as the screen powered down. His mood had improved after his brief chat but didn't stop the thoughts swirling around about Demitrova.

I can't afford to think about her anymore. Stop it! Come on. It's done.

Willing his internal dialogue to change his train of thought, he decided to do some chores, as his place was a mess. Dust was piled up around his room and office. One clean swipe of the desk on his finger left black smudge of dirt, which he now cleaned properly.

He paused his house cleaning and pulled up his laptop, searching the Dark Web for Walkers. There was little general information on them however he came across a private forum where there were people requesting a Walker to swap IP addresses to venture beyond their neighbouring LGAs.

William continued with his search until he stumbled across a Walker registering their location at the local bar. He tried looking for this person's information but a photo was all that was available. He ran a photo scan of the Walker through the Dark Web at considerable cost, which he paid.

I have to be certain this person is clean. I can't afford for them to be working for the police.

He left the search and resumed his cleaning, then stopped in front of his wardrobe, looking at his limited collection of clothing. He pondered the evening ahead with Kristie, and wondered what to wear. Nothing he had spoken of a man with confidence or one that knew what he wanted aside from the fact that he was easy-going and cared little about most things. He decided on his grey work blazer and navy-blue jeans—suitable enough for dinner with a jumper or something light underneath the blazer.

It's better than nothing, I guess.

Three hours later, he was appropriately clothed and ready for dinner, putting out food for Ramses before leaving.

'I'll be back soon,' he said.

He'd saved the address to Kristie's place on his GPS and headed for home which was luckily within his local government area. He didn't want another breach on his record. His walk lasted around twenty-five minutes until he came across a building of old architecture with lights shining from the inside of the various rooms. He hit the number to Kristie's room and the entrance door opened. He went through a cleansing tube, then made his ascent via elevator to the fifth floor. He searched for room 509 and found the door partially open with jazz music playing.

He closed the door behind him as he entered. The dining room held more items than his, and an 'L' shaped sofa sat along the white walls, accompanied by a long mahogany coffee table. Upon the walls were three digital portraits of artworks similar to Picasso's Cubism style.

While there were also wall-mounted shelves and a Zerya's hotspot, William's attention barely moved from the portraits. Something about the disjointed faces and obscured shapes reminded him of himself—an idea he wasn't sure whether he wanted to explore or not.

'You made it,' a familiar voice said from behind.

William turned to see Kristie standing by the kitchen door, wearing a black skivvy, blue jeans, and caramel boots. '*Hey.*'

'I thought for a moment today that you wouldn't come.'

'I thought for a moment today you would call it off.'

'I will admit, I had my concerns. I didn't know if this was going to work. It's so new for me.'

'You're not alone there.'

'Come.' She extended her hand.

He approached her, taking her hand and embraced her in his arms. 'How did you come by this place?'

'This is one of my parents' places that they lease out. They're overseas investors and had this place bought many years ago. I liked it so I asked to live here.' She placed a hand on the wall. 'It's only temporary until I get my own place, although I don't know how much of a chance given my working visa status at the moment—even then, I'd have difficulty finding something here as the market has basically outpriced everyone. Anyone would be lucky to find something within their borrowing capacity these days.'

'That's why I rent. Getting property will only happen either through being really rich or inheriting it through really rich family. That's why I rent now.'

'I'm thinking of doing that myself too. It would take the pressure off having to worry about a mortgage. But let's not talk about property buying. You're here now. I can actually see you, even hold you.' She smiled. 'You must be hungry.'

'I could eat.'

She went quiet for a moment, looking at his face. 'Everything okay? You have a bruise.'

'I do?'

'Yeah, here.' She placed a gentle hand on his face where a mild purple swelling showed across his temple.

'Oh this. Funny story. Today I was at home doing some cleaning when I slipped on my tile floor and hit the wall nearby. I'm surprised there's any swelling.'

'It doesn't hurt?'

'It hurt when I fell but not now.'

'You sure?'

'Yeah.'

'Okay... I thought we could have takeout pizza and watch something on the projector. Believe it or not, I'm not a good cook. I tried cooking something earlier today. This is the result.' She showed him an oven baked meal seared into charcoal with barely a piece of vegetable or meat surviving the heat.'

'Pizza is fine.'

'Cool.'

Ding dong!

Her face brightened. 'Right on time. That should be the pizza.'

Moments later, William sat on the sofa with Kristie lying against his chest as they watched a movie. His hand was interlocked with her hand. Not much attention was given to the movie as he kept looking at her. He couldn't believe the fact he was in the presence of another person, physically speaking. Everything until now had been virtual apart from his run-in with Demitrova and her friend, and the run-ins with the police.

As he sat with Kristie, her presence overwhelmed him.

Kristie turned around to face him, catching his gaze. 'What's wrong?'

'I'm just surprised.'

A look of confusion crossed her face. 'At what?'

'It's just I never knew if I would ever actually be with someone again. Yet here I am. With you.'

She smiled, gave him a quick peck on his lips. 'Let me pack this up. I don't like leaving things lying around.' She left the couch and removed the items off the table.

CHAPTER 10

William watched her leave, then returned to the movie. He soon lost interest and grabbed the remote to switch channels. *Click!* He arrived on a news broadcast with footage showing a familiar house in flames. The location didn't register at first until another camera gave a different perspective.

Suddenly, he jumped up, panicked. The house was the place where Demitrova lived with her friend. It was on fire.

'Authorities from the state police,' the news anchor said, 'report that a raid earlier today took place in No Man's Land to capture a woman known as Demitrova. Reports indicate that she was in affiliation with the terrorist group Gaia, devising attacks which would have brought about significant harm to the lives of the people in the areas they were targeting.' The screen changed the footage to the energy emitters. 'These were weapons Demitrova was creating and planning to place in key strategic locations in the city. But luckily, the hard-working protectors of our city and their dedication to their work served the citizens well, as Demitrova's plans were thwarted.'

'The hell?' William said.

'Reports indicated that Demitrova was fatally shot down in crossfire between law enforcement earlier. It seems our troubles are now over. Here's Lieutenant Baladin with further information.'

'Will?' Kristie said.

William snapped out of his shock.

'Everything alright?'

'I—I—uh,' he said, eyes riveted on the news. The camera showed two black bags lying on the concrete with personnel picking up one before loading them into a truck. He sank onto the couch breathing heavily, sick at heart. *What have I done?*

'Hey, hey.' Kristie rushed to his aid. 'What's wrong?'

'I—I killed them.'

'What?'

'*I* killed them.'

'Are you talking about this person on the news?'

He didn't say anything.

'What makes you say this, Will?'

'Because I was with the police this morning. They took me in... to talk about her.'

'You're not making any sense? Why were you with them?'

He sighed deeply. 'I wasn't completely honest with you yesterday when you called.'

'You weren't at work?'

He shook his head. 'I was with her.'

Kristie slowly moved her head away from him, appearing concerned. 'What are you talking about?'

'Not in *that* way though.'

'But you were with *her*.'

'I was with her because I was trying to understand something.'

'Understand what?'

'Why she was the way she was.'

'What the hell does that mean?'

'She's an Allocron. She didn't have a neural port. Everything she had in her place was *real*. There were books. There were plants. Even actual paintings at her place. Things you could touch and see history. Why would someone live like that?'

'Because she *was* an Allocron. She was a defect. There's a reason why they are separated from us, and you find most of them away from the city. Their bodies are not capable of synchronising to the technology. Ours are,' she gestured to him and herself, 'That's *why* she lived the way she lived. Plus, you found her walking around in the open, risking everyone to contamination. Who knows for how long she has been doing that? That's not the right way of living.'

He stood up, walking away from her—not wanting to snap at her. 'How is it *not* though? Look at the way we live. We have Zerya where it's *supposed* to connect with people yet it's just a front for everyone to use to hide their true selves. And I'm not denying I didn't do it myself but there's still something wrong about that. And this,' he walked to the window, pointing at the Smog, 'why isn't this over? Why haven't we had any announcements about ending this goddamn Smog that kills people, and lets the authorities use it against us to keep us in our boxes? Why?'

She approached him, troubled by his response. 'Where is this all coming from, Will? You never struck me to worry for such things.'

He paused. 'I guess... with the way things have been these past few months, I just wanted out. And when I saw this person, something seemed different about the way she lived and did things. I wasn't attracted in any way. Believe me when I say that. I wasn't. But there seemed to be something this person had that I didn't have.' He looked at Kristie. 'The freedom to be human again. She was different to us all, who was even trying to help us. I know because I was there. She wasn't a threat, and yet she was killed.' His eyes welled with tears and his mouth quivered. 'And it was because of me... it was because of me.' He sank into the wall.

She embraced him, bringing her face right up to his own. 'You listen to me, Will. You're not a bad person. What happened has happened. It can't be changed. But all you have now are the moments that will follow. This woman—threat or not—she's gone and I won't let you keep remembering her if you're going to be like this. It's making you miserable.'

'But—'

'No buts. Let it go. You're with me, Will. I'm the one standing here in front of you. Not her.'

William looked at Kristie, trying to fight off the thoughts rapidly emerging in his head.

'Do you not care for me? Do you not care for us?'

'I do.'

'Then let it go... let it go.'

William approached her, looking at her lips. Overwhelmed by his troubles, he threw himself at her, kissing his soft strawberry lips, and she seemed to respond in kind.

She broke from his lips for a moment, placing a caressing hand along his face. She smiled. 'It'd be better if we did this somewhere else.'

William followed her to the bedroom. He quickly undressed himself and hopped onto the bed.

Kristie turned off the lights in the room. The street lights burst upon the ceiling, casting a soft ambience to the place.

'You won't be able to see me,' he said.

'It's okay.' She grasped his hand and placed it into her chest. 'You need only feel me.'

Trusting her, he made his move and another passionate kiss sparked their night of love. He caressed her skin, letting his hand trail along her body.

Suddenly, his hand caught coarse scarred ridges along her lower abdomen and nether regions, and he wondered at the cause until Kristie quickly changed positions and he forgot about it in their passion.

When it was over, William lay against his pillow, taking in the moment, relaxing as Kristie lay pressed against his own body. He couldn't imagine things getting any better for them, and his mind for the first time saw some clarity and peace. He'd found someone real for the first time in his life, someone who truly understood him and didn't question him as a person for his habits and hobbies. He had feared his life was slipping away without someone with whom to share his life. He put aside any thought about Demitrova and fell asleep.

Later in the night, he got up and went to the toilet to clean himself off. It had been some time since he'd been with a real woman. He looked around the bathroom until something in the cabinet caught his attention. A packet of estrogen and hormonal tablets. It seemed like serious stuff but he didn't really understand it, so read the instructions, and suddenly suspected something about Kristie he didn't know how to deal with.

He held the packet in his hand, his mind racing. When he thought he had himself under control again, he returned to the bedroom doorway, watching Kristie sleep. He turned around and went to the second room letting the door swing open to show an office desk in the middle with white curtains hanging towards the floor with a hologram projector installed against the ceiling.

He crept in to find a set of closed sliding doors, moving them aside to find high fashioned clothing suspended on hangers. There were half-opened cardboard boxes, one in particular which held scans and photos of a man's body with black lines running along their lower abdomen and genital regions. This seemed to be the before images of a procedure, with the following images showing female genitals replacing the male ones. He looked at the date of the picture, which dated back fifteen years ago.

'Will?' Kristie said.

'Yeah?' he said, startled.

'Everything alright?'

'Yeah, I'm fine. Just umm... washing up. I'll be there in a—'

'Will?' This time her voice seemed closer, like she was standing behind him.

William remained still, then turned around to see her.

'What are you doing here?'

He showed her the images of the body. 'I think there's something important you forgot to tell me.'

'I can explain.'

CHAPTER 10

'Explain that you're not the person you pretend to be? That there's been... *changes?*'

'I am me. I didn't lie to you.'

'Then explain this. *Seriously* explain it. Explain the hormone tablets that just so happen to be in plain sight.'

'You saw them?' Disappointment crossed her face.

'Not by intention. But they were lying about by the basin.'

She went quiet.

'You didn't think to ever tell me about this?'

'I didn't think it mattered.'

'*How* can it not matter? Please tell me that. How? You were once a completely different person.'

'You're telling me now you don't care about me anymore because you know about my past?'

'I—I don't know what to make of this.'

'I accept you for who you are, Will. Can't you accept me?'

William didn't answer. Deep down he wanted to say 'yes', but at the same time 'no'. He sighed, then silently he placed the photos back in the boxes, stood up and exhaled.

'Come back to bed.' She grabbed his hand. Her eyes were filled with pain and longing. 'Please.'

He followed her to bed. He lay his head against the pillow, while Kristie lay beside him. He was troubled by her past but he closed his eyes, trying to ignore everything around him so he could sleep. He knew Kristie was looking at him but he didn't want to invite a conversation.

Just go to sleep, Will. Think about this tomorrow.

CHAPTER 11

AS WILLIAM WATCHED Kristie leave the bedroom for her morning ablutions, the events of the last twenty-four hours ran through his mind. The sleep hadn't helped him. The revelation of Kristie's past bewildered him and he decided it would be better not to share it with anyone. But the single question plagued him all morning: *What was real now?*

How to even speak to Kristie confused him. Apart from those marks from her transition surgery, there was nothing else to suggest that she had ever been someone else in the past—she must have had an excellent surgeon.

Once she was done in the shower, William raced into the bathroom, avoiding any awkward conversations. As he washed himself, he looked at the basin to see if the tablets were there. They weren't. He focused more on rinsing himself to fight off unpleasant thoughts in his head.

Five minutes later, he was dressed and suited up to return home. He stood in the living room, looking at everything and anything to distract his mind.

'You got everything?' Kristie said, walking out of the bedroom.

'Yeah, got everything,' he said.

'Your oxygen mask seems low. Do you need a spare?' She handed him his respirator mask.

'No, it won't be necessary, I have enough to last me at least two trips, back and forth from here to home.'

'Okay.' She embraced him. 'I want to apologise again for yesterday. Even though my past was... discovered, I had a lovely time with you last night.'

He paused for a moment, then said, '*Yeah*... it was nice.'

'Will you come over again?'

CHAPTER 11

'Sure. Why not? Although I don't know when I'll be free. This coming week will be busy. I'll let you know.'

She smiled and gazed admiringly up at him.

'What is it?'

'Thank you for understanding.'

He smiled in return. 'I gotta go.'

A quick peck on her lips and he was off. He power-walked home, brewed a pot of coffee and spent the rest of the day doing nothing except looking at Kristie's photo on her Instagram, trying to imagine what she looked like before her surgery. He glanced at Zerya hotspot every once in a while, but he wasn't interested hopping on. It wasn't enough for him now to keep him engaged. This continued late into the night.

He grew tired at some point and went to sleep until Monday morning came, where it was expected that the results from the recalibration program were to be released.

It was judgement day and he didn't anticipate anything good to come from the meeting. He was already in the video conference, staring a black screen, alongside many others who were waiting for their managers to join and give them the results.

Bing! Ensemble chat chimed with an alert as he sipped on his cup of coffee.

'Today's the day,' Marlene messaged.

'Yes, today's the day,' he messaged back. 'I wonder what we're supposed to do while we wait for the results.'

'Your guess is as good as mine. But it shouldn't be too long before the results appear on our workday portal.'

He paused. 'Listen, I'm sorry about before. I didn't mean to hurt you if I did. It's just—a lot has happened.'

'It's okay, Will. I'm sorry too. I shouldn't have pushed too much. It was wrong for me to have lost it at you. Like you said before "it's a shit situation", eh?'

'I probably had it coming anyway haha.'

'*Probably* did.'

'What are you going to do in the meantime?'

'I'll just sit in the corporate chat until the higher ups come join. I have nothing else better to do.'

'Is there anyone in the meeting already?'

'Quite a few actually. No doubt they're concerned about the announcement. A lot of jobs hang in the air now.'

'*Yeah...*'

William continued to sit on his desk chair, holding his cup of coffee in his hands to warm up his fingers. He glanced at the corporate chat to see if any executives had joined the meeting. None had joined yet although the number of participants grew by the hundreds every time he looked.

Anxious with the waiting, he checked his facial search on the Walker. He wanted to know more about him after he sent his request on the Dark Web. There was a 78% hit on a person—Kieran Webbster—who'd been convicted for setting several fires on properties and churches. *Oy vey.* He continued to read but nothing indicated he was a police officer, or ever had been. This relieved William.

Suddenly a face appeared in the corporate chat with three other people joining the meeting with their cameras on. All of them were executives of Pinnacle Funds—people he'd seen in emails, corporate banners and videos.

'Hello everyone!' the Executive General Manager said. 'It's good to see so many of you here. It's an important day for us all—for the bank, for us, and for the people who contribute to the bank's success on a daily basis.'

William observed the executive as he smiled but everything seemed off. The other three held similar expressions. Something unpleasant was about to happen.

'We'll just wait for another minute or so before we get started. The meeting won't take too much of your time. I'm sure you all have busy schedules ahead.'

'Are we going to be losing our jobs?' one employee asked, sounding impatient.

'Umm... we have news that we'd like to share with everyone in one go.'

'It's just a yes or no response. I don't want to lose my job here. I've been with the bank for so many years.'

'And we appreciate your loyalty alongside everyone else's, and the work you've all done. The program has come to an end and those who have completed the marking will have your results on your workday portal in the coming moments. If not, possibly within the next hour or so after the meeting has ended.'

Sly devils... William thought.

About a minute passed before things were finally in motion.

'Alright!' the Executive General Manager said. 'It looks like we can go on from here and begin the meeting. Now, most of this talk will be about the future of this organization and how our current services will improve the outcome for our customers.'

William tuned in and out of the executive's talk about statistics and responses to the recent addition to the organization's services—Illumina. He cared little for the news or anything that they discussed for the next fifteen minutes. Then finally came the main topic of concern for all of them: the results of the program. His heart began to race. It was the moment of truth.

'With the recent addition of Illumina and its significant improvement on processes, there's been an executive decision to embed the AI permanently.'

'What does that mean for us?' one employee asked.

'With the recent changes and Illumina's capability to see much of the work completed without errors or delays, we will commence the lay-off of staff.'

'Lay-off?' another employee asked. 'When the hell does that begin?'

'Today... and it looks like the results have just been released for the reskill program of those who have participated.'

Silence ensued.

William quickly refreshed his workday page—having had the page open on the ready should he be asked to look at something. The page refreshed with a shining blue icon worded, PROGRAM RESULTS. Hands shaking as he clicked on the link, taking him to another page where a PDF document with a marking checklist, he scrolled through the two-page document to the end to see a score of 86% with a grade, FAILED, next to the mark.

The fuck? That's a good mark. He looked at the comments on the corporate chat where people were posting similar remarks about their score and grade.

'I got a score of 92.7% yet I failed,' one employee said, sound confused and upset. 'Isn't that a good mark?'

'It's a good mark, indeed,' the executive said. 'However, the benchmark to pass was 95%.'

'Let me do the test again. I'll get the mark then. There has to be some sort of exception in place.'

'Unfortunately, there won't be another program in place. Hence the reason why your trainers were advised about telling you consistently to study for this exam.'

'But this is bullshit! It's a good mark.'

'Yeah, what the hell?' another employee said. 'I got a mark of 94.8%, yet I still failed. Can't you make an exception? I was only point two off the benchmark.'

'There won't be any exceptions applied. Where the mark stands, the outcome will remain the same.'

'That's it, I've had enough,' one of the employees said, 'I'm coming into the office. I've had it with the bank and this fucking AI thing. I've got bills to pay. I can't afford to be laid off.'

'Please message your line manager,' one of the executives said, 'if you have any enquiries.'

'You are our managers as well. What the hell is this bullshit?!'

'Once more, you'll have to—'

'They're not in the office anymore,' another colleague said. 'Ours opted to work from home due to the situation. But I do know where he lives. Let's go visit him.'

'What are you guys doing? Don't think about doing that.' The executive manager suddenly sounded concerned, even panicky.

'We need to inform the unions,' someone else said. 'There's gotta be something we can do to stop this.'

'Already have,' Marlene said.

'I've been working with Pinnacle for years,' a familiar voice said, 'and now to think that the bank doesn't want the help anymore—wanting to cut loose employees who have contributed so much to them for the sake of cutting costs for this goddamn AI.'

'For those who are still part of the organization,' one of the executives said, 'you can talk about other opportunities. You can go through it in your one-on-one talk about your career development plan.'

'What will there be to develop?' another employee asked, 'if there's an AI doing all of the work? I may have kept my job for now but who is to say that you won't decide to do another layoff in the future. My hours have been reduced to half already from what they were at full time. But now I'm considered permanent part time but with half the work and half the pay. What the hell is that about?'

William read the messages filling the chat of complaints from employees who worked in the same and other departments, coming through like a waterfall. He browsed through the participant list to see if any of the managers were online. Some were online but non-responsive to the messages—particularly those having their names tagged.

Bing! A message came through from a private chat from his closest teammate.

'Can you believe this crap?' Marlene asked.

'I don't really know what to say,' he replied.

'Are you going into the office?'

'Office? What's happening?'

'We're going to protest and fight this. It's not just us from the department, but lots of people from other departments are going to be there.'

'I don't think that's going to be a good idea.'

'What are you talking about? This is a great idea. We're protesting for our right to work and not lose our jobs.'

'The bank will stop anyone from going into the office. All our messages are recorded. They will know what's going on.'

'They should know. Now are you in?'

He sighed and typed, 'Yeah.'

Thirty minutes later, he sat in the backseat of an automated cab heading towards the office. His right leg shook uncontrollably. He knew the police would be alerted to his latest breach but he didn't care.

The day was spiralling out of control. He was in freefall, and didn't think his day could get any worse after killing Demitrova and her friend, followed by Kristie's revelation. And now he had to add his name to the unemployment list alongside many other people—something he'd once thought inconceivable. It'd be a matter of weeks before he found himself sleeping on the streets.

'GET RID OF ILLUMINA!' a many-voiced angry chant echoed. 'GET RID OF ILLUMINA!'

William looked ahead as the chant grew louder and the bank's headquarters came into sight. The car veered right onto the main road leading to Pinnacle Funds, avoiding a crowd of people carrying banners, and storming the streets in their hazmat suits and masks. He had the cab park nearby, tapped his bankcard over the sensor to pay from his rapidly diminishing funds for the fare and the door lifted open. His phone chimed with an alert for his now overdrawn account.

Shit!

Security barred the entrance stopping the employees entering the building. Those chanting close to the building instigated a fight with the patrolling officers and Enforcers. Batons against bats. The soon-to-be former employees of the bank charged forward but couldn't make any ground against the Enforcers looming over the people and pressing them back with ease.

Brrng, brrng! His phone rang in his jacket pocket. He had his earpiece attached and accepted the call.

'Hello?' he said.

'Will!' Marlene said. 'It's Mal. Where are you?'

'I just arrived. Doesn't look like we're going to be able to get inside.'

'I found a way in. Meet me by the underground car park area on the east side of the building. Do you know which one?'

'I think I do.'

'Wait by the entrance for a moment. The area will be guarded but that's alright. Just keep a lookout for the diversion.'

William ran around the building, looking for the entrance to the underground car park. He arrived and found sinister-looking security personnel standing guard behind the shutter fence.

What did she mean by diversion?

Engines roared from behind William. He turned to find two hover cars flying directly for the shutter fence. The cars rode straight through the doors, sending the guards into a frenzy for cover. As they dispersed one of the cars exploded followed by a group of protesters rushing inside.

William rushed through the entrance, slipping past security officers who appeared solely focused on the protesters. Once he passed them, he acted normal and headed towards the elevators. He entered one, ascending to his designated work level. Not since his last hub day had he visited the office. Everything was the same. The elevator soared eleven levels, reaching the top, where the elevator doors slid open for him to exit. He followed through the department floor, where rows and rows of emptied desktop stations gleamed with barely a person in sight. Kitchen areas to the floor witnessed the same emptiness aside from the occasional beeping and whirring of fridges and coolers.

He spotted a familiar blue-eyed blonde by the window, looking down at the protest happening outside. He quickly crossed a platform to get to the other side.

CHAPTER 11

'Mal?' he said.

'Will!' she said. She embraced him, holding him tight as if for the first time. 'You made it.'

'With some luck. How did you get in here?'

'I know someone inside.' She showed him a pass with a different name and staff number.

'Neat.' He looked over the protest below. 'How were you able to get this many people involved so quickly?'

'I've been talking to a lot of people since we last spoke. There's a lot of us who care about this more than you think. Although I had help from the unions.'

'I'm sorry. I should have been there helping you.'

'It's okay. You're here now. And I'm glad you are.' She offered a gentle smile. 'Come on. We need to find Raj.'

'What good will it do, Mal? Most of us have already been given the axe.'

'Yes, but it's the Line Manager's decision to allow exceptions. He could change the outcome.'

William doubted the chances of Raj helping them but he followed Marlene through a corridor, passing the toilets and small meeting rooms to arrive at another open and emptied work area.

At the corner side of the floor, by the building edge, a workstation seemed occupied by an actual human body sitting behind the monitors. He could hear a male voice like a soft murmur becoming clearer as he approached the desk. Raj was there with other people. It seemed like they kept their jobs. Black hair and brown skin, he seemed to have put on weight since their last in-person meeting.

'Raj?' Marlene said.

There was no response. Raj was wired into headphones, his eyes fixed upon the screen.

'Raj!'

This time Raj noticed.

'William? Marlene?' he said. Surprised crossed his face as he pulled his headphones down. 'What are you doing here?'

'What do you mean? We work here.'

'I mean how did you get into the building? There's security all lined up around the building to stop those idiots coming into the buildings.'

'Idiots?! What are you talking about? Those are our colleagues including our teammates fighting for their right to work here while they still can.'

'What work? Illumina has taken over as our designated operation. There's no need for them anymore.'

'And how about you?' William asked.

'What about me?'

'If there's no team to manage, then what will be done with you? Are you going to be made redundant like us?'

Raj chuckled. 'Don't be silly. I'm being reassigned to another team. The bank still wants me to operate in another space where I can still work.'

'While the rest of us get the axe?'

'I tried to get the team reassigned to other teams or projects but there wasn't any availability.'

'So that's it? That's as far as you go in helping your team?'

'Pretty much. My delegation has been removed.'

'Fuck delegation! What about the people who have worked for the bank for years? They are being let go while others, who have worked for less, still get to work here?' His voice caught the attention of those nearby. They popped their heads up to the side to see what was going on.

'Why do you care? You didn't like this job to begin with.'

'The hell should that matter to you? I was good at my job and at least I contributed.'

'Well, now you have an opportunity to try something different. Perhaps there's another place out there where you can do something you really want to do. I hear the disability sector is in need of people.'

'Nearly every other place is going through the same shit,' Marlene said.

'That's not my problem.'

William's blood boiled and his skin grew hot from frustration at Raj's lack of care towards them.

'You could at least get us exceptions. You owe us that. You know we're good workers.'

'Like I said before, that's not up to me. I've given my exceptions to the higher ups.'

'And?'

'Hey Raj, we have a meeting, you good to—' Everett said, 'Well, looks like the cat dragged in some misfits that don't belong here anymore.'

CHAPTER 11

William turned around to see Everett standing by the entrance door to one of the meeting rooms. 'You let *him* through?'

'Hey, it's not my fault that you weren't good enough.'

'Say what?' Marlene stormed up at Everett, who quickly scrambled away from her. 'Come say that again to me—right here—to my face. I dare ya.'

Marlene exhaled and faced Rajesh. 'Tried to help the team? You fucking dickhead.'

Heavy footsteps hitting the floor carpet echoed nearby. Everyone turned to find a pair of security officers approaching them. They appeared stern-faced, sturdy and immovable.

'What seems to be the problem here?' one of the officers asked, looking at the four of them.

William and Marlene remained quiet.

'We have protesters here,' Raj said, 'who broke through the parking entrance on the east side. Please take them away.'

'You're not going to get away with this,' Marlene said.

William bit down, feeling his jaw tighten in anger. His own temperament matched Marlene's but he couldn't do anything about the situation, so he left with the officers. The entire time his mind ran wild with ideas on what to do about the redundancies.

He arrived on the ground floor and left the building for perhaps the last time. The chants had continued and the protests had caught the attention of the media. News reporters set up posts by the crowd, reporting the news or speaking with people who worked for the bank.

William hoped he'd be noticed by the reporters because he was ready to unleash a rant exposing everything about the bank. As he passed the revolving doors, a bomb suddenly exploded on the other side of the building, sending people into a frenzy.

He looked over to see debris and bloodied, mangled bodies spread across the ground with black hazy smoke rising to the top of the building. Screams of terror and helplessness rang through the field. Their cries resonated with the turmoil he was experiencing within himself as well.

Fuck...

William left the area quickly with Marlene before the police and Enforcers began arresting protesters or anyone they deemed to be involved. He found a street bench and sat down while Marlene paced angrily.

'This is ridiculous,' Marlene said. 'The hell happens now? I have no job. I can't support my family. My baby boy.' Her voice trembled like she was on the verge of crying. But she didn't break. 'Are we *that* expendable now?'

'We always were, Mal. It's just that technology has finally caught, and is now able to do things like take over and replace us on a far greater scale than ever before. We can't stop it.'

'Screw that! There's got to be something we can do. We can't just be discarded like this.' She sighed, and finally sat down beside William.

Silence passed.

'Does your husband know now?' he asked.

'Yeah, I had no choice,' she said. 'I broke down a few days ago... I couldn't take it anymore... he just happened to be there when I did. Definitely wasn't a conversation I wanted to have.' She looked at him. 'What will you do?'

William looked at her. He knew his answer but it wasn't one he was happy with.

Whoop, whoop! A police siren rang as the car drove past them, racing away towards Pinnacle Funds.

'We should go. It isn't safe here anymore.'

'Yeah, I'm going this way.' She embraced William. 'We'll be in touch. Good luck with everything.'

'You too.' He watched her leave before he headed in the opposite direction.

An hour passed since the events at the bank, William did nothing but lay on his bed in silence. His phone buzzed and buzzed. Multiple calls came through from people he knew who most likely wanted to talk about the layoffs at Pinnacle Funds. When he reached his limit, he grabbed his phone to turn it off. One message from Kristie caught his attention as he went to switch settings.

'Hey, I heard the news,' Kristie messaged. 'Everything alright? Call me when you get a chance.'

He stared at the screen, not sure what to do about Kristie. The idea of having someone's past to be so different to who they were now troubled him. He knew he couldn't avoid talking to her forever as he was committed but for how long he would remain committed was unclear. William pulled her number up and called. He didn't know what he was going to say. The phone rang and when there was an answer, he ended the call. He waited a moment to consider calling again, then did but again, ended as soon as she answered. He couldn't bring himself to call Kristie yet. Not till he had some words.

CHAPTER 11

Brrng, brrng!

William looked at his phone. Kristie's caller ID appeared on the home screen. He let the phone ring and ring, and at the last second, he answered the call.

'Will,' she said. Her soft voice was gentle and concerned.

'Hey,' he said.

'Everything alright? You called before. I didn't know if there was something wrong with the connection.'

'I—uh—I'm alright.' He sighed. 'I did call... There wasn't anything wrong with the connection. I just didn't really know what I was going to say... given what's happened to me in the last few days, everything's been like a wild circus.'

'Because of my past.'

He hesitated. 'Yes, and because of the assault by the police, and now that I've lost my job.'

'What do you mean "you lost your job?"'

'Many of us were made redundant after our results from the program. The benchmark was way too high. Many of us didn't make it. Myself included, but they never told us the benchmark. Had I known...' He sighed.

'Surely the unions can do something about what the bank's doing? This is ridiculous.'

'Doubt it.'

'What will you do?'

'Try and survive, I guess.' He sighed deeply.

Both went quiet for a moment.

'I'm sorry about before,' she said. 'I should have been upfront from the beginning.'

'It's a lot to process, Kristie. After learning about your past, I—it's just— you struck me so convincingly as you are that I didn't think twice about you being someone different in the past.'

'But I *am* a woman.'

'I'm not saying you aren't.'

'Then what *are* you saying?'

'I'm saying it's a lot to take in!' Another sigh followed. 'Just give me a few days... please. I need to think things over right now. The last thing I want to do is make things worse, okay?'

'Okay.'

He ended the call shortly after, and tossed the phone aside. He didn't want to think or do anything. He closed his eyes, letting sleep take over. It was lights out within a few seconds.

CHAPTER 12

THE TIME PASSED, and notice followed notice, alerting William to his late payments for rent, utilities and breaches. He threw aside his phone several times. He knew money would resolve many of his issues but the real problem was work. Every place he called had no vacancies as artificial intelligence had now taken over most of the work. Any work which remained resided with the owners of the companies, and the people they knew. He knew nobody.

Brrng, brrng! His phone rang beside him as he browsed the internet for work. Sasha's name appeared above the ringing icon. It didn't look like another invitational call to the family so he accepted it.

'Sasha,' he said.

'Will!' she said. 'I've been trying to get in touch with you for ages. Everyone from the family has been trying to get in touch with you. They're worried sick about you.'

'Yeah, I've seen the missed calls and messages. Sorry for not getting back. Is everything alright?'

'I think I should be the one asking.'

'I'm alright, Sasha.'

'Be serious, Will. I heard about the news. The layoffs and stuff. What happened?'

'Something out of my control.' He sighed. 'Sasha, I do appreciate you calling, but I really have to go.'

'Don't hang up, please!'

William remained silent and waited for her to speak. Desperation in her voice.

'I know things are tough right now, Will. Why don't you come back home? Stay with Mum and Dad and me. There's plenty of space. You'll be fine here until things settle down.'

'Everyone in the family is different. My way of living will rub some people up the wrong way as will theirs' with me.'

'You mean Mum and Dad?'

William didn't reply.

'Why do you hate them?'

'I don't *hate* them, Sasha. I never did. It's just—it's just better if we weren't in the same place because they have their expectations, and I have my own. None of which are the same or even remotely similar. I'm sorry. It's a nice idea but not likely to happen.'

'Well, they think you hate them. That last call we had together really affected them.'

'Look, I'm sorry you had to see that, but I don't regret what I said to them. At least now they know what I think.'

'Why don't you speak to them again? Surely you don't want to have your last memory of them be an argument.'

William considered her words.

She sighed. 'What are you going to do now?'

'I don't know but I'll figure out something... Look, I have to go. There's stuff I have to get a handle on.'

'Alright. But don't do anything stupid... please... I don't want to hear of another call about you in the hospital with a note left behind for us.'

'I'll catch you another time, Sasha.' He ended the call before she could say another word. He couldn't afford to.

Her last remark triggered a memory he hadn't thought about in a long time. He glanced at his right wrist, running his index and middle finger over scarring. Fragmented memories of blood, alcohol, and depression played on his mind.

He immediately got up and left his office to forget about the memory. Deep breaths. He didn't want to go there again. He slapped his face several times to shock himself out of it.

Get out.

Minutes later, he had regained his composure somewhat. He returned to his office and continued browsing the web to find work but to no avail. With the possibility of not having a job in the coming weeks—possibly for months—he needed to budget. He accessed his bank account to see his savings. He didn't have any. He cursed himself for spending money on virtual women and unnecessary distractions.

Knock, knock!

William approached the door. Anxiety crept up on him again. He didn't know who it was. No invitation had been sent out by him to have someone visit. He looked through the peephole to find two men in suits. The logo across their right chest read, DUTYPACK. They were transporters and removalists for Pinnacle Funds. The company's equipment he had needed to be collected.

'Mr. Kepler?' one of the packers said.

He exhaled and nodded. 'The stuff is in the room on the right.' He stepped aside, letting the two men inside.

Afterward, William lay on his bean bag. He had no idea what to do for the day. Having no work, and being confined to an apartment with no way out, didn't help the situation. He pulled his phone towards his face to look at recent news. Pinnacle Bank was one of the main trending topics, alongside similar situations reported at other organisations.

The articles spiked his anger and adrenaline. It was a shit situation and he knew he couldn't do anything about, which made him angrier, as the videos showed conferences of executives from other organisations stating their own reasons for their staff layoffs.

One particular situation resulted in the staff striking against the company and locking themselves inside the premises, refusing to leave the buildings. Police officers and Enforcers had stormed the place, taking the people away. A fight had broken out between the two parties but it hadn't lasted long. By the end of the video, footage of people in black body bags were being shown.

What the hell?!

A second later the video went black with the reporters asking people to disregard the 'misleading' footage.

Brrng, brrng! He jumped in surprise as his phone rang. Kristie's name appeared on the screen. He stared at it, letting the phone ring until the last moment, then answered.

'Kristie,' he said.

'*Hey...*' she said.

'*Hey...*'

'How are you holding up?'

'Things could be better. You?'

'Same. Things could be better... Listen, I—I, uh... I didn't know what I was thinking when I picked up the phone to call. So much of it was *second nature*, you know? I just—wanted to hear your voice. I didn't want my last conversation with you to end like it did.'

'I will admit, I've had the same experience in a way but I worried that if I start talking the moment we spoke, some things would have been said that I don't think either of us wouldn't have wanted to say at all.' He paused for a moment. 'Times are not good for us at the moment. There's been such a shift in everything that I really don't know what to do.'

'Well, at least you have someone who *is* going through the same thing. Sort of lessens the discomfort in a way, don't you think?'

'Maybe... I should apologise. What you shared with me is something that is common now, and is important to you. If you believe who you say you are or feel you are, then I should be able to accept that... but it'll take time.'

'Thank you.'

'Anyway, I'm going to head off.'

'Before you go, I wanted to ask, if you think it might help, I'm hosting a small gathering at the rooftop of my apartment building. I think it'd do everyone some good to wind down a bit and just have a relaxing time. Come over.'

'Umm... sure. I'll come.'

Kristie sounded happy when he agreed to attend the party. The party was set for that night. A party during this time was ill-advised but not illegal. As long as everyone in attendance was carrying a mask and adhering to the social distancing rules to avoid the spread of the virus if exposed to the Smog.

For William, he hadn't been to a party in over seven years—even the last one he attended wouldn't be considered a party as it involved everyone who'd attended sitting around a table, eating junk food and talking about trivial matters. He went to his wardrobe and check his clothing to see if he still had something deemed fashionable for an outing with other actual people. He didn't have anything of the sort but he did have his work suit from which he removed the logos.

He put on his suit to see if it still fit. It was a little tighter around the back and chest. He was thinner back in the day.

CHAPTER 12

Thanks to the lockdowns, his diet had worsened and his weight increased. Although it didn't matter as much to him since Zerya grew exponentially with its features and capabilities, which allowed him to mask his actual appearance with his own customized avatar.

Hopefully one day it gets better... Hopefully it all gets better. Can't afford to be living like this for long.

When the time came to leave for the party, he grabbed his belongings and fed Ramses. He left the building in his hazmat suit, mask and gloves, and booked an automated taxi to Kristie's place.

After ten minutes in the cab, he arrived at Kristie's place. He received a message to use the staircase after using the elevators to the top floor as there was no direct route to the rooftop. He followed the instructions, completed the detoxification, and within five minutes, he stood before the rooftop door and heard voices in lively conversations.

Do I really have to talk to these people?

He stood there for a moment. Conversing with people, especially small talk, had always been his weakness, which was why it was easy to work in a call centre because there was scripting and he didn't have to say anything aside from stating facts about products and procedures. But all that was gone now.

He shook off his anxiety, took some deep breaths and pushed the door open. Before it could swing forward, someone from the other side pulled the door, startling him. There stood a slender girl with purple short hair and ring piercing on her nose.

'Oh hey,' the girl said, in a lively tone. 'William, right?'

'Ah, yeah?' William said.

'It's so nice to finally meet you. I've heard a lot about you.'

The hell could that possibly mean?

He wondered if Kristie had mentioned to this person about his reaction to her past. 'Okay, and—um—you are?'

'I'm Kristie's friend. We work together—well, I should say—we *worked* together when we were in our old jobs. Gotta love AI, you know? We all got the axe.'

'*Yeah...* gotta love AI. I didn't catch your name by the way.'

'Angelina. But you can call me Angie. My full name is only reserved for my family or someone who I really care about.'

149

'Right.' He looked around and saw Kristie, who waved when she noticed him. 'Nice meeting you.' In his mind he said, *Not!* He left Angelina and crossed the glass-enclosed rooftop, looking at the ventilation channels hanging down from the ceiling, before spotting a Zerya hotspot stand in the centre. His mind played possible scenarios behind its presence but forgot them when he embraced Kristie.

'I'm so glad you're here,' Kristie said, who appeared to have gone the full nine yards to appear the most attractive girl there. She appeared to have curled her straight hair, wearing a retro orange dress and white heels.

'You look good,' William said. He gave her a peck on the lips, and nothing more. He still couldn't fight off the idea of her past.

'As do you. Have you eaten?'

'Not yet. Is there food coming?'

She laughed. 'Of course, there's food coming. How could there be a party without food? It should be arriving in about twenty minutes. We ordered pizza. Again. Can't afford to have me cooking or anyone here for that matter. Anyway, I have some things to finish up before everyone arrives. Just leave your suit and mask by the door. You don't have to keep them on your person. After that, feel free to chat with a few people. I'll catch up with you later on.'

'Sure.' He watched her head over to her mini bar, setting up lights and bottle racks with a shaker bottle for cocktails. He looked at the other people as they socialized amongst each other. Knowing he had little to say or any interest in talking to anyone else, he headed towards the rooftop windows to look over at streets below and neighbouring buildings—similar sight to his own place. All haze and nothing to see anywhere.

'Can't seem to talk to anyone?' a voice said.

William turned around to find a blue-eyed man, trimmed blonde hair so white, it was blinding. He wore a checked shirt and blue jeans, and held a small glass of alcohol against his pants. 'Well, it's not actually common nowadays to have people so close together now.'

'We do it all the time in Zerya. How is it any different?'

'Because no one's really there.'

'Hmph... I digress.' He approached the window as well, standing a meter away from William. 'So you haven't spoken to people in a setting like this, then, have you?'

'Not for a long time.'

150

CHAPTER 12

'Well, you won't find too much joy looking out the windows. Barely a sight to see. Just the depressing air that is so trying to get us.'

'It's enough to pass the time.'

'Perhaps... but if this is how you're going to spend your time, I wonder how you're going to react then, when we all engage in carnalites.'

'Carnal-what?'

'Carnalities—well that's the name we give for... you know.' He smiled cheekily.

'I don't.'

He pointed to the Zerya hotspot. 'Why else do you think that's here?'

'In case someone gets bored.'

'Now that'd be a waste.' He stood closer to William. 'I'm surprised Kristie didn't tell you about this. It's her kind of thing anyway. On a regular occasion.'

'It was her idea?'

'Well, yeah. It's something she believes in—how did she put it?' he looked away as if recalling a memory. 'Something that resonates with her identity.'

'And what's that?'

'I think you should ask her yourself. But anyway, you don't need to worry about her. I think I can look after you while you're here. She wouldn't mind.' He placed his hand on William's. 'After all, wouldn't it be better for someone to look after you who knows what it's really like to be a man, rather than Kristie?'

William removed the man's hand. 'I think I'd like to be alone right now. If you don't mind.'

'Of course.' The man didn't seem offended by the gesture. If anything, he seemed to treat it as a tease.

William's heart beat through his head and ears. As he looked around, he noticed the numbers were growing. He saw Kristie socializing and greeting people who were arriving. Some wore exaggerated clothing which screamed 'drag queen' to William. He couldn't take it and saw the bar where a lady was preparing a drink with a shaker. He marched right over to the benchtop.

'What would you like?' she asked.

'Anything that's going to take the edge off.'

'Depends on your state. You need to give me something I can work with.'

William looked at her with confusion. 'What the hell does that supposed to mean?'

'You want a drink or not?'

'Yeah!'

'Then give me a story.'

'Fine. How's this? It's been two years without a single meeting with anyone until a few nights ago. I have a girlfriend who was once someone else completely, and I just found out that this is the gathering of some sort of virtual orgy. Plus, I've lost my job to AI and will most likely be out of work for a long time. And I have been assaulted by the police. Would you like me to go further back than the last seven days?' He looked at the bartender questioningly.

'No, I think I got just the thing for you.' The lady slapped a glass on the benchtop, collected two bottles from the shelf, pouring both two liquids into the shaker—one was white and the other red-brownish. She placed the bottle into a contraption, which shook the shaker quickly. Within thirty seconds the bottle appeared to blur from the speed.

What is she making?

As the machine continued to shake the bottle, the lady popped a spherical ice cube into the cup. *Beep!* The machine completed the shake. The lady poured into the cup the blended liquors and passed the glass to William.

'Now, before you try this, you need to have it with this.' She took a bottle of granulated salts, or something that appeared like salt and passed it to William. 'Open this and inhale this at least twice.'

'What is it?'

'Salts with blended aromatic oils, and an added spice of my making. It should take the edge off.'

William examined the bottle labelled *Stardust*. It seemed like an approved recreational drug but it wasn't the case. He opened the bottle and moved the opening towards his nose. A sweet, pungent scent assailed his nostrils. He inhaled another round without conscious effort, as if his body wanted to absorb it all. He coughed uncontrollably for a moment.

'Holy shit!' he said.

'Strong, isn't it?' She pushed the glass towards him forcefully. 'Now, drink. It won't work if you don't.'

He obeyed and downed the alcohol quickly with minimal burn along his throat. There seemed to be a thin coating around the alcohol, allowing it to run smoothly into the drinker. He hammered the glass on the bench. Luckily for him, it didn't break. He exhaled, taking a moment to observe the effects—if any. He waited. Nothing happened. He looked at the bartender, disappointed. 'Is that it?'

'Give it a moment.' She smirked.

He waited. Still nothing happened. 'I'm sorry. I think that beverage sizzled to a dud. I think you're going to need to add something that's really going to pack a pun...ch...' He did a take back. He felt his stomach churn and mind crack open into something he hadn't experienced before. 'Oooooohhh...'

'There it is.'

William found himself sucked out of reality. His surroundings gleamed with life and vivid colours. He looked at the people in the courtyard. Their features were clearly accentuated now as he sank into the high chair, letting the substance take hold and watched their physical bodies transform into clouds of energy moving across the floor until they blurred together. He looked back at the bartender. Her body had disappeared but her energy remained, or so it seemed like energy, he thought. It was like another dimension of life he hadn't seen before.

'The hell did you give me?' he asked.

'Something to loosen you up,' she said.

He closed his eyes and shook his head. He waited a moment, hoping it would stop. He wanted it to stop. The experience was overwhelming. The very sensation of sweat beading through his pores multiplied tenfold as did every function of his body.

His journey took him through the unknown places of the universe. Stars, planets, and obscure shapes and colours passed his way while he moved through space at lightning speed. At some point he found himself falling through darkness and clouds, then plummeting towards a sky-blue ocean below. He became a water drop before hitting the ocean.

'Will?' a voice said.

His mind fired on all cylinders as everything turned inside out. His vision warped his reality into another dimension as if he now viewed something in his mind to see the universe through a different lens.

'Will!'

William finally heard the call. He looked up and saw a ball of energy in front of him. Then transformed into something that appeared like a woman and resembling the rooftop again. 'Kristie?' He looked around to see himself crouching in a corner.

'Are you alright?'

'You tell me... I just got a space-hit of mind-bending shit.' He kept blinking to see if his eyes would adjust to the lighting. They were, slowly. 'The hell is this, Kristie?'

'What do you mean?'

'What was the point of this gathering?'

'It was for us to get along. And to—' She went quiet.

'And to what?'

'To connect with people on a more *intimate* level through Zerya and be who we really are.'

'You mean play an avatar?'

'You say that as if a person can't experience something real through Zerya.'

'No, you can't. It's mind manipulation. It's not real. None of this can be. Believe me, I've tried.'

'It's as real as you can experience when we were intimate. Why not give it a go?'

William looked around and realized the position of the room had changed. He found himself buried away in the corner. He got up and followed Kristie, taking her by the hand. He arrived in the centre and could see nearly everyone connected to Zerya.

All of them lay on a sofa, chair or bean bag with a bottle of stardust and similar looking beverages beside them. They all appeared to be in a trance.

'How long was I out for?' he asked.

'Close to an hour. I spoke to Frida.'

He looked at her, confused by the name.

'The bartender. She said she gave you your first hit. I took you away because I thought you may need time to process everything. It can be something when you haven't had it before.' She stood beside a recliner chair. 'Come.'

I was out for an hour? That felt like five minutes...

William, reluctant, took his time. He dropped onto the cushioned seat. His body and his mind still raced with uncertainty. Something about the whole thing didn't sit well with him.

'Just relax.' She placed a consoling hand on his shoulder as she gathered the neural port to Zerya.

William sat motionless as his eyes darted around the room from person to person. Men and women moaned or gasped in pleasure. Their lips curled around their mouths, biting out at the end in enjoyment. Some massaged their legs and sounded out of breath. From where he was, it seemed they were already in the act, although he couldn't tell who was engaged with whom. He didn't care for it, and as Kristie approached him, holding the cable to Zerya, dread filled him. Where was he going? Was it something he really wanted to know or experience or do? Could he really continue doing this with Kristie? She said it was real—but...

'I can't do this,' William said, as he sat on the sofa with Kristie about to insert him into Zerya. 'I can't.'

'What do you mean? You said—'

'I know what I said.' He stood quickly and marched away from the area. He staggered away as his bearings were still under the influence of Stardust. He reached for things to support him which aided his balance.

'Will, where are you going? Will?' Kristie rushed ahead of him, trying to stop him from leaving. 'I thought you wanted to stay here and be with me. You said you'd give it a go.'

'Is this something you do regularly?'

'Well, yeah. It's the only way to be who we really are.'

'Who you *really* are? What are you talking about? There's only one real world. It's this shithole.'

'But who I am here isn't me. I don't identify with this—' she gestured to her body, 'as I see it every day. I see the marks and everything that came with the change and I can't be accepted for who I really am.'

'You're not making any sense.'

'Just give a go, please.' She grabbed his hand.

William glanced back at the people lying around. Then looked back at Kristie. 'I can't... I thought I could deal with this. I seriously thought I could... but I'm sorry. I can't do this.'

William released himself from her hand and walked away. He gathered his belongings, closed the door shut behind him and quickly descended before anyone else could stop him. However, he figured with his last comments, she wouldn't come after him as his position was clearly final and he believed she understood that.

He arrived at the ground floor of the building and headed for the exit when a bottle splattered across from the floor, startling William as he couldn't tell where it came from. He stumbled to the ground as the drug still affected him.

'Screw you, you goddamn asshole!' a voice yelled from above. 'What the fuck do you think you're doing?'

William looked up to find Kristie's friend, whose name he hadn't bothered to remember, launching another bottle. He moved away in time to avoid getting hit.

'You get back here you piece of shit! This woman fucking loves you and you treat her like dirt.'

William raced towards the exit. He'd had enough and didn't want the matter to escalate. He needed to take his mind off everything. He placed his mask on and marched off into the city, not caring anymore about whether he was outside his LGA. With a tram, bus and a bit of walking he was in the heart of the CBD.

The city nightlife took over when he arrived. The streets were filled with people in defence suits, entering and leaving buildings as if there was no cause for concern from the Smog.

What the hell is going on here? There are more people going out and about here than my area. Where are the police? Why aren't any of them being questioned?

Deciding not to think about it anymore, he headed straight for his destination—*Rem Haven.* A place where he could replace his troubles with a good time, and more importantly in a real place. The establishment resided on the seventh floor of a particular building with a blue holographic projection of a woman whose figure bordered on the voluptuous. She twirled and acted innocent-like but the more someone looked into her eyes, the more they were able to see behind the act. More often than not, men would venture here. The occasional woman might be seen trying out the scene but it mainly attracted men.

William removed his mask and took an elevator to the seventh floor. He had frequented the place in the early years while the virus slowly moved up the gradings of catastrophe. It had been more than several years since he last visited and he hadn't considered coming back but today of all days seemed like a reasonable excuse to visit again to regain some sort of normality, he thought.

Ding! The elevator chimed. He arrived on the level. The door slid aside to show a gorgeous brunette in a grey blazer, tight skirt and string-strappy heels. The immediate sight of the woman sent a rush of excitement through him. But he ignored the feeling. No good to go off before he got into the room. He approached the woman but remained at a distance as two tall, hulking men, wearing black suits, stood guard.

'Hi there,' the woman said, voice smooth and classy.

'Hi,' he said. 'It's been sometime since I've been here. I don't suppose,' he took a platinum membership card and passed it to the woman, 'this still works?'

She took the card, inspecting it for a moment before walking around the concierge desk to look into the matter further. William followed her as she tapped the car over a sensor, which beeped. Within seconds, information about William and his history with the establishment appeared on screen. He could see his last dated time for a visit posted on 31 January 2034. He tried to remember the night but his memories blurred together. He couldn't remember the dates but he did remember the women and how he'd felt after his visit. Mostly satisfied. Something he wanted to feel again.

'Mr. Kepler?' the woman said.

'Yes?'

'It's definitely been some time since your last visit. With this card, while there's credit in the account, the card itself has expired. To make use of it, you'd have to sign up again as a member to get access to the credits.'

'That's no problem. If you can reissue the card and throw in an extra thousand credits, that'd be greatly appreciated.'

'Certainly.' She assisted him with membership reactivation and passed him a new card. 'Everything's good to go now.'

'Thank you.' He stood for a moment, looking at his card, then looked at her. 'You're not available by any chance, are you?'

She smiled. 'I'm not.'

He left for the entrance. The guards standing by inspected his card before letting him in.

The sound of old school jazz and slow dancing music reverberated through the entrance doors as he made his way inside. An instant switch to dim-purplish lighting took over as he looked around to find men sitting around runways of lewd women stripping and performing pole dancing movements that would send any ordinary person to the chiropractor should they dare to attempt them.

Men followed women into private showrooms, while others followed women to the second floor to engage in far more intimate affairs.

'Hey love,' a woman said, who was wearing silver all over. 'Are you looking for a good time?' She brought herself into a close embrace with him.

'I'm definitely looking,' he said, 'But I just got here. I want to enjoy the show first. We'll talk later.'

'Don't keep me waiting.'

He watched the woman leave, then headed further inside to find a free table to sit by undisturbed. He ordered fried food and his usual choice of alcohol whenever he was here—XO Hennessy. He sipped on his alcohol, letting the warmth and smooth burn course down his throat. He twirled his cup as he watched the women dance along the poles, until commotion from behind him caught his attention.

He turned to find a hostess and a man engaging in a minor argument which wasn't quite audible to his ears. The pair continued to exchange words before the man slapped the woman, who fell against the floor as the man tossed alcohol on her.

'Oi!' William said, running to the woman. 'The hell are you doing?'

'You want some of this as well?' the man said.

William unexpectedly felt he was ready to fight the guy despite having Stardust in his system.

Before anything else could happen, guards arrived and escorted the man away. One of the woman's colleagues came to help, but she was already on her feet.

'Hey, are you alright?' he asked.

'Don't worry, she'll be fine,' her colleague said.

'*I* was asking her.'

'I'm okay,' the woman said.

She still had her back to William, until she turned around. That was when everything about the moment changed for him. It was the girl from the district. She was alive.

No way.

CHAPTER 13

'YOU'RE—YOU''RE ALIVE?' he asked.

Demitrova's face seemed to register shock and anger at the same time. But she did nothing as if not reveal their history—little as it was.

'What are you talking about?' the other woman asked. 'She's always been here.'

'Renae, let me handle this,' Demitrova said.

'You sure?'

'Yeah, I'm fine.'

'Okay, but if something happens, you ring me up right away, you got it?'

'Got it.'

William watched Renae leave the pair for a moment until she disappeared elsewhere. Then he returned his attention to Demitrova.

'What are you doing here?' Demitrova asked.

'I could ask you the same thing,' he said.

'I'm working.'

'I thought you were dead!'

'Say it a little louder. I don't think anyone else heard you.' She stood closer, speaking soft but aggressively.

'Listen, whatever happened, I didn't mean to—'

'Hey lady, I'm getting a little excited over here,' a middle-aged man said. 'I'm gonna need some butt cheeks to clap and some credits to pass on if you're interested. I have lots of it.'

'Can we talk somewhere else—' William's question fell short as Demitrova pulled him into a kiss. Stunned by the act, he completely froze.

'Sorry boys,' she said. 'I'm a little bit occupied at the moment with this geezer.' She placed her arms around his neck, then whispered, 'Follow me.'

The man scowled.

William didn't utter a word and made no move to protest. He followed her away from the common area into a private lounge room. The same dim purplish glow illuminated the room as he sat on the sofa, waiting for the girl to follow around and sit beside him. 'You're going to have to start—'

'Shhh,' she said, gesturing her head towards something in the ceiling.

William took his time, moving his gaze up. When his gaze arrived at the purple fluorescent lights, he spotted a tiny black circular device about the size of a baseball—it was a camera. He looked back to see the woman enabling a feature on her phone. The word, INCOGNITO, appeared temporarily before the screen went dark.

'We can speak now,' she said.

'Where do I begin?' he said. 'How is it that you're alive? I saw your house in flames on the news, and then there were two black body bags on the ground.'

'Those were for the two officers I killed. It wasn't intentional but they left me no choice.'

'How about your friend? Charles.'

'He's alive. But wait a minute, I got questions: how is it that they were able to find me? I've been hiding in that place for several months, and as soon as you show up, my place is suddenly ambushed within twenty-four hours. And in addition to that, your IP signal was masked the moment you got closer to my home, which means they shouldn't have been able to find me.'

'How was that possible?'

'Never mind how. They were still able to find me.'

'Perhaps you underestimated your enemy.'

'*Perhaps*... or maybe I misjudged you.'

William went silent. Her words and aggression irritated him but he couldn't dispute her claims.

'Either way, I'm without a home now. That's the third time you've inconvenienced me. Are you planning to make this a regular thing?'

'Listen, if I could go back in time to change my actions, I would. I never meant for you or anyone else to be hurt or bothered simply because of my curiosity,' he raised his right hand, 'something I know I should *really* fix.'

Demitrova didn't look convinced.

'In any case, I got taken to the police headquarters after we split that morning. And I mean the *big* one... I spoke to some guy who really has it in for you. I got smacked around for information because he suspected I was working with you in some way.'

'Did you say anything?'

'What? No! I don't even know you. The only thing I mentioned to them which I'm going to tell you now, was I thought you were an Allocron and I was curious. I wanted to know you and figure out how you lived life.'

'Well, you caught wind of some of it. It's one heck of a life, isn't it?' she said, sarcastically. She sighed, appearing frustrated and exhausted. 'Seriously, why did you follow me back then?'

'I thought... given how nearly all of our interactions nowadays are virtual or accompanied by a machine—with some exceptions of course—I might be able to find or learn something real with you.' He paused. 'And given how my life has completely turned upside down in a short space of time, I thought it might be possible to still find a purpose in life... still do.'

The woman seemed to relax. Her face lost some of its strain and she lay back against the sofa, silent.

'What happens now?' he asked.

'Don't know about you but I have to work. I'm on the clock so I'd imagine someone will be knocking on the door very soon.'

William looked around the room to take his mind off the subject with little success. 'How did you end up here?'

'A girl's gotta eat.'

'But you could have found work anywhere else. Why here?'

'Because people come here as evident right here.' She gestured to him to illustrate her point. 'And because more money can be made here than just about any other place. Perhaps more so now than ever with what's happening with AI.'

'It's dangerous here though. I mean I could only imagine police officers raiding the place from time to time.'

'I'm aware. But I don't really have much of a choice.'

'Are you still being followed?'

'What do you think?'

'I think you're crazy for being here, and that you should be figuring out a way to get out of here.'

'Same could be said about you with that thing in your head.'

'What are you talking about?'

'*That* neural port. Did you just think it was a port and nothing else?'

William scoffed in disbelief. 'This is only a port. Nothing else.'

'Oh yeah. Then how is it that the police were able to track me and burn my place?'

'Drones?'

She chuckled. 'I've eluded those things for years. Besides, even if they were able to use one on me, they still would have had to be quick with their operation. No Man's Land is treacherous. Too many eyes survey the area. Any indication of the authorities would instigate an all-out fight with the outlaws. They wouldn't have made it far. Hence the reason for them finding me was that.' She pointed at his neural port.

'But you said when I got to your place my position was masked. How was that even possible?'

'Charles developed a contingency. If ever we were to have had someone with us coming home, we would activate our mask to protect that. However, I think the police might have been able to figure out a way to overcome that now.'

'All the more reason not to be anywhere near here then.'

'That's what I'm trying to do.'

'And you need Gaia to help you?'

'Gaia?' She seemed dejected by their name. 'No. I don't even work for them, as the media might have you believe.'

'But you are in some way connected to them, right?'

'No, I'm *not*. I've tried to reach out to them in the past. I thought they would be able to help with the mass production of the emitter. At least there would be a common goal temporarily to make things better for all of us.'

'Did you manage to?'

She went quiet. Disappointment crossed her face. 'I wish... anyway, I think it's best you—'

Knock, knock!

'Who is it?' she asked.

'Dreyfus.'

'I'm a bit occupied at the moment.'

'So, it would seem. The boss would like a word.'

CHAPTER 13

'It's best you leave this place while you still have time,' she told William, 'And in one piece.'

'What will you do?'

She opened the door to find three men in black suits. In the centre stood a bald man with a war tattoo along his right temple. By his demeanour, he didn't seem like the social type. She turned around to face William, and said, 'Survive.' Then she disappeared with the men, closing the door behind her.

What the hell is going on here?

He left the room in pursuit of Demitrova. He arrived back in the common area, scouring the room for her. He couldn't find her but did spot the bald man heading backstage. He moved closer to get a better look but saw only maroon curtains.

'Hey hun,' the silver-haired woman said, 'you ready for that catch up now?' She embraced him intimately, coiling her silver right leg along his thigh.

'Not now,' he said, letting her go and returning to the entrance. He approached one of the closer private showrooms and found an emptied one. He hid there, waiting for Demitrova to return. His attention was fixed on the backstage area. Seconds turned to minutes. Minutes turned into an hour. Eventually, she reappeared. She had her duffle bag, and was wearing a trench coat, before she left the establishment. He wanted to approach her but didn't believe acknowledging her again here was wise. He followed her outside.

'Did you have a good time?' the concierge said.

'Sure did,' he said. 'Thank you.'

'See you next time.'

Demitrova had boarded an elevator with the doors closing as he approached. He hopped onto the adjacent elevator, heading for the ground floor, assuming the girl was also heading in the same direction.

The only thought in his mind for her sudden departure would be for her to get right away from the noise and everything to do with the establishment, including him. He watched the numbers descend from seven to one, then stopped at *G*. He exited the lifts and scanned the entrance, trying to find her through the crowds of people congregating around the front desk and concierge.

Even when he stood on his tiptoes, he still had no sight of her, before catching a glimpse of her flowing hair as she left the building. He placed his mask and hazmat suit, and followed her outside. Within seconds he was drenched by the pouring rain. He unzipped his pouch to cover himself with the poncho.

Where did this come from?

He caught up to her when suddenly a car appeared, driving straight for her. He rushed afterward her, and as he got closer, he yelled, 'Demi!'

His voice caught her attention and she turned around as he pushed her out of the way. However, the car collided with him. The force sent him hurtling overboard and crashing hard against the ground. He laid motionless, as his vision blurred and blurred, until everything went black.

Sometime later, William woke up to the smell of sterilized cleaning products. He moved his head right and left, both of which hurt. His vision was still blurred and was taking time to adjust. When his eyes finally returned close to working order, he found himself in a hospital room filled with four patients' beds, including his own.

He tried to get up but his wrists hit metal. Confused by the abrupt halt and heat radiating from his grazed skin, he turned to find his wrists handcuffed against the bedside railing. He tried to break free from them. Nothing happened.

'I think it'd be unwise to do that,' a man said from the other bed on his left. The man appeared elderly but seemed to have the use of all his mental faculties. His gaze lingered upon William.

'What are you talking about?' William said.

'You're making too much noise for me and the others.' He motioned to the other patients sleeping.

'There must be a mistake.'

'Yet here you are.'

'Who put this on me? And how did I get here?'

'You don't remember?' The man's right eyebrow rose as if unconvinced by his response.

'No, I mean... the last thing I remember was walking...' A memory flashed into mind: *He was out in the rain, following Demitrova from the establishment... A car collided against his side, then nothing.* William stared down at the bed sheets. 'After that, I don't remember.'

'I guess you'll have to thank that girl then.'

'What?'

'My word. I guess it must have been a heck of a hit if you can't remember the pretty girl who saved you. She came with you and stayed for a bit watching you very closely before leaving.'

'Mr. Kepler?' another person said.

William saw a police officer slowly approaching him. Uniformed and masked around the mouth and nose. The awkward yet menacing-looking Ulyanov stood several meters away. William could see Ulyanov's expression was more troubled than ever compared to their previous encounters. He swallowed as his throat suddenly dried up from fear.

'Why is it that my path has crossed with yours more than any other person I've dealt with in the last month?'

'Beats me. By no means is it intentional nor can I think of a reason as to why.'

'Oh, no. I think it is. You brought about a great deal of inconvenience for me, Mr. Kepler. So much so that your actions have warranted an arrest. Fortunate for you, I'll be overseeing the process.'

'I haven't done anything wrong.'

He smirked. 'As the guilty always say.' He crept closer. 'I'll read your rights in a moment, but I'll lay down your offences first for your consideration. Something to think about.'

'Just forget the reading.'

'Good, I'd rather spend my time on more important things.' He examined William's leg before looking at him. 'Must have been a nasty hit although luckily nothing's broken... for now.' He approached William standing a meter from his face. 'You know? I heard about your work situation. Must be tough now living with little to survive on. I guess that's what you and Demitrova have in common, right? I'm guessing you know more about her, eh?'

William swallowed again. Anxiety built up but he remained silent, giving nothing away.

'I'm surprised nothing has loosened your tongue after all our meetings. Resistance is good, I guess. Same for the resistance that was held up at the bank for however long it was. Your friend was responsible for that, wasn't she? Marlene, right?'

William still remained quiet.

'I think I should pay her visit.'

'Don't you dare.'

He smirked.

Footsteps approached from outside. A bespectacled man in a hazmat suit, wearing a respirator and latex gloves, walked into the room and breezed past the officer without acknowledgement.

'I take it that you have the results, doctor,' Ulyanov said, grabbing the doctor's arm, stopping him.

'Any results I may have, *officer*,' the doctor said, 'are for my patient's considerations first.'

'I have authority here to hear the results, doctor.'

'Not unless my patient consents. Now if you don't mind?' He gestured to the hand.

The officer didn't seem impressed. He cast a stern look at William. 'I'll be outside waiting.'

The doctor grabbed the blinds and sealed William's section away from the attention of others in the room. Then he sat himself beside William, crossed legged, cleaned his glasses and pulled out the report from his holographic tablet and swiped through the information.

'What's going on?' William asked.

'It seems you've had your run of misfortunes, Mr. Kepler.' He shared a look with William before returning his attention to the tablet. 'You're lucky to have sustained minimal injury from the car hit, although, when you were brought in, you had a fever and displayed symptoms similar to that of the pathogen living in the Smog.'

'Do I have it?'

'A variant of some sort, I think.'

'Is it serious?'

'Hard to say... thankfully with the antibodies circulating in your body from the immuno-booster, it's warding off most of the effects for now. That being said, given the severity of the virus, we all know the end result. It's hard to say how effective it will be.'

William went quiet.

'Is there anyone we can call for you?'

'No. I'd rather not let anyone know.'

'How about family? Or anyone at work?'

'I doubt they'll be of any help.'

'And what about your police friend over here?'

William glanced over at Ulyanov, who was talking to his subordinates. But he got the impression, the officer was still watching him. 'I guess I don't really have much of a choice in whether you tell them or not. I'm a Contaminant now. You're meant to tell them anyway, aren't you?'

The doctor didn't say anything.

'If you tell them, just ask them to remove these handcuffs and leave me alone. I really don't want to talk right now.'

'I'll do what I can.'

'How much time do I have left?'

'By this time, you would have already displayed symptoms at the later stages of being a Contaminant. You'll probably have 24-48 hours. As for the grace period, I don't think you'll want to be around to find out.'

'They're bringing an Enforcer here?'

'Yes.'

A knot tightened around William's neck. 'My last moments can't be here, doc. You gotta help me.'

'There's nothing I can do, Mr. Kepler.'

'They're going to kill me. It may not be now but in the coming day or two, I will be gone... please.'

The doctor seemed to toy with the idea. His eyes glanced over at Ulyanov for a moment before returning back to William. 'I can't promise anything but I'll try and get your handcuffs removed.'

'That'll be enough.'

William watched the doctor converse with Ulyanov. The two stood firm against one another until Ulyanov gestured to his subordinate and left. The officer approached William and removed the handcuff from his right hand only. 'Hey, come on!'

'I did what I could,' the doctor said. He passed two puffers to William. 'The rest is up to you.'

'What's this?'

'Alleviants. Inhale this once every two hours. It's not a vaccine. It'll only slow down the progression. May even give you a few more hours. Good luck.' The doctor scurried away.

Half a day later, William found himself shaking his leg uncontrollably. He worried for Marlene. If Ulyanov knew of her, then it was only a matter of time before something happened to her. He tried calling from his phone but she didn't answer which worried him even more.

He looked at his food tray, staring wide-eyed at the salad sandwich, jelly carton and biscuit packet. He didn't want to eat. His appetite had disappeared shortly after learning about his latest complication.

He looked at the other patients in the room who were still asleep. Two of them were still on ventilators, machines ticking and puffing air into their systems. The more he looked at them, the more he wanted to get away from the whole situation and be free of it all.

Ring, ring! His phone vibrated. He grabbed it. Caller ID: Sasha. His gaze lingered on the screen for a moment before the call ended. He caught sight of himself on his phone and saw his sunken eyes and dark eye bags against pale white skin. He hadn't been sick in a long time; he had forgotten what it was like to be sick.

Suddenly an itch tickled the back of his mouth. He couldn't tell if it was from the alcohol he'd consumed the previous night, or if the variant coursing through his body had already begun to invade his immune system. He drank water from his bottle. His throat was soothed for a moment but was still scratchy. Worried, he continued to monitor his body for further symptoms.

Bing! His phone chimed.

'You need to get out,' the unknown person messaged. 'You have thirty minutes to get back to your place.'

Confused, William replied. 'Who is this?'

'Get out. NOW.'

William didn't know what to do. He cast a look at the entrance to see if any officers were stationed nearby. There weren't. Now was his chance to get out. He tugged at the handcuff on his left hand, wriggling the metal bonds but nothing happened. He toyed with the position of his hand to work it loose. The size of his hand had to be smaller, which meant a broken thumb.

Oh, dear.

He knew what he had to do. Gripped by fear and anxiety, he stared at his hand as he considered the idea for the whole of a minute. He bit into the sheets, then pushed his thumb out of its socket. The pain almost knocked him out. He groaned loudly into the sheets, taking long breaths to regather himself. He freed his hand from the handcuff with his thumb wriggling around. He left a pillow under the sheets to create the impression he was still there.

Doubt they'll fall for this but whatever...

Once done, he left the room, limping from one place to another. He found a change room and discovered one locker open with a doctor's uniform, lab coat and folder. He pushed his thumb back into place before he put on the uniform, collected a mask hanging on the wall and raced out towards the entrance doors.

As he passed through a corridor, a pair of police officers sprinted past him. They didn't notice him. An alert ran through their radios—he had escaped. Realizing his chance to leave the hospital through the front doors were low, he sought out another route.

Emergency entrance, then.

Without delay, he followed the signs to the emergency area. On his way there, a sharp high-pitched ringing shot through his ears. He shook his head in response to the pain. The ringing continued to sting his eardrums as he passed through the exit where emergency personnel raced in and out to tend to the patients. His immediate desire was to stay in hospital to get himself sorted out but there wasn't a remedy in place to combat the virus. Only the puffer the doctor gave him seemed to have stalled the spread. As he marched out of the building, his eyes bounced everywhere to find a vacant vehicle to make a quick getaway. There were masked people in hazmat suits pushing patients in hazmat suits in strollers into the building while hospital vans drove away for another emergency call, and others drove in to deliver yet another patient.

'Hey, we need a hand!' one man asked. 'Can you help?'

William turned to face the person standing by the rear door of a hospital van, his assumption being the man had addressed him. He was wrong as another person went to their aid but he went on full alert as the van was prepared for departure. He waited for the man to enter the driver's seat and leave. When the opportunity came, he jumped onto the rear of the van, grasping hold of the railbar above the rear doors, and keeping clear of sight from the side mirrors and rear windows. He glanced back at the hospital to see if anyone had noticed. No one did. He breathed a sigh of relief but he knew it wasn't over. Word would spread quickly of his escape. He had to get home before the police found him.

I don't like this.

The moment was disrupted by sirens wailing nearby. William didn't look at the origin of the sound but instead readied himself to jump off the van as the vehicle set course to turn right. Without delaying and thinking about his next course of action, his feet carried him away onto the pavement. He stumbled onto the ground, then staggered back up as he raced up an alley. He looked back to see police cars driving somewhere.

After running past several blocks, he found a tram docking at a station. The banner on the tram read, DISTRICT 13. As the door closed, he launched himself through the narrow gap and sat by the exit in case he needed to leave at a moment's notice.

Ten minutes later, he was standing at the corner of the street where his apartment building resided. He stood watch as police cars and a hospital van parked beside the sidewalk while workers entered and exited the building several times. One particular sight caught his eyes—a black bag was rolled out of the building. Another poor bastard dead. He wanted to get closer to see but couldn't risk getting caught. He knew the police would come after him anyway as his position would already have alerted the authorities of his breach. Yet something was off. He should have been caught by now.

Why haven't the police found me yet? I have a tracker on me after all, don't I? His hand hovered over his port.

When the police and paramedics had left, he raced into the building to get into his apartment. He arrived on his apartment floor to find everything in order until he passed his neighbour's open door. He peered inside to see an elderly lady sitting with her back towards him, hand on her forehead, looking at a small glass of clear liquid and some tablets beside it.

'Mrs. Watson?' William said.

Startled by his voice, the woman turned around to see him by the doorway although he didn't proceed inside. 'Who are you?'

'Oh, sorry.' He removed his mask.

'Oh, my dear boy.'

'Is everything alright?'

'It's best if you come back another time. I don't want to talk right now. Better yet don't come at all please.'

'What—what happened?'

She paused then spoke. 'It was too much for him in the end. He couldn't take it. He saw another Purge nearby. It was his friend he was visiting. Enforcers checked them... and...' She went quiet.

'Will you be alright?'

CHAPTER 13

'It's getting hard for us older folks. He was one of many others who were suffering from this confinement.' Her eyes lingered on him, appearing morose. 'You should get out before it's too late.' Then she pushed a button and the door hissed closed for privacy.

Not Mr. Watson, William trembled. His eyes watered and his breathing quickened. He took a moment to regather his composure—little that remained, of course. He wanted to talk more but he didn't have time. He had to leave. He headed for his apartment and slid his access key over the sensor. The door hissed open.

A plastic sheet covered the entrance door. Confused by its presence, he pushed the sheet away, making flapping noises. When he arrived in the living room, a sterile scent invaded his nasal cavity and throat. He coughed and coughed as he headed back to the building corridor for fresh air. He looked back at the room and noticed his furniture covered in plastic sheets with a yellow stripe along the centre that read, WARNING. The haze from all the chemicals used to bomb the entire place made the scene looked like a filtered photo.

Just how many times did they bomb the place?

He put his mask back on to assist with the oxygen. His breathing became normal but the back of his mouth and nose still itched. He entered his emptied office.

Surprisingly, he didn't seem bothered by the empty space. If anything, he was happy the equipment was gone. It wasn't fulfilling and he had no care in the world for the people he was supposedly *helping*. It had just been a job to pay the bills, even though he had defended it to his family. Then he remembered Ramses.

Fuck! He looked around the place but couldn't find his cat. He was about to call an agency to find out what happened to his cat but stopped himself at the last minute, afraid of alerting the authorities to his location.

As he left the room, William found his breathing was laboured. Each time his chest expanded and contracted an ache shot through his chest and ribs. He dropped to the ground, gasping for air. He reached for the puffer in his pocket. With his hands clammy from the sweat, it slipped out of his grip.

Come on! He launched himself over the floor to get the puffer and punched the button to send the chemicals into his lungs. Nothing happened. His chest still ached from the contraction of his lungs. The virus was taking over.

Suddenly, his vision went dark and he scrabbled on the floor before passing out from the pain.

Minutes must have passed as he woke up again groggily. He looked around to find everything the same. His vision was still blurry when he spotted a shadow hovering over him. He couldn't make out who it was.

'Will...'

William pushed upright to see Demitrova kneeling beside him. 'It's you.'

'Yeah, it's me.'

'How did you—'

'Talk later, we gotta move.'

Woop, woop! Police sirens rang through the apartment.

William and Demitrova stood up and spotted a police car pulling up alongside the curb in front of the building.

'We have to go,' she said.

'I know,' he said. 'But my cat.'

'I got your cat.'

'What?! How?'

'I'll explain later.' She rushed out.

Without delay, he grabbed his duffle bag and stuffed in his hazmat suit, spare respirators and battery charger. He cared for little else as he didn't expect to survive beyond the next two days but he wanted to make sure Ramses was okay.

He raced out of his apartment with Demitrova, taking the elevators to the parking levels below. Just two officers exited the car with no backup. He suspected someone had tipped them off about him being home or possibly they had been ordered by Ulyanov to check his apartment.

Once the elevator arrived, they raced outside, where a car pulled up in front of them.

Hesitant, William stopped dead in his tracks.

'Get in, Will,' Demitrova said.

'I don't even know who the driver is,' he said.

'It's Charles.'

'That doesn't help.'

Woop, woop! A police car drove past the elevators on the opposite side. The driver inside seemed to have spotted him as the car sped around.

CHAPTER 13

William jumped inside the car and Charles powered away, barging through the boom gate, swerving onto the road and accelerating. He turned around to see the police officers, momentarily stunned, unholstering their firearm and unloading shots.

'Keep your head down!' Charles said.

'No shit!' William said.

CHAPTER 14

THEIR ESCAPE RACED ahead in feverish haste.

William watched Charles drive through the traffic, speeding past red lights, giving little regard for the other drivers, automated transports, or cameras flashing shots of the car.

He looked at both people who were dead quiet in his company but darting glances left, right and center. Clearly, they were unsettled by the venture. Then Charles wheeled off the main road onto quieter streets. His attention still lingered over the mirrors.

'Where are we going?' William asked.

No one answered.

Demi unzipped a bag and removed a similar looking contraption which the Walker used for him when he was at the TAB. 'Turn around.'

'What?'

'Turn around!'

He turned around and his head was pushed down, chin to neck, as Demi had her hand firmly on it while she injected his port. The contraption whistled as if drilling something into his port. Tightness around the neck formed as it did. It lasted several seconds until she released him. She took his phone and hovered it over hers, completing a function he didn't recognise.

'What did you do to me?' William asked, passing his fingers over his port.

'Mask your position.' She toggled settings on her old digital wristwatch—one of the very first types from many years ago—and set a timer for thirty minutes. The countdown started, dropping one second at a time. 'We'll have to do it again soon.'

CHAPTER 14

The sirens continued to wail behind them until the car was positioned in an alley behind two other cars that seemed in need of a good car wash. They were layered with dirt and dead Smog particles.

Demi raced outside and grabbed a dirty, worn-out tarp cover and tossed it over the front of the car.

'Get out!' Charles ordered.

William obeyed. He collected his belongings and exited the car. He stood in confusion like a helpless bystander. Eyes bounced between Charles and Demi, who were finishing up the cover of the car.

Demi approached him and said, 'Start walking. Head towards the end of the alley. Then turn right.'

'What?' he asked.

'Walk! And head right until you reach the following alley that connects to this street. We'll meet there.'

'You can't be serious?'

'I won't tell you again.'

His legs buckled into a run from the adrenaline pumping through his body. He forgot about his injured leg. He was making quick progress.

'Walk!'

William stopped running and followed her instructions. *But why? The police are right behind us. They will know. How stupid does she think they are?* He doubted the plan. It was so simple that it seemed ludicrous to test the intelligence of the police with it. Yet, he couldn't challenge the idea otherwise he would get barked at again. Or worse, he would get captured. Neither of which he wanted.

He reached the end, turned right and walked. The first alley that came had stretched halfway inside, blocked off by adjoining buildings. It wasn't the one he had to go through. He continued walking.

Sirens wailed and blasted the area with its presence while passing through. It stayed around before it went quiet instantly, as if the officers had parked the car and scoured the area for their three wanted suspects—him being one of them. His heart pounded. He didn't know how long they were going to be in the area looking for them. It didn't help his anxiety. His body trembled in fear. He didn't want to be captured now.

Not a way to go out. End in captivity and shot in the head... NO THANK YOU... there's gotta be something different...

All the while talking in his head, he arrived at the next alley which connected to the adjacent street. He headed inside and picked up the pace into a brisk walk. He squinted, trying to find his fellow acquaintances in crime but there wasn't a soul lingering around. About twenty meters from the street, his breathing quickened. His mask was fogging up and obscuring his panoramic mask.

Shit! Not now. Come on.

He tried his best to calm his breathing. It helped. The fog was clearing away. As he took another step, an Enforcer suddenly appeared. He almost soiled his pants on the spot. Caught dead in his tracks, he simply watched the robot walk. Heavy steps stomped the ground with its heavy weight. His eyes stayed on the robot until it was on the other side, and out of sight.

William breathed a sigh of relief before the stomping went silent. He remained in position for a moment, focusing his listening skills—weakened as they were—to figure out what was happening. The stomping had resumed, however, was growing louder. It was coming back. Not knowing what to do, he froze. As the Enforcer's body was coming into view, William found himself yanked from behind into a small space. He turned around to find Demi there with her index finger over her mask, as if telling him not to make a sound. She gestured at him to follow her into a dark passage below.

He followed her, closing the door behind him, as the robot sounded like it was marching into the alley.

Blinded by the darkness, William struggled to get his bearing as he moved forward. There was a click. Light flashed in front of them from the torch Demi had in her hand.

'Where are we going?' he asked.

She didn't answer as she had made her descent through the stairway. Her footsteps reverberated inside the narrow passage. Not liking his questions getting ignored, he followed her, waiting for the right opportunity to find what exactly was the plan. He didn't know what it was or how the place existed underneath.

'Demi,' he said.

'Shh!' she said.

'Just tell me where are we going,'

'Refuge.'

'*Refuge?* For who?'

'You asked where. I gave you an answer, now please be quiet. I need to focus on what's ahead.'

William had more questions. Sure, he got an answer but it just raised more questions than it answered. He wanted to ask the questions circulating in his head but opted to stay silent until Demi seemed less tense and more approachable. *If she ever is*, he thought. *Plus, where is her friend? Where the hell did he go? Did he get caught?*

He looked on, trying to see light in the darkness, while walking through the passage. He started counting the steps taken as it didn't seem to end.

Eventually, after what seemed like fifteen minutes of walking an endless stairwell, an EXIT sign caught William's attention. He wondered where he was until she pushed the door aside, and he realised they had arrived in an underground stadium. Barely a person was in sight except for food delivery drones flying away, carrying packages.

'This way,' Demi said.

He followed her down the walkway, then veered into a restaurant, heading straight to another exit. It led to internal passage behind the shops. He struggled to keep up as Demi carried herself efficiently, covering a lot of ground in quick, long strides.

Demi stopped by a white door, knocking on it like she was giving a code. The door opened with a man in his chef uniform. He was clean shaven and brown eyed. He cast a look at both of them before looking back at Demi. He seemed apprehensive toward the two at first. 'You're late.'

'We had company.'

'Hmph... this way.'

The pair accompanied him until they arrived in front of a floor hatch. The man opened it, revealing a man-made tunnel with bar handles mounted on the wall for descent.

'Thank you,' Demi said, sounding sincere and grateful.

'Good luck.'

'You too.' She smacked William on the shoulder. 'Go in.'

Why don't smack harder while you're at it? William thought. His neck inflamed in anger. He was getting tired of her. He spotted two other people who were dressed like them. *Decoys?*

He made his way down the bar. They were unstable but seemed to hold him without popping out until he arrived at the bottom. He dropped off the last bar and waited for Demi. More darkness laid ahead and he didn't want to venture onward into the unknown with her, especially as she was the lead.

'How long has this been here?' he asked

'Ever since the lockdowns became permanent,' she said.

'It must have taken years to get this made.'

'It *did* take years. We thought something bad was going to happen considering the state the world was in. So we planned ahead. We just didn't think it would have been a virus that would cause all of this.'

'You were a part of it?'

'Not for long.' She walked ahead with her torch, flashing it forward to reveal timber logs holding up everything above. 'I had to help Charles with the Emitter. He couldn't do it on his own, nor did he trust anyone else for that matter except me.'

'We're not there yet, are we?'

'No, but we will be.'

Step by step, William strode beside Demi. There weren't any more questions asked by him as she stopped giving answers. She didn't talk except for when she had to mask his Zerya port, resetting it again for another thirty minutes.

It must have been several kilometers when light ahead emerged from being a white dot in the air to being a staircase leading towards a warehouse filled with the high-standing shelves and emptied workstations. The place seemed abandoned long ago. The howling wind passed through cracked windows above and along the gaping holes in the ceiling.

He stayed close to Demi, who had her torch replaced with a firearm, as he anticipated a gun fight.

Demi stopped, placing her back towards the shelf as she got closer to an exit. She made a tapping sound like a two-beat signal. There was nothing. She did it again, then waited.

William waited with her. He didn't know what she was waiting for. Then there was a different two-beat signal replied in kind.

Demi sighed.

'You can come on out now,' a familiar voice said. It was Charles.

William left the shelves with Demi and approached him. There were two other people standing guard with assault rifles.

'You made it,' Demi said, sounding relieved. 'Looks like your detour worked after all.'

'As did yours, kiddo.' He embraced her. 'He didn't slow you down, did he?'

'There were a lot of questions... but no, he didn't.'

'Where are we?' William asked.

'Doesn't look like he's going to stop.'

'Old wholesaler building,' Charles said. 'Used to be a place many people, including myself, frequented for tools and equipment.' He looked around, as if recalling a memory. Then cast a glance back at William. 'How are you feeling?'

'Like I could call it a day of walking.'

He chuckled. 'We're almost there.'

'We're *still* not there?'

'This is a checkpoint.' He led him outside and pointed towards greyish buildings, looming high, away from the city. '*That's* where we're going.'

'What is over there?'

'You'll find out by tonight.'

An itch crawled up William's throat like it dried up from the lack of water. He coughed. He couldn't stop it. His chest hurt like it was collapsing on itself. He sank against the wall. He reached for his inhaler but couldn't find it.

'Whoa, whoa!' one of the guards said, coming around and aiming their weapon at William. 'You said nothing about bringing a Contaminant.'

'He isn't one,' Charles said. He looked at Demi, concerningly. 'He isn't one, right?'

William spotted Demi's attention on him. He could see it in her eyes that she knew he was. Although he didn't know what he was going to do if she blurted out the news to the others.

'No, he isn't,' she said, and approached the guard with their rifle trained on William. 'He's asthmatic. The respirator masks aren't enough to help with oxygen, especially under stress.' She looked back at William. 'Obviously we've been running around a lot. For an able body they can take it... his can't.'

'Then what's the point of bringing him along?' the other guard asked. 'He's just deadweight.'

'He saved my life. I'm returning the favour.'

The two guards exchanged concerned looks but ultimately decided to let the matter go.

'We better leave now,' Demi said. 'Thirty minutes are almost up, and he needs to be at the refuge before then.'

'Come on,' Charles said, extending his hand to him. 'We gotta go.'

William took his hand, then resumed walking.

Eventually, William arrived at the location. It was a former college or university but had lost itself magnificence from weathering as it looked like it was a rundown, decaying prison or correctional facility as they entered.

'Stay behind me,' Demi told William.

He sighed and did as he was told. Again. Not knowing the reason why behind the order and he obediently followed instructions like a good dog to its owner otherwise he won't get fed.

William searched the place. None of it seemed familiar to him. He never went to college or university. He just took jobs whatever he could get from fast food outlets, cafes and tending bars. Although the only job he considered a *real* job was when he was with Pinnacle Funds. And now he was made redundant. He continued to look around when shuffling footsteps came out of nowhere.

'Halt!' a male guard said.

'Easy, Harrison!' Charles said. 'It's us.'

'Normally there's only two. Who's the third?'

Charles paused. 'New party member. I needed more hands to make the emitter work.'

'Never seen him before. Is he cleared?'

'Yeah.'

William saw about six guards in different locations, directing their firearms at them. Their unwavering attention fixed on them like trained soldiers ready to rain hell the moment the order had been given.

'It's good to see you, old bud,' Harrison started laughing. 'I thought you were dead.' He embraced Charles in a brotherly hug.

'I thought I was for a moment. Though, I was fortunate enough to have had help.' He looked at Demi.

The three of them were escorted by Harrison and another guard underground—their access point through an elevator. Three floors it took before they arrived in a massive hall-like bunker. A Column of pillars stretched fifty meters or more with rows of retractable military beds.

People from all walks of life had taken refuge here. Spanish, Indian, Asian and other ethnicities were present. Adults, teenagers and children. It was a community. And most notably, none of them had a Zerya port upon a closer look at their necks.

William walked beside the group, eyeing the children playing with each other and men and women staring at them with curious eyes—mainly on him as if they hadn't seen someone with a Zerya port.

'What's the situation been like here?' Charles asked.

'Worsened since you left,' Harrison said. 'More people are trying to leave the city. They hear of this place and spread the word. We've grown double in numbers in the last month. It takes more food, more water and space to keep it going... and we're running low. Though morale is still in good order. But the moment that last water drop hits or last meal is eaten, morale won't mean jackshit then.'

'What about the plan for another refuge in the outskirts?' Demi asked. 'Surely by now there are people there that can hold more numbers?'

'It's been set up already. Razia's there. She's holding the fort but she'll end up having the same issue here if we don't get support from Gaia asap.'

'That's what we're trying to do as well.'

They headed into an office room away from the community gathering around. The door slid aside revealing a command room with three officers staring at screens and communicating to unknown parties.

'So, how can I help you?' Harrison asked.

'We just need a place to stay for the night. We have plans already to head up North.'

'Trying to reach Gaia yourself?'

Charles nodded.

'It's risky. The two of you, and,' Harrison looked at William. 'I don't think I caught your name.' He stood closer to them.

'William... sir,' William said, not sure if he had to add 'sir' after his name.

'No need to call me "sir"'. He chuckled. 'You can call me 'Harrison'. Nice to meet you. It's been some time since I've seen a Zerya port. What did it take before you called an end to it?'

'Too many things... but if it had to be one thing. Staying locked-in.'

'Same here. I couldn't take it myself. I grew depressed pretty quick.' He shook his gloved hand with William's hand, then looked back at Charles. 'Well, if it's a place you need to stay low for the night. You got it. There are spare beds. You can take them. Showers won't be in use as we're rationing water so I apologise in advance for the body odour. People haven't had one in a few days.'

'It's fine,' Charles said. 'We just need a bed.'

William watched intently at the people communicating through their headset while reading information on their screens. *Who on Earth are they talking to?* he wondered. He glanced at the surveillance footage of the ground areas above. So far it didn't seem like police officers and Enforcers were following them. The footage didn't offer comfort as he knew from experience, nothing is ever certain with the law. They were relentless.

Hours later, William rested on his assigned bed. His chest ached but thankfully he used the Alleviant to relieve his lungs. He tried to get some rest until dinner came but his curious mind didn't allow him to shut off completely. Everything was new for him and his mind wanted to know what it was like here.

He was left to his own amusement and thought while Demi and Charles offered their help around the place. He caught sight of Charles talking smack with the people assembling the tables and preparing dinner, while Demi sat with young girls and braided their hair. Their interaction with people was so personable, tears welled up in his eyes. It was as if his own body yearned for the same type of interaction in his life. He did try to find it before but it had pulled him back into Zerya, which he didn't want.

He took out his phone and scrolled through his contacts, stopping at Marlene. Fear struck him instantly as he remembered Ulyanov's threat. *Shit! Marlene!*

He dialled her number. It rang and rang. There was no answer at the end.

He tried again.

'Will?' she answered.

'Marlene!' William said. 'Thank God. Are you alright?'

'Yeah, I am. Is everything okay?'

'Not really. You need to get out.'

'Get out? What are you talking about?'

'I mean, the police know about the protest at the bank.'

'Of course, *they* would know. It was all over the news. Plus, they were there as well.'

'Marlene, you don't understand. They know it was you.'

There was silence on her end before she asked, 'How do you know that?'

'Because I was threatened with it.'

'*Threatened?* By the police.'

'Yeah.'

'Why were you threatened?'

Not wanting to draw attention from the people nearby, he walked towards a quieter area, and then in a low voice, he said, 'Because I'm a Contaminant now, and I'm trying to get out of the city before they can catch me. I was lucky once. I don't think I'll be lucky a second time.'

'You're a Contaminant? But how?' Her concern for him was more apparent than his warning. 'You've been indoors, haven't you?'

'Never mind how. It's done already. I don't have much time and the last thing I want to know before I go out is you and your family being hurt because of me.'

'There's nowhere I can go, Will. My home is here. My family is here. I don't know anyone else. Where would I go?'

'Think of something. Anywhere is better than where you are right now. They're going to come after if you—'

'Let them come.'

William did a take back. 'What?'

'Let them come. It was my decision to lead the protest, and I would do it again if given the chance to.'

'Mal, please...'

'It's okay, Will. Don't worry about me in your last moments. I'll do what I have to do. You do what you have to do, alright? If something happens, don't feel guilty. Don't.'

William hung his head. Desperation was sinking in.

'Will?'

'Alright.'

'Take care of yourself.'

'You too.'

She ended the call.

William put his phone away, staring into nothingness as he didn't know what was going to happen now. The actions of the police were beyond him. The actions of Marlene were beyond him. If he had the power to move his friend to safety and stop the police from looking for them, he'd do it without hesitation.

He turned around and looked back at the people who were in their company, minding their own business.

'Is everything okay?' Demi asked, walking towards him. Her cautious eyes fixed on William.

'My friend is in danger,' he said. 'I tried warning them but they decided to stay where they are.'

'Why are they in danger?'

'Because of me.'

'Anything we can do?'

William considered the idea. It might help to get someone to her, but then what? Where would she go? He thought about his options. He looked back at Demi, then sighed. 'No, I'm going to respect her decision.'

'Fair enough.'

Harrison walked into the area, clapping his hands together as if to make an announcement. 'Alright, everyone. Dinner is served. You know the drill. Each person gets their own serving. Seconds can be given to those who didn't get any yesterday if there's any left, okay?'

'Usually there's always seconds,' Charles said, who appeared beside them. 'Let's eat.'

'One moment,' William said, then looked at Demi. 'What's happening about my port? I thought we were supposed to update it every thirty minutes.'

'Didn't need to once we got here,' Demi asked. 'This place hides everything, including your port. Law enforcement won't be able to find us here.'

'How can you be certain?'

'I'm not certain but they've not found this place yet. And it's been a few years.'

'Come,' Charles said. 'Eat. You'll feel better once you get something into your system.'

He gathered around with the others after getting his meal—potato bake pie with a serving of corn soup and garlic bread. He kept to himself as he ate but the people around him conversed amongst each other with such wit and care, he couldn't help but be drawn to them. None of them seemed to have a shroud of concern at all about the dire situation they were in. Not a word of the Smog, the police or anything else was uttered.

Interesting...

He turned his attention to Demi and Charles engaging in their own conversation about their idiosyncrasies while living with each other.

CHAPTER 14

'Hey,' Demi said, 'it's no picnic having to follow your insistent rule about using two sponges to wash the dishes. I mean, come on, there *has* to be one for the cups, and there *has* to be one for the dishes. Seriously?'

'Well, yeah,' Charles said. 'It's about having your cups smell like cups, and like the sponge used to clean your plates.'

'And what exactly does a cup taste like?' She looked at him. Her eyes fluttered as she looked amused. 'A serving of carbonara?'

'As long as they are separated, they won't taste like anything.'

'*As* long as they are *washed* properly, they won't taste like anything.'

'Interesting theory, but I won't be changing the rule.'

Demi exasperated as she rolled her eyes.

William chuckled in amusement.

'Something funny?' Demi asked.

'Yeah, but don't mind me,' William said. 'It wasn't so much about the subject the two of you were talking about.'

'Then what was it about?' Charles asked, chewing on his garlic bread.

'It's just... I miss this... or so I think I do. I've been cooped up in my apartment all this time. It's funny for me now as it took so long to realise.' He looked at them. 'Having family dinner.'

'You're not in contact with your folks?'

'Not really. We haven't been on good terms for a long time which usually resorted in my siblings or other family members to bring us together.'

'Why's that?'

'Unmet expectations from both sides. They want me to be a certain person and I want them to be different people.' He smirked. 'It's not going to change though. Parents won't change. It'd have to take something bad to happen, or at least get into an argument for them to at least listen—that's if they listen at all.' He went quiet. 'Like I said, don't mind me. Listening to you and everyone talking reminded me of the times when we were able to have conversations with each other without having expectations for one another.' He paused. 'I'll just stay quiet and enjoy the moment.'

'That's one of the rules when having dinner here. To have a conversation about something else other than the life we're in. Sometimes the break here, however long it is, does help.'

William nodded. 'It's a good rule. Although I haven't been at the dinner table in a long time as most of my time was spent in Zerya or in bed watching something on my phone. I think I forgot my manners.'

Harrison approached the table with a guitar, wrapped with a scarf around his neck and thick brown jacket, looking like a busker from the old days.

'Anyone with a recommendation?' he asked.

'Dealer's choice,' one of the women answered.

'Very well.'

Harrison grasped the guitar as if holding a lover with gentle hands and giving it care and attention. He strummed his nails against the nylon strings and projected his voice with passion and sincerity.

William listened to the man. He hadn't heard the song before. He simply sat in awe, coming to understand what a person is capable of without modern technology of any kind. Wood, six strings and a voice were all that was needed to produce something special.

He listened to the lyrics as Harrison sang about a time lost to them, where a person could choose what he or she wanted to do without fear or need to use technology to make life better—something about what Harrison was doing spoke to William's need for connection.

When he was done, everyone clapped, including William, and asked for another song to be sung. He obliged.

'That sounded like an original,' Demi commented.

'He writes his own songs now,' one of the little girls said.

'How about that.' She looked at William. 'What did you think?'

'It was good. I haven't been a part of a dinner where someone sings. Usually, we just have the radio or our own playlist playing in the background.'

'We have that as well. Not everyone can sing, you know?'

'Amen to that,' Charles said.

'What are you talking about?'

'You sound like a squeaking jukebox.'

'I do not.'

Charles impersonated her singing, which cracked up William.

Later, when dinner was done and everyone went to bed, William kept looking at Marlene's name on his phone. He couldn't help but worry for her. Ulyanov's threat at the hospital weren't just spoken words. Something was going to happen. He simply didn't know how or when.

CHAPTER 14

An itch rode up the walls of his throat like a rocket that he broke into a coughing fit. He covered his mouth to not wake up anyone and collected his inhaler. He pushed the button and took in the substance. The effects worked shortly after and his fit had disappeared.

He sighed as he gazed up to the ceiling.

'Can't sleep?' Demi asked, who was lying on the adjacent military bed.

'No,' he said. 'I didn't wake you up, did I?'

'No, I've been awake for a while. I can't sleep here properly.'

'Why's that?'

'I just have this fear that something is going to happen wherever I sleep.'

'Well, something can *always* happen.'

'I mean in the sense that the floors above can collapse on us at any given moment, or the police could find us here and most would be stuck here with only a few who would be able to get out, or someone here may let slip the knowledge of this place to the police which will be make us question our loyalty to one another.' She stared at the ceiling. 'God knows we don't need that right now.'

'You don't think you're not overthinking it?'

'Maybe... maybe not.' She looked at him. 'You? Worried for your friend?'

William nodded his head. 'Yeah! She's perhaps my only friend. Ever since the breaches at home, the police have been nonstop in trying to figure out who is an Allocron or working with Gaia, and whoever has a suspected relationship with them. Which they tangled me into it. It's been nonstop. And since she knows me, it makes things worse.'

'And they think you're one?'

'Well, up until the night at your place, it was suspicion... Now they're downright certain of it. Anyway, there's this officer who has it *in* for you guys. A real asshole. The guy doesn't stop. Don't know if you've met him.'

'Probably.'

'Well, I got beaten up, and *threatened* with interrogation and having someone I know be killed, if I didn't give this guy information about you. And don't *worry*, I didn't. Anyway, my silence on the matter hasn't stopped the threats.'

'Does your friend know?'

'She does, but she decided not to do anything.' He sighed. 'I'll probably give her a call tomorrow just to see how she is.' He looked at Demi. 'I'm sure you've had your run-ins with the police.'

'I've had plenty. I think everyone here has had at least one encounter with the police... but in my case, I've tried to keep a low profile as often as I can.'

'Like going to the shopping center to stare at photos while buying goods? All of which can be done online.'

'Well, that's all there is to do. I liked going to the supermarkets where you could see the things you were buying. Hold it. Smell it. It was the best way of figuring out if it was good quality. You can't do that anymore. All you have are the images and scanners, all the while hoping what you get is something decent.'

'And yet you still go? Why?'

Demi went quiet. For a split second her face contoured into sadness before she covered it up. 'To remember what life was like before all of this.' She grabbed her blanket, covered herself and turned the other way.

'*Sorry.*'

She sighed. 'Try to get some sleep.'

William darted in and out of sleep, when he heard shouting and people running around him. His eyes fluttered as the lights to the place were on again. Some people were throwing on their hazmat suits while others were packing up their belongings. Nothing seemed of concern to him until...

Boom! Boom! The place trembled violently by what seemed like explosions happening on the ground level above.

The hell is going on? he wondered, as he jumped out of bed and ran towards the center of the room to find Charles or Demi. He needed to find out what was happening. Eyes bounced between faces until he found Demi helping one of the children pack their belongings. 'Hey!'

'You woke up,' she said.

'No thanks to—' He stopped midway. *Boom! Boom!*

'That sounded closer.' Concern underpinned her voice. She looked at the ceiling as the place rattled.

'What's going to happen to us?' the child asked.

'Nothing, dear. We're going to get you safe.' She zipped up the child's bag and handed a teddy bear to the girl. Seemed like it belonged to her. 'Now, follow the guard to the exit. Stay with him and listen to him all the way. Understand?'

The child nodded and went to the stairway exit. The door closed behind them.

'What do we do now?' William asked.

'We regroup on the ground with Charles. He's up there at the moment, fending off the police.'

'How did they find us? I thought this place was hidden.'

'I don't know.' The thought appeared to trouble her as well. 'Look, the longer we stay here, the more risk we take. Now, I don't know about you, but I don't want to be here any longer than I have to. Do you?

'Well, I—'

Suddenly a red laser pierced through the ceiling, and between William and his new acquaintance. He fell back while Demi retreated. Another laser pierced another part of the ceiling, striking one of the guards in the head and split him in two as it whirled in a circle, in a swift, precise manner before disappearing. Debris fell down, toppling the guard, while other holes formed above.

'Look out!' Demi said.

Once everything cleared, an Enforcer fell through, landing onto its feet, head facing the floor. Suddenly a red light emitted from its head. It was set to exterminate someone. Or perhaps everyone. It raised its head and surveyed the area, as if locking on targets, while more Enforcers emerged through another opening in the ceiling.

Then a robotic body landed in the Refuge. This one was different but familiar. When it looked up and disengaged their helmet, there stood the sickly-looking Ulyanov. His face wreathed in anger.

Shit! William thought.

'Enforcers!' the nearest guard yelled, as he fired his assault rifle at their newly, unwanted guests. More guards joined in the firefight.

Shots whistled past in all directions. Men and women groaned in pain after getting shot. Enforcers crashed to the ground after sustaining extensive damage towards its head and legs. Casualties were piling up on both sides.

William turned his attention to Ulyanov, who fired a quick succession of shots at guards, killing them instantly, as he marched towards him. His body didn't move. No matter what he wanted to do at the moment, his body had other plans—to accept its fate and die.

'It's over, Mr. Kepler,' Ulyanov said.

Not like this...

Before anything else could happen, Demi jumped on top of Ulyanov and struck a screwdriver into the neck of his suit. Upon impact and fierce striking, the suit lost power, causing him to drop his firearm. She leapt off but Ulyanov caught hold of her arm. She tried to yank free but he brought her closer, face-to-face, now holding both her arms.

'Where do you think you're going?' Ulyanov asked.

William remembered a similar sight from weeks' ago, when his neighbour was Purged, as a contraption appeared beside his head. He got up and sprinted to her aid. 'Demi!'

Then, the side of Ulyanov's head was struck by bullets. He dropped to the ground, groaned in pain.

William looked back to see Charles by the stairway exit, his assault rifle trained directly at them. Dry bloodstains painted his face and body, which he knew best not to ask about if ever the opportunity arose.

'We have to go,' Charles said.

William helped Demi up and ran for the exit. He covered himself as Ulyanov raced after them, firing shots. Luckily, the officer dropped to the ground when Charles barraged him with bullets to the ankles. The armoured suit crippled in beneath its weight from the damage.

'KEPLER!' Ulyanov roared.

William paid zero attention to the officer as the door was sealed shut.

'You're right,' Demi said, 'He's an asshole.'

William smirked. He made his ascent to the ground, struggling with breathing as the effects of the virus was digging into his lungs. He coughed several times. Pain like a thousand needles striking his chest fell on him. He dropped to knees, unable to move.

'Will?' Demi said.

William clenched his chest, groaning from the severe pain. It took his inhaler and shot another dose into his system. 'I'm okay.' Although he clearly wasn't.

The three of them arrived on the ground floor. Suits and masks were on. They ran through the area, where another firefight was taking place. But by the emerging presence of the police and Enforcers, it seemed like a losing battle.

'We need to get out of here,' Demi said.

CHAPTER 14

'Harrison is waiting for us,' Charles said, still holding his rifle in his hands, ready to hammer the trigger at a moment's notice. 'We'll be fine.'

They moved away from the area, heading for the pickup site, where they found a wounded and unmasked Harrison, alongside three other dead refugees. None of them were alive except him. Bullet holes ruptured across his body. He wheezed and convulsed.

'Harrison!' Charles said.

'Sons of bitches,' Harrison said, smiling. 'Really did a number on me. Especially *that* officer.'

Ulyanov... William knew immediately. His anger boiled to the surface. He wanted to be rid of him once and for all.

'Take it easy,' Demi said. 'Catch your breath.'

'I got none to catch.' He looked at them. 'I'm sorry... old friends.' He dropped his head onto the ground, letting out his last breath as the life in his eyes disappeared.

Charles dropped his head over his fallen comrade, while Demi approached Harrison's face and closed his eyes.

KABOOM!

William shot his attention to the sound where fiery flames engulfed the air. Silence eclipsed the area afterward. The last line of defenses had been defeated.

'Charles, we must go,' Demi said.

Charles didn't respond.

'Charles?'

'Get in the car,' Charles said. His deep voice registered in anger. 'I'm driving.'

CHAPTER 15

THE CAR ZIGGED and zagged between the traffic as the police raced after them in hot pursuit. Sirens rang through the area with more joining them from nearby streets.

Fighting the urge to look back, William forced his attention forward. Better to find a way out than to worry about the people who were pursuing them.

Bang, bang! Shots whistled past the car.

'We need to get out of here, Charles!' Demi said. 'We can't afford to be on the road much longer. Enforcers will be here shortly.'

'I'm working on that,' Charles said, 'but as you can see, I'm a little busy at the moment.' He veered the wheel left, swerving the car to a hard left around the bend onto another street. As the car resumed position, the view became clear, two police cars with flashing blue and red lights emerged through the haze.

'That's not promising,' William said.

'We need a diversion.'

'We have none,' Demi said. 'And they're not going to let us go until they have all of us or at least one of us.'

'Then maybe we'll have to give them what they want.'

'I'll go,' William said. 'I mean I'm the one who got you into this mess to begin with. All you were trying to do was to get away. Let me help with that.'

Bang! A shot struck through the window, grazing Charles in the right shoulder. The car swerved between lanes until Demi took control of the wheel.

'Charles!' she said.

'I'm alright,' he said.

CHAPTER 15

'The hell you are.'

The police cars loomed ahead. The vehicles emerged through the haze, driving at full speed.

'Don't think of jumping out, Will,' Charles said. 'After all we did to get you out, just to have the plan upended moments later wouldn't make it a successful operation, now, would it?'

'You call *this* successful?' William asked.

'It's about to be.' He looked at Demi. 'You know what to do, right?'

Demi hit the glove box and passed several brown packages to William. 'When I give the signal, throw these out the windows towards the police cars.'

Not wanting to know what these packages held, William followed her instructions. He threw his mask on quickly to avoid absorbing any more of the pathogen in the air and braced himself for action.

Charles hit the brake and spun the handwheel right twice clockwise, moving the car into reverse position, then drove backwards.

'Ready...' she said.

The cars got closer.

'Set...'

William sat close to the window in preparation. Hands firmly grasped hold of the package. He trained his attention on the cars when suddenly something heavy landed on the roof leaving two concave dents above their heads.

Dzun, dzun!

William's heart rate doubled. He'd recognized that sound and shot concerned looks at the others.

There was movement atop the roof, followed by a shot that whistled through the metal, hitting William in the shoulder. 'Ah!'

'Will!' Demi said.

'Take cover!' Charles swerved the car around to shake the Enforcer off. It didn't work. Another shot came through the roof, hitting Demi in the thigh. She yelled in pain. 'Demi!'

'We need to get out of here!' William said.

'There's no way out at the moment,' Demi said.

'No, there is,' Charles said. He looked at Demi. 'I'm sorry.'

'Charles... don't...'

'You don't have much time.' Suddenly he hit the door open and jumped out of the car. 'Look after each other.'

'Charles!' both of them said, trying to yank him back inside the car but the door closed on them.

In response to him leaving, the Enforcer leapt off the rooftop and pursued him.

William and Demi didn't have time to respond as the car collided against another car, spinning around in the air before smashing onto the ground.

William laid on the car rooftop for a moment, trying to shake off a sudden weariness. He heard muffled gunfire as he checked his mask and noticed cracks and tears across the cover although it still held together. He heard police cars getting closer, and moved with haste, reaching for Demi who seemed to have taken a blow to the head. Blood dripped through her mask.

'Demi?' he said.

She didn't respond.

He listened for her breathing and checked her pulse. There was one but faint. He strapped his bag around his chest before he pulled Demi outside. He heard a barrage of guns nearby. He immediately shot a look at the direction of the sound to find Charles coughing out blood down on the concrete; his body punctured by bullets and blood pooling around him. Seconds later he froze.

William wanted to do something, anything, to help him but then a spark burst from the engine. He pulled Demi into his arms and sprinted away as quickly his body would allow before the car caught fire and exploded.

Once they were far enough from the scene, he settled in an alley to hide. He placed Demi against the concrete wall to check her wellbeing. She was conscious but he didn't know for how long. Her O2 compactors were damaged which triggered a red emitter on the respirator—she was running low on oxygen. Plus, blood from her wound was seeping through her pants.

Come on, come on, come on.

He replaced one of her compactors with one he had in his bag and tore off strips of his suit and bandaged her as best he could.

Once done, he covered her with cardboard to hide her presence. He was happy with his work, so he left her to tend to a more urgent matter. He went to call Marlene about Ulyanov but worried the police might be able to trace his call. His finger hovering over her name, then he withdrew it.

First, he needed to get his neural port removed, then needed another phone. It was the only chance he had to slip through the city without detection to help her and himself. He stood motionless in the centre of the street pavement, wondering what he could do. He considered his options. Speaking to his family was the last thing he wanted to do. Speaking with Kristie since their fallout he believed she wouldn't appreciate his call; and speaking to his former colleagues wasn't going to happen either as they were most likely monitored as well.

He checked his account balance to see if there were enough funds to get a train ride out of the city. His access was denied. His credentials weren't accepted with an alert popping up on the homepage to visit the police if he wanted to get his situation fixed. He exhaled and walked out of the situation. He knew he didn't have much of a choice aside from seeing the police.

He checked his phone. Battery was low at 12%. There was little time to consider his options now as he either had to turn himself in, risk being Purge and Archived, or leave the city completely. But even if he left the area, news would be passed onto other police stations. Drones and Enforcers would be sent out to bring him back to his area, then to the station. He glanced at his phone again. It was at 11%. The clock was ticking. He needed to find someone who knew where he could get his neural port removed ASAP.

Ten minutes to get to the city. Phone would have to be left on extreme power saver mode, he thought. *That would give just over an hour or so. Not a lot of time but it's better than nothing.*

He didn't know if his legs would carry him. A body weakened from the virus, a gunshot to the shoulder, and a car crash had set his energy back considerably. As he wandered, he thought of one person who might be able to help him.

'Hey Janyce,' he called—the woman from his carnal endeavours. He didn't know if she would know anyone but considering her line of work, which was illegal, she might possibly know someone or something.

'Hey hun,' she said, 'Have you finally changed your mind about seeing me?'

'That's definitely changed, but listen, I can't talk for long. I was wondering if you could help me with something else other than the normal service.'

'Which is?'

'Do you know anyone who knows anything about removing neural chips?'

'Are you in some kind of trouble?'

'Breaches. However, I don't know the full extent of them right now. I have to go to the police to find out more, which is something I don't want to do.'

'Well, I could only imagine that it'd have to be pretty bad if you're asking me for help.'

'It is.'

'Where are you now?'

'Ten minutes out from the city.'

'Head over. Let me know when you're outside.'

'Will do.'

As he placed his phone on extreme power saver mode, a hand clapped on his shoulder. He turned to find Demi standing beside him.

'Did you really think,' Demi said, 'you were going to leave me behind there for the police to catch me?'

'I didn't think they would. We're far from where the car crash happened.'

'And what of Charles? Did you see him?'

He didn't want to answer the question. He looked at Demi, struggling to find the words.

'Did you *see* him?'

'He—he didn't make it.' He could see Demi's eyes redden and fill up with tears. 'I'm sorry.'

She coughed, swallowing a sob, then yelled out in frustration.

'Listen, I know someone who might be able to help me get my neural port removed. Now, I'm going there. Don't know if you want to join me but I must go before I have more cops coming after me.'

She sighed. 'Then let's not linger around here anymore. After all, it wouldn't be a successful operation if you got caught.'

'Are you sure you want to come? After you were shot in the leg?'

'And you shot in the arm. We don't have much of a choice, now do we?' She kept on walking.

William followed her and hopped onto a tram heading to the city. They arrived at his destination shortly after and headed towards a set of apartment buildings. Both buildings stood seven storeys tall. He buzzed for entry to the building which Janyce permitted.

A minute later he was standing with Demi in front of apartment number 708. He remembered his first encounter with Janyce. Not much talking had taken place at the beginning but when everything was over, he remembered the pair in each other's virtual arms. Despite it all being virtual, in that moment he'd felt was at ease and cared for—something he seemed to have lost.

CHAPTER 15

Knock, knock!

Soft footsteps approached the door from inside the apartment. The door hissed aside and there stood Janyce, wearing a gold silken robe.

'Hey,' he said.

'Hey, yourself,' she said. 'You look horrible.'

'You have no idea.'

Janyce went quiet, running her eyes over them as if considering her options. 'I see you brought company. What do I get out of this?'

'I can pay you.'

'I figured your phone is locked and most likely all of your other accounts as well, like your money.'

'Not all of them.' He paused. 'But if you're thinking I'm going to fall short in delivering on my promise, then I really shouldn't be here. I figured you know people, and considering you're slightly on the other side of the law, I thought you'd be a little more flexible.'

'Oh, I am. But it's not me I'm concerned about. You've fallen short at times, performance-wise.'

'Am I missing something here?' Demi asked.

'We have a history,' William said without looking at Demi. 'Look, we've shared our moments together and you've been respectful of my privacy, as have with yours. I think you can trust me not to say anything about this. Now, will you help me or not?'

She sighed and moved aside. 'You're lucky that I like you, you know? Come in.'

Relieved, William walked inside as the door closed behind them. He watched her pass by to collect her phone. 'How much is it going to cost?'

'Triple the pay.'

He choked. 'You're kidding, right?'

'Honey, I'm not kidding. I've been on this side of the law much longer than you'll ever be, and I know the price it takes, especially when you're asking someone to direct you to people who happen to know how to remove neural ports.'

'Fine.'

'Good. By the way, do you know the kind of trouble people can get themselves in once the *law* gets wind of them wanting to get their neural-link removed?'

William was lost for words. He didn't know nor had he ever considered the consequences. 'No.'

Janyce got her projector remote and switched on the device. In an instant, a live feed shot upon the empty wall of a news broadcast. The paused sign 'II' sat on display towards the top right of the screen. A banner screamed 'INDIGNANTS' across the bottom. The stream played footage of people with faces pixelated during an interrogation and getting beaten up by Enforcers.

'What are you—' he said. 'What the hell is this?'

'This is what happens.'

'Where did you get this?'

'Anyone can find this online if they know where to look.'

William looked at Demi who didn't appear surprised by the footage.

'Do you really want to go ahead with this?'

He looked at her. 'Make the call. I'll get your credits.'

'This will take a while. In the meantime, you can figure out how you can get your credits. Also, there are some bandages and a first aid kit in the pantry.' She turned off the news and left for her room.

William collected the items from the pantry and tended to his wounds alongside Demi. 'You knew about this, didn't you?'

'About what the police do?' she asked. 'Yeah.'

'Just imagine if everyone knew about this?'

'I can't imagine it. People are too afraid. And in that fear, it has allowed for abuse to such a degree that they're now living in boxes with nothing but a virtual life without truly *living* a life.'

'Is that why you were living with Charles in No Man's Land?'

Demi's eyes reddened and welled with tears again. Her breathing quickened. 'Charles was like a father to me. I didn't really have one growing up. Mine was absent. Charles saw joy in things we made and did as humans but always had serious concerns about technology, and those who may potentially want to abuse it. He thought life was about truly getting out of your comfort zone and embracing the uncertainty that comes with it—a life outside a safe box and without technology. Something I agree with.'

'Which is why you're trying to get out, right?'

Demi looked away, not giving a definite answer. 'It's just better that way. There's a price to pay with everything. This way of living is harmful in ways most people can't see at the moment... or choose not to see.'

'You're not wrong there.' He exhaled, taking a moment to consider his thoughts. 'I'll do what I can to help you.'

'Why?'

'For the same reason you came to help me.'

'You don't owe me anything. It was our decision to get you out. Not yours.'

'I know, and I'm grateful for that. Which is why it's my decision to see it through till the end.' He finished cleaning his wound and removing the bullet with Demi's help.

'How did you learn all of this?'

'Charles. He was once in the army. He learnt a lot of things, which were passed onto me.'

'Thank you.'

She nodded in acknowledgement and continued to clean her own wound. 'We need to reset your location again.'

He let her mask his position, then left her alone, and reached for his phone to access his drop-box. He raced through websites to get to the main page of his account. He input his credentials and found his savings still there with only a monthly account keeping fees deducting from the balance. The balance read as 12,893.26 CREDITS. He sighed in relief as he might make it after all.

He also kept a drop-box in another bank under an alias. It was for when he wanted to engage in activities, he didn't want the authorities to be aware of. He got Janyce's account information ready but waited to get confirmation from her before sending the credits. This was money he didn't want to part with unless absolutely necessary.

Let's hope this works.

He waited. Five minutes passed. Ten minutes passed. Twenty, then thirty. Eventually, William glanced at the digital clock: 2:34PM. He was starting to worry and wonder if he should have come here in the first place.

'It's been a while,' Demi said. 'Don't you think?'

He stood up and called for Janyce. There was no response. He approached the door, knocking for a response. Still nothing. He manually opened the door, detaching the emergency lock to slide the door away. He found her lying flat on the bed. He knew right away something was wrong. Her smooth beautiful face was stricken in pain and trembling. Her veins stuck out from under her skin, running widely from her neural chip across the right of her face. Her breathing was ragged.

'Janyce,' William said, rushing to her aid. He picked her up, putting a pillow under her head, moving her to her side.

'Number...' she said, sounding like she struggled to utter single words. 'On...' She took another breath. 'Phone...'

A whirring sound rang from outside the apartment. He approached the curtains, moving them aside only enough to get a view of the outside and making sure not to reveal himself behind the curtains. A mechanical black, tactical drone hovered in the air about twenty meters away from the window.

Shit! He rushed to Janyce, kissing her on her forehead. 'I'm so sorry. I promise to pay you back.' He took her phone and rushed out of the room.

'We need to go now!' Demi said.

Something whistled through the window, missing William by an inch as it hit the kitchen wall. He looked back at the balcony to see the drone fast approaching. 'Move!'

He stayed low and ran behind Demi, holding his mask as he left the apartment. He could hear footsteps coming from the end of the corridor. An emergency door was to his right. Without deliberation, he ran inside. *Stomp, stomp!* Heavy boots rushed up the emergency staircase together with loud shouts of instructions by the police. He quickly descended three levels, while he half-dragged Demi who struggled to run with her injured leg. 'Come on. We're almost there.'

They exited onto the level and headed down the corridor, taking the elevator. They put on their masks and stopped by the entrance as the door slid open.

William walked in before Demi pulled him back.

'Hang on,' she said, pointing at something on the ceiling panel in the elevator.

William turned his attention to the corner to see a camera. 'So what?'

'We can't risk it.'

Someone from behind opened an apartment door. An old man with white messy hair and a beer gut stood by the entrance looking curious.

They threw him into the corridor as police officers burst onto the floor. They shut the door before heading straight for the balcony. The doors were sealed.

'Put your mask on!' Demi said, while throwing a chair at the glass door. It didn't break at first, but by the third throw, the glass shattered.

CHAPTER 15

William followed her onto the balcony and saw another drone descending rapidly down the apartment floors. He heard Demi groan as she went over the balcony, holding firmly to the railing. 'The hell you doing?! You've been shot in the leg.'

'Do you have a better idea?' she said, then released her grip and caught a cable wiring, dropping three floors below. The line halted, bringing her in full swing as she collided into the building wall. She didn't fall off but she groaned heavily. She dropped again, landing on her shoulder before she looked up at William. She appeared okay as she cleaned off the dirt and leaves off herself.

You're nuts! William leapt out over the balcony for a moment, staring at the ground which was seven stories below. What caught his attention was cable wiring out in the open, hanging about three floors away. He leapt off while his body screamed at him for his stupid decision, his brain wanting to shut down NOW to avoid being overwhelmed. He resisted the urge to close his eyes and suddenly wiring came into view, and he grabbed it. The locks in place to hold the wiring immediately broke out of their sockets. William continued to fall until he was flung away from the apartment building into neighbouring trees. This time he closed his eyes, hands held in front to stop anything sharp from hitting him. His body ricocheted off the branches before crashing to the ground.

Oh, damn. He gasped for air as he heard the drone still looking for him. He pushed himself up. Several seconds later, his arm hung motionless, pain radiating from deep inside. He tried to move it. The arm didn't respond except for aggravating the pain further.

'Hey, you alright?' Demi said, fast approaching him.

William pushed himself up. 'Do I look it?'

Bang! Bang! Shots rained down on them as police officers emerged onto the balcony.

'Let's go!' Demi said.

William got up with Demi's aid and ran away. He grabbed up the phone. It was still unlocked, and in one piece—wonder of wonders. He went to the settings and changed the password so he could access the phone later. He found the last number texted.

Janyce's contact had texted her the address of a place to go where he could get his chip removed but he didn't have time to read further. It was only a matter of time before he ended up like her and he needed to keep moving.

He limped away from the area, supported by Demi. His eyes scanned the area for authorities and for a way out. A tram about a hundred meters away docked at a station. He had to get to the next stop. With his broken arm, and residual pain from the bullet graze, he struggled to fight the urge to not stop and give in. He had to keep moving. *Don't stop. Remember, don't let them break you.* Then, at some point, the pain was receding as he'd reached the next stop, just before the tram was due to depart.

'We're almost there,' Demi said.

When he arrived, he saw a familiar face. The Walker who'd helped him with moving through LGAs stood in line for the tram.

'Let me go for a moment,' he said.

'You sure?' she asked.

Will nodded. He stood upright for a moment as she released him. He removed his mask and bumped the Walker softly to get his attention. The Walker turned around to face him, looked away then did a double take as if remembering who he was.

'The hell you doing here?' the Walker asked, grabbing William by his coat and shoving him against the hologram billboard.

'Oi!' Demi said, trying to intervene.

'It's alright,' Will said, raising his functional arm to stop her from getting any closer.

'You have some nerve showing up around here.'

William shoved him back, and pulled his jumper closer to hold his injury in place. 'I wasn't looking for you. It was a coincidence but I may need your help.'

'Are you freaking serious?'

Whoop, whoop! Police sirens wailed in the distance, racing through neighbouring streets. Red and blue lights flashed along the building walls.

'Get in!' William pushed the Walker into the tram while fighting the pain that shot through his shoulder again. He followed behind and sat two rows away from the exit in the event he had to make a quick escape.

'They're for you?' the Walker asked.

'For anyone looking to get their neural link removed.'

The Walker raised his head as if understanding his point. 'So why are you here?'

'I need to get out to the city but I need a distraction.'

CHAPTER 15

'Why would I help you? What makes you think I wouldn't tell the authorities where you are?'

William chuckled. 'You have some nerve thinking that.'

'Is that right?'

'I know all about you, Kieran.'

Kieran seemed taken aback. 'The hell you know that name?'

'You think I don't do my work when I get into business with people I don't know? I know of the convictions. Most recently an assumed arsonist of the bells and halls of a church. Something about the end of all things including religion. Although, the authorities don't know where you're residing at the moment. Lucky for you... but I know.'

'What do you want?' he asked.

'Weren't you listening? A distraction.'

Police sirens wailed past the tram, causing an abrupt halt to everything.

'We need to move,' Demi said.

William left his seat, hit the emergency button and exited the tram as the doors slid aside.

'What the hell did you get me into?' Kieran asked.

'Nothing you need to concern yourself with,' William said. 'I just need you to make me disappear.' William pulled up to an alley, getting them away from unwanted attention.

Kieran looked around, his face pulling tight behind his mask. 'Fine. How much time do you need?'

'As much as you can give me.'

'It'll take me about fifteen minutes to get to a hotspot. Then another about a minute or so to switch your IP.'

'How will I know?'

'What's your number?'

William passed his number to Kieran, then watched him leave.

'You trust this guy?' Demi asked.

'No, but he doesn't have a choice but to help us.'

Kieran continued walking to the police officers. One of them pulled him aside, asking some questions. When a holographic picture of William appeared on the display, Kieran raised his hand, as if readying himself to point somewhere, then pointed directly at William. The police officers looked right at him.

'So much for trust,' Demi said.

'Son of a bitch!' William veered left as he exited the alley. Shouts from behind alerted him to the presence of officers catching up.

The pair raced into a shopping centre and ran through an empty floor. As they continued to move, an Enforcer appeared up ahead, which sent both hurtling for cover behind a pillar.

'This isn't going to go well if we stay here for much longer,' William said, he cast his attention around for an escape.

'You don't think?' Demi said, sarcastically.

Brrng, brrng! William's phone made him jump as he scurried away from the attention of the Enforcer. He checked the caller ID. It was from an unknown number although he had an idea who it might be.

'Hello?' he said.

'Your address has been changed,' Kieran said.

'You fuckwhit! Your stunt before didn't really work well for us, you know that?'

'That's not my problem. I had to get them off my tail, and you seemed like the best way of distracting them from me.'

'How can I be certain the change will work?'

'You don't. Much like I don't know how certain you'll be in keeping *your* word about my side of things.'

William went quiet for a moment. He'd made a valid point. 'How long will this last me?'

'Unless authorities have figured out a way to trace positions after an IP switch, which they haven't yet, however long you need.'

'Thank you.'

'Hmm... this will be the last time we meet. I don't want to see you again.'

'You won't.'

The call disconnected, leaving William standing beside a pillar, as he watched law enforcement officials stroll through the floor on the other side. A glimmer of hope emerged but he didn't want to get ahead of himself. He may have bought himself time to slip unnoticed by the police and Enforcers but he couldn't outrun the effects of the virus plaguing his body.

'Did he, do it?' Demi asked.

He took out his phone and dialled a number.

'What are you doing now?'

'Warning a friend?' He waited until Marlene answered the call. 'Mal! You answered! Thank God.'

'Will...' Marlene said.

'Listen, I need you to listen to me very carefully. You need to leave and get out of the city now. You don't have time. You need to do it right now.'

'Will... I can't.'

'What do you mean you can't? I can help you. Just tell me where you are. I'll try to make something work.'

'*They*... are here.' Her voice trembled in fear and sadness.

William paused. 'Mal... who is there?'

'I'm sorry.'

Suddenly a gunshot fired through the call followed by the sound of someone dropping onto the ground.

'Mal! Mal!'

'What's going on?' Demi asked, looking concerned.

'No, no, no, no, no.'

'Will?'

Heavy footsteps approached the phone from Marlene's end, then an audible sigh passed.

William recognised the voice.

'Understand now, Mr. Kepler?' Ulyanov asked. He ended the call.

William wreathed in fury. He stood still in silence.

'Will?' Demi said.

'GODDAMMIT!' He kicked a nearby shop's shutter door, creating a dent. He sank onto the floor, defeated and heart-broken.

'What happened?'

He paused, thinking of Marlene's smile and bubbly personality whenever they spoke over the phone. 'My friend.' Tears rolled down his face.

Suddenly, a high-pitched ringing shot through his ears. He groaned in pain.

'Will, are you alright?' Demi asked, looking concerned.

William tried to respond but the ringing increased tenfold. He struggled to catch his breath as the pain burst through like a knife piercing through his head.

'Will, what's going on?'

Then an Enforcer showed up and spotted them.

'We gotta go!' Demi said, grasping hold of him.

William's weakened state meant he had to force every step. He pushed on until they managed to escape the building as more police and Enforcers could follow.

The pain subsided a little as he got away. He checked the address on the message and input the coordinates into the GPS. They were fifteen minutes away via car. He requested a cab with Janyce's phone. A self-driven car arrived by the curb. He sat beside Demi as the car took off. Eventually, the car pulled up to his destination, and the car door slid open for them to exit.

William looked around to find they were at the city district which seemed like the wrong place to have such a service around for all to see.

'You sure we're in the right place?' Demi asked.

William checked the GPS, which said they were in the right place. Then, the high pitch ringing came back. The pain intensified to such a point his vision darkened just before he crashed into the pavement.

CHAPTER 16

MURMURS AND BLURRED vision dragged William away from his trance-like state. He couldn't tell where he was or who he was with. Two black figures went in and out of his room as he noticed himself lying on a cushion chair.

'What's... going on?' he asked.

He heard a muffled voice speaking yet couldn't tell if it was directed at him. He shook his head to focus, thinking the virus was blocking out his hearing. 'What?'

A figure emerged by his side but he couldn't tell if it was Demi or someone else who looked like her. Darkness took hold of him again, transporting him, to an unknown place.

'You're... friend is...' a man said, who sat beside him looking at something. 'Treatment... have to worry...'

'Worry about what?'

'I said you don't have to worry. Your treatment went well.'

William went back to sleep and woke up later. This time his vision was clear. All he could see in front of him was a grey wall. A machine hummed as the chair he laid on returned into an upright position. His surroundings became clearer as did his realization that he was somewhere unknown. It was a tiny room, similar to a doctor or dentist's surgery.

He fought a sudden urge to run when he heard someone enter the room. Their footsteps came around his right until a man sat beside him, wearing a blue mask, hazmat suit and latex gloves.

'Who are you?' William asked.

'Somebody you'll do best to forget shortly after leaving my clinic.'

'You're a doctor?'

'Of sorts. But I have a question for you; have you told your friend that you're a Contaminant?'

'What do you mean?'

'Even a child could tell you are sick. The symptoms are as clear as daylight.'

William went quiet.

'Since when?'

'Yesterday...'

'So, about twenty-four hours or less now. Then what was the point of it all coming here?'

'I wanted to get that neural port out of me.'

'Well, it's definitely out.' The man passed an opened container with a bolt-like device inside.

William went to touch the back of his neck.

'I wouldn't do that if I were you.'

'Why is it that I can't feel anything at the moment?'

'Anaesthesia hasn't worn off yet.' The man stood up and approached a cabinet. 'A good thing too. Procedure does leave lingering pain which is why you'll be needing this for that and the shoulder which has been cleaned.' The man passed William a box. 'It's painkillers. Should last you... well... however long you have left.'

'Do I have hole in my neck now?'

'No, synthetic glue was applied to the area. It acts like a bind holding the skin together until the body repairs itself. You will feel tightness around the back soon, however the good thing is that it won't break—even under strenuous circumstances. Some blood might seep through but that's normal. You can wipe it off or wash it.'

William pushed himself off the chair, taking a moment to gather his thoughts. His vision spun around. He reached for a nearby cabinet for support.

The doctor rushed to his aid. 'Take it easy. Your body hasn't flushed out the propofol yet.'

'Thank for the help.'

'Don't thank me. Thank your friend. She brought you here. Had you stayed several minutes longer outside after fainting you wouldn't have woken up.'

Both went quiet.

CHAPTER 16

'Wait. You still didn't answer my question from before.' The doctor approached him. 'What was the point of all this?'

William stopped by the door as he was leaving. 'I guess... what time I have left I would like to keep for myself... even if it's just for a day or so. Tell Janyce, "Thanks", the next time you see her.'

The man looked at William as if considering. 'And how does your friend fall into this?'

'She's not my friend...' He left the room in search of Demi. Arriving at a corridor, he headed towards the end where he found a waiting area in front of a desk where a lady receptionist sat in silence looking at her phone. He approached the building window behind the waiting area to find the clinic positioned away from the main road in an alleyway.

A door hissed aside on his right where he glanced to see Demi enter the clinic from the lobby outside.

'Hey,' she said, sounding relieved. 'Did it go well?'

'I think so,' he said.

'Well, congrats. You're an Allocron now.'

He smirked. 'By the way I wanted to ask before—was that you messaging me when I was in the hospital.'

'I thought my presence at your place was more than enough to give you your answer.'

'How was that possible to have had my phone or my port not tracked?'

'Had help. But we couldn't make it work for long as we're doing yesterday every thirty minutes, otherwise, we would have been caught.' He sat on one of the waiting chairs. 'I never did ask why you helped me?'

She joined him. 'For the same reason you did when you pushed me out of the way that car hit me...'

'I had to do something.'

'Exactly.'

'Even after knowing I was Contaminant?'

'Yeah.'

'Why didn't you say anything? You know I'm a risk.'

'Because all this would have been nothing. I figured I'd help you get something control or freedom back in your life before it ends. I thought maybe that's what you were after.' She looked at him. 'Was I wrong?'

William shook his head. 'Thank you.'

She nodded in understanding, then spotted a similar looking homeless person, walking into the clinic, heading straight to the back office. 'You have Walkers working here?' she asked the receptionist.

'You could say it's more of a joint venture,' the doctor said, approaching the front desk.

'What do you get out of this? They can't really pay anything to you without the system deeming any of those credits as suspicious or fraudulent.'

'Which is why I don't ask to be paid. I do this out of goodwill. There may not be many of us right now but it doesn't take a genius to figure out that there's something deeply wrong here.'

'I guess I should be thanking you.'

'It's fine. In any event you should—'

'Incoming!' Demi yelled, tackling William to the ground.

A hovering missile blasted through the window, straight at the receptionist. The entire room erupted in flames, sending everything and everyone hurtling in all directions.

William scrambled to his feet, pulling away the debris that piled over him. His ears stung from the high-pitched ringing. He spotted the receptionist lying crushed beneath the desk and chairs. Only muffled noises now registered through. He spotted Demi beside him and rushed to her side. Her eyes fluttered as if she was regaining consciousness.

'You need to go now!' the doctor said. His voice sounded muffled as he approached the pair.

Suddenly a police officer emerged through the gaping hole.

William grabbed Demi by the arm and ran. As he ran, something caught hold of his arm. He turned to see the officer.

'Let them go!' the doctor said, charging directly into the police officer.

The police officer front-kicked the doctor away, sending him flying across the room.

William struggled to break free from the forceful grip as Demi threw a chair at the police officer, who just caught it and threw it back at her at a faster speed. She groaned in pain.

Then the officer yanked William by his throat with one hand, suddenly sighing as if disappointed or frustrated at the situation.

William instantly recognized the voice—his pale, relentless stalker as he struggled to free himself from the chokehold.

CHAPTER 16

'How disappointing this is,' Ulyanov said. 'This has been most inconvenient to find you always on the move.'

'No one... asked you... to follow,' William gasped.

'No, I was obliged to.' He disengaged his mask to reveal himself behind a plastic cover. He looked paler and sicker than ever. 'Had you only followed instructions, everything would have gone according to plan.'

'According to plan?' Demi said, frustration in her voice. 'Chasing innocent people and gunning them down before they have a chance to defend themselves?'

'What need is there for defense if they are already guilty? There are consequences for rules broken. No one is above punishment, and if punishment isn't delivered, what's to say an uprising won't happen?'

'One will happen—whether you want it or not,' Will gasped.

The officer took a moment to consider. 'If it does, I'll make sure you're not around to see it.' His mask re-engaged into position, he looked hard at William as his fingers dug deeper into his neck.

William flailed around, kicking in every direction, sending a few at Ulyanov. He could feel the muscles tear aside as the fingers slowly squeezed his neck.

'Will!'

'Oi!' the doctor said, grasping a grenade launcher in his hands.

A grenade shot directly at Ulyanov, which he caught with lighting reflexes. A second later the area around them flared in a flash of white light. He groaned and released William from his grip to cover his eyes.

William dropped like a stone. His neck and throat hurt as did his battered body. The energy in his extremities was gone. His eyes were almost closing from sheer fatigue falling over him.

'Will!' Demi picked him up and he watched himself follow the doctor who had another weapon around his neck—a black automatic assault rifle. He cocked and loaded the weapon, leading them away through the back alley of his clinic.

'Take this!' the doctor said, passing them his car key. 'Give him this as well.' And hand two small blue tubes with white caps at the end.

'What is it?'

'Adrenaline.'

'What about you?'

'There's not much I can do now. I just shot at a police officer.'

Ulyanov yelled in rage, staggering into the walkway before he regained balance and stormed towards them.

'Go!' The doctor fired his weapon at Ulyanov and another flash grenade exploded right in front of the officer.

William, half-dragged by Demi, hopped and limped down a flight of stairs to an open parking area, where they found the doctor's car. He fell into the passenger's seat while Demi ran to the driver seat, fumbling over the controls.

Blam, blam! Shots whistled past them.

William could see Ulyanov hot on their tail, and spotted blood stains over his forearms and chest—belonging most likely to the doctor. He watched Ulyanov jump on the bonnet, holding his firearm at them. 'Demi...'

'I know, I know!' Demi said. 'Do you think this car has voice control?' She still fumbled all around the controls and buttons before hitting one that roared the car to life. 'Reverse!'

The car reeled backward, bursting out of the parking lot and onto the road with Ulyanov gripping hard to the car. The car automatically maneuvered into the air on a backward trajectory towards the skyscrapers, catching the attention of two Enforcers that followed after them.

'We have company.' William looked back at Ulyanov who appeared to regain position on the car and aimed his weapon at them.

'I know!' Demi spun the wheel down and around to shake Ulyanov off, while making the car fall now. It wasn't working as he fired a few close shots. 'Stop!' Demi commanded. It didn't work. 'Brake!' In an instant the car came to an abrupt halt in mid-air. Ulyanov fired another shot and missed the pair as he disappeared overboard.

'Fuck!'

'Can you see him?'

'I'd rather not.' She hit the manual control button and wheeled the car around into the sky traffic, heading away from the city. 'He's probably still alive if those Enforcers were following us before.'

'Where are we going?'

'Rendezvous point.'

'Well, we can't be in this car for long. Odds are against us if they're able to use the GPS on this thing to find us.'

'That's alright. I'm not flying us there.'

CHAPTER 16

The trip lasted about thirty minutes before the horizon to the coast appeared in the sunset. The sky ahead was clearer compared to the intense blur of the city. Blue sky beyond the haze could be seen in patches as they landed on the sand.

William's jaw dropped as he exited the car. He approached the shoreline, staring at the sky and sea. Everything seemed fresh but as he looked harder, he realized the area wasn't far behind the city in pollution. He glanced at the waves crashing and spotted plastic, discarded pieces of furniture and areas of extreme blackness like oil spills on the water.

'Not a pretty sight, isn't it?' Demi asked.

'Not at all,' William said sadly. 'For a moment, I thought the sea was free from all of this.'

'Nothing is.'

William continued to stare at the water as the sun slowly disappeared below the horizon.

'We should go.'

'What will happen with the car? We can't just leave it here.'

'There's nothing in the car that can be traced to us.'

'You can't be that certain.'

'Oh, but I am.'

A second later, a soft thud came from the car. The lights flickered, then shut off while smoke seeped out.

'Can we go now?'

William walked away from the car, fearing he was within range of the blast radius should the car explode. It didn't, as he followed Demi away from the beach. He jabbed himself with the adrenaline the doctor gave him, which immediately made him feel better. William moved onto the next area, looking at the streets and people strolling through. The area wasn't much different from his own. This continued until night fell over the Earth. He listened for sirens when they were close to a town although his concerns changed once they arrived in front of a forest range.

'You can't expect me to go in there,' he said. 'We've been walking for a while now. If I go in there, I won't even make it halfway.'

'Would you prefer a ten-kilometer hike around?' Demi asked.

'Well, no.'

'Then you're going in.'

He sighed in disbelief but didn't complain. He limped behind Demi who flashed a torch around as she led the way.

William's eyes wandered about from left to right as he wanted to see what was lying in the dark as nightfall took over. He didn't think anything alive was lurking behind a rock or tree while they trekked through but he couldn't fight off the anxiety creeping up his back.

The adrenaline wore off and the trek through the forest range took its toll on William's weakened body. He slumped onto a log, taking deep breaths while holding his broken arm. His chest hurt and his head throbbed in pain.

'I can't keep going,' he said.

'What do you mean?' Demi asked. 'What's going on?' She approached him quickly. Eyebrows furrowed with concern across her face.

'I *can't* keep going.'

'But we're almost there. I mean look.' She pointed to the sky beyond the trees. Stars in the sky glistened like white gems upon the cosmos. 'We're not far away now. I promise we will have time to rest and clean up really soon.'

He sighed, pushed himself off the log and followed Demi until they were out in an open area of rock and patches of shrubbery. Shades of black and white cascaded throughout the field as he trudged ahead. He stopped alongside the edge of the cliff where the black ocean lay fifty meters below like a dark living mass. The crashing of waves and the slight breeze of the wind filled William with wonder but not as much as the magnificence of the moon high above the Earth—seen through clear skies.

Where are we? William wondered. He couldn't remember a time when he'd seen any place free of the Smog.

Bang! A loud clash of metal and rock made him jump. He looked back to see Demi pulling a tightrope to pull open a door. He approached her to find a human-sized hole inside the ground with mounted grips for descent into an underground space.

'Come on,' she said, limping over to the hole. 'I think there's someone in here you want to see.'

'What do you mean?'

He waited for a response but Demi ventured down the ladder without answering. She grimaced from the bullet wound on her leg. He followed slowly behind, his shoulder close to useless, to a passage in full darkness. Space between him and everything was a void of nothing as he slowly took one step forward at a time. He could hear Demi dragging her foot against the rock floor in the dark but couldn't see where she was.

Click! Soft light from the ceiling lit the passage in an instant. The light bulb appeared close to the end of its shelf life but remained functional enough to show their surroundings.

The walls around seem untouched by human hand and more likely made by nature and time. Cracks and crevices ran off in all directions but William was more interested in what lay behind the metal door in front of him.

Demi punched a password onto a keypad. Seconds later the door hissed and slid aside. It was dark inside until she turned some lights on.

William stayed by the door until the room light revealed a small bunker.

Two shelves of food supplies stood on the right and a desk sat in front of two mounted monitor screens on the left side. Further down was a single bed with a metal cabinet as its end. His eyes immediately shot to a welcome and familiar sight—his cat.

'Ramses?' he said. He ran to him for a cuddle, even though Ramses appeared far from impressed by the smothering. 'How are you here?'

'I brought him here,' Demi said.

'But how?'

'I checked your address on your license. I figured I'd take a look around at what life you lived. It wasn't until I took my third or fourth step that your cat appeared in the living room, crying for something. I was assuming he was hungry or looking for you.'

'I'm surprised he didn't attack you.'

'Why would he? I'm harmless.'

William snorted.

'Anyway, I didn't know how long you were going to be out of commission, so I had him brought here. Couldn't risk him living with myself and Charles in No Man's Land. At least he was safe, and we could worry about you after.'

'Thank you.'

Demi nodded and resumed unpacking. 'By the way you should get yourself cleaned up.' She pointed to the bathroom opposite the bed. 'There's a shower with hot water and a clean set of towels. The water tank doesn't hold a lot so use it sparingly. I'll be using it myself afterwards so I'd like to get some hot water as well. And in the meantime, I'll get you some clothes.'

'Will do.'

He placed Ramses on the bed, put his phone to charge and entered the bathroom. There was enough space for a toilet and shower. He undressed and jumped under the hot stream of water, letting the dirt, grime and sweat roll off his skin. He reached for the soap when his chest suddenly seemed to squeeze all the oxygen out of his lungs. He dropped to the ground, coughing and gasping for air. The cough became unbearable until he saw spots of blood on his hand. He stared at the crimson splatter, realizing his time was almost up. He rested against the tiled wall, not knowing what to do.

Knock, knock!

'Will? Will, are you alright?' Demi asked.

'I'm alright,' he said.

'You sure?'

'I'm fine.'

After his shower, he dried himself and gathered up the clothing Demi had left on top of the basin—black cargo pants, white shirt, beige jumper. Beside the clothes was a note which read, 'Do not put on the jumper yet. Come see me first.' The clothes fitted him well. He collected his phone and left the bathroom to find Demi absent from the room.

'Demi?'

There was no response.

He walked around, looking at the books on leadership, surviving in the wild, world history, and much more. Then he inspected the food and supplies. Some packages were opened. By the looks of it, recently. Some fire starters, coal, timber, and instant noodles in a cup. He lost interest and left the room.

After climbing painfully back up the ladder with his one functional arm, he walked towards the cliff edge to enjoy the moonlight view. He caught sight of a beach towards the left region several kilometers away. He'd wondered when he'd last visited the beach but nothing sprung to mind. Everything he'd experienced recently was in Zerya—none of it had been real. Every touch or sensation had been simulated.

As he stood atop the hilltop, he felt the cool wind brushing against his cheeks and the smell of salt water. He found it strange to be outside, wearing nothing but casual clothing. He had become so accustomed to wearing his respirator mask and hazmat defense suit that he found himself worrying that he didn't have them on.

CHAPTER 16

He surveyed the area and spotted a small fire burning with Demi sitting beside the light, cooking the noodles inside a pot. He approached her and felt the comforting warmth of the fire, giving strength to his cold aching extremities. He came around the fire to see what took to be a person but on closer inspection, he realised it was a statue made of straw and wood. 'The hell?'

'Don't mind the statue,' she said.

'I'll try not to,' he said.

'By the way, come here.' She took out an arm sling and dressed his shoulder wound. 'Now you can put on the jumper. Also, take this.' She passed him a zip up blanket. 'It's going to get cold later.'

'Thanks.'

'It's alright.'

'Do you need help?'

'No, it's all good. I hope you don't mind noodles in a cup.'

'I don't mind. I'll eat whatever.' William sat away from the statue, to the right of it, but still within range of the fire to absorb the heat. His bottom slumped against the rock. 'What's with the statue?'

'It's whatever you make it to be.'

'Did you bring it here?'

'No, Charles did.'

'Why?'

'To ward off unwanted guests. Not that there are ever any.'

William remained doubtful but let it drop and waited for the food. He watched until Demi poured the soup in a bowl with some seasoning and broth. He took the bowl with his functional hand and dug in right away.

Both of them went quiet as they ate the food and watched the fire crackling in the night.

'I want to ask,' she said, 'how long has it been since you've...'

'Become a Contaminant?' William sighed and took a moment to consider his answer. 'Ever since I woke up in the hospital.'

'That was like two days ago.'

'*Nearly* two days.'

'How much time do you have left?'

'Perhaps only a few hours at most.' He took out his puffer. 'This was given to me by a doctor. It somewhat stalled the effects but... it's not enough.' He offered a weak smile. 'How did you know?'

'Because it's not the first time I've seen the symptoms in someone who contracted the virus.'

'If you realized then why didn't you do anything? I am contagious after all towards the end.'

'You are but a friend of Charles devised a failsafe to shield me and Charles from the virus.'

'How did they make that work?'

'They were part of the vaccine program. However, they realized early into the program that the vaccines weren't showing promising results. There was a lot of contention between the manufacturers and the people actually developing the vaccine which stalled the progress for a long time. Charles's friend, Nicholas, worked off-record to see the results of the research for himself. He was able to get promising results but the government caught wind of it and he was sentenced to jail.'

'So, it's like a vaccine?' William was curious.

'Not quite, but it's more to do with an increase in production of white blood cells. Nicholas's theory was that certain blood types have a stronger response to the vaccine, and therefore, increasing white blood cells in each type may help. I'm an O-positive blood type. Also, the virus has to be detected early in a person before they're coughing blood or experiencing severe migraines. It's their best chance of surviving the virus. Otherwise, it's just...' She went silent for a moment, then looked at him. 'You've already been losing blood, right?'

William averted his gaze, avoiding giving a definitive answer. 'More than I'd want to.' He looked back at Demi. 'I take it that you don't have anything stored inside the safehouse, right?

'Unfortunately, no.'

Both went quiet. Their attention turned to the fire and they threw on more wood to get it to stay strong and warm.

'Are you expecting Gaia to come here?' William asked.

'Yes.'

'How certain are you that they will come tomorrow?'

'I'm not certain at all,' Demi said. 'But I'm willing to believe they will come.' He looked away. 'It's all I got.'

'What happens if they don't show up?'

'Well, that's tomorrow's problem. Right now, I'm going in with the belief that they will come.'

'Where do you think they're based?'

'Don't know. There were rumours they set up base inland but moved over to the ocean as they were getting a lot of unwanted attention. There's been reports of ships passing through waters close to the shore in the event they had to complete a mission... but they're just rumours.'

'Hmm... I hope they come for your sake. And I hope they let you take Ramses with you. I can't imagine him being left alone.'

'I won't leave him. You have my word.'

'Thank you. I'd definitely like to see you make it to them.'

'You speak as if you don't believe you'll survive the night.'

He looked at himself. 'I can feel it.' He exhaled deeply to expel the air but there was still pressure in his chest. 'Even now as we speak, something's not right... But that's okay. If I can at least hold out until you and Ramses are with Gaia, that'll be something worthwhile that I have done with my life.'

'But why help?'

'Life makes sense the way you live it. There's a connection. People are real—well, they *were* once real. I mean you had a meal with your friend in person. No Zerya, phones or gimmicks. You have—well, *had*—things actually created by people that speak history.' He paused. 'There's a sort of energy you put out in your company that you don't get with people living in the city these days.' He looked at her. 'Which is why we can't continue living in a box or hooked into Zerya anymore.'

'It won't change, Will.'

'Not at first, of course. And it may not change completely but something has to happen. Maybe you, and that energy emitter might be the very thing we need right now.' He went quiet. 'That's *why* I want to help.'

Silence came over Demi as if his words had sparked something inside her. 'Thank you.'

William continued to talk with her until both grew tired.

'Are you going to come and sleep inside?' Demi asked.

'No, I want to sleep outside,' William said. 'I've been cooped up inside my own apartment for so long, I just want to lay here for the night until morning comes.'

'Okay, sleep tight.'

He watched her disappear from the light and become a shade in the dark moving before vanishing completely.

On my own... again.

William stood upright and gathered the branches and small logs, placing them beside the fire. Those that were dry he threw into the centre and around the side.

About five minutes later, the fire grew in brightness and warmth. Concerned it was now too big, he moved the wooden statue away from the fire to avoid burning it.

He turned his phone on, looking for Marlene's name. He burst into tears upon the sight of her name. He tried to stop himself as his body ached the harder, he cried but he couldn't stop it.

I'm sorry. I'm so sorry.

His grieving continued until he opened a message for his Mum and Dad, and recorded a video message of his apology and a farewell. He needed to leave one last thing for them—something positive before everything was over. Then he repeated the same to his brother and sister. Last on his list was to pay Janyce. He sent her the money he owed, and he switched off his phone and laid beside the fire, placing his head on a pillow Demi left for him. He looked to the stars.

From this place he actually could see more of the night sky than any other places he had ever been to. If one were to look up to the sky in the city now, there would only be a haze. You'd be considered lucky or wealthy if you were able to see a star or two. The more he looked to the sky, the drowsier he became until he fell asleep.

CHAPTER 17

SOME TIME LATER, William woke up. His breathing quickened as he realized he was still alive. The pain in his chest wasn't as bad as it normally was. Although he was ready for it to hit at any given moment.

How much time do I have left?

The sun hadn't yet risen but he could see his surrounding areas. To his surprise, the fire continued crackling under two small pieces of wood. He had no memory of adding stock to the fire during the night. He continued to glance around and noticed the wooden statue was missing. He stood up in a panic and looked around to find it. He didn't want to be remembered as a person who loses other people's things.

He continued to search the rocky terrain with no success until he heard footsteps approaching. Demi appeared, looking refreshed.

'Morning,' she said.

'Morning?' he said.

'You alright?'

'Yeah, I was just... stretching.'

'You look worried.'

'Well, I can't find your statue. I was looking around before you arrived. I have no idea where it went.'

'I put it somewhere else. I think it would serve its purpose better away from here and have it not scare you.'

'Oh, there's one mystery solved for the day.'

'There are others?' Demi smiled, amused by his comment. She walked past him, and sat beside the fire.

'No, no, just the one.' William hadn't seen her smile ever in all the time they've been together. It seemed genuine enough that he wanted to see her smile again. He followed and sat beside her. 'Thanks for putting the wood in the fire. I remember tossing some into the fire during the night, then nothing. I crashed asleep after you left but I don't remember putting more wood in the fire.'

'It's alright.'

'Did you get some sleep?'

'I did. It was much better than most nights I've had leading up to today.'

'I think it was from all that walking.' He chuckled. 'I might have to invest in—' He realized he couldn't finish the sentence.

'You okay?'

'I—uh—I'm alright.' He sat in silence and watched Demi push the ambers around with a stick. Curious to learn more about her before his passing, he tried to think of something to ask but his mind drew blanks.

'If you don't mind me asking—I know it's a bit out of the blue but you're a Dota fan, right?'

'For Esports?'

'Yeah.'

'Sure am. Are you?'

'No, I'm a Valorant fan.'

'What? How's that possible? Dota is so much better. You guys have just been lucky with crossover world championships.'

'Valorant is so much better. Going on the last ten series, I'd say it's been close to domination, as they have won eight out of those ten series.'

'Historically speaking, it's about fifty-fifty. No way are they better. And besides, had it not been that wrong call the refs made for the Dota team in the last series, it would have been seven out of ten.'

Demi laughed. 'Oh, excuses. Admit it, the only thing you have going for the Dota is Mitchell Till, and even he isn't what he used to be. He's way past his prime.'

'Fair point about Mitch, but we have other players that have definitely taken on the mantle.'

'Like who? James Gunther? Lukehold Strong? Esau Isse? They're upcoming players. They haven't really made a mark.'

'At least we don't have cheats on our team like Reeds Iona or Tank Pritchard.'

CHAPTER 17

'You take that back.'

'No can do there,' William smiled. 'Anyway how did you know I was a Dota fan? And why are you asking me this?'

'When I was at your place, I looked around. it was quite obvious you were a fan when I found your jersey in your wardrobe. And to answer your second question, I just wanted to know a little about you.'

'I see. Well, I'd imagine you know your history on the game.'

'Other among things.' She chuckled, then went silent as another mood took over her. 'I'm sorry about your friend.'

William sighed. 'Me too.'

'What she was like?'

'Fun to be around. You could muck around and talk to her without getting judgment. And when you had her support, you had it one hundred percent. She was there.'

'They're the people to have around.'

'Yeah, they are.' He smiled at memories of Marlene. 'Although she worried a lot about things—and in hindsight, they were quite trivial. Then again, who am I comment? I worried about a lot of the same stuff as well.'

'We all worry. We do it to ourselves.'

Beep, beep! Demi checked her phone. There was a message. She walked away from the fire and went quiet. She stood with her back towards William for a bit before facing him.

'Everything alright?'

'It was Gaia... they're coming.'

'That's good news. When will they be here?'

'Just before sunrise. So that could be in the next hour or so. I really don't know. This is a first for me.'

'Do you have everything ready to go?'

'Yeah, it was done many days ago.'

'Then, what's wrong?'

Demi appeared stunned. 'Nothing. It's just—I can't believe it's really happening now. I've been planning for this for so long and to have actual confirmation, it's such a relief. I don't have to hope anymore.'

'Then let's celebrate. It might not be anything big but it's a step in the right direction for you.'

'Isn't it a little early for a celebration?'

'I'm not saying we should drink, but maybe we can have breakfast... together.'

'I'd like that.'

'Then it's settled.' William headed into the safehouse with Demi. He cuddled Ramses and fed him for what he believed was his last time. He caressed the fur over his neck.

'I'm going to signal our position to Gaia first. Better to make sure they know where we are just in case.' She approached the mounted computer. Applications popped upon the desktop screen. She input several short text commands.

'You sure they will be able to find this place?' William looked at the screens, having no idea what the application did nor what the information meant.

'Before sunrise, definitely.' She input another command, then left the desk. 'I'm going to get ready to cook up something by the fire. It'll probably be the same as last night but different flavour. It's not fine dining or anything but it'll do.'

He chuckled. 'It's okay.' He went to gather some items, when he heard a woman's voice singing nearby. He turned to find a small, portable speaker beside Demi. 'Who is that?'

'It's Don't Know Why by Norah Jones,' Demi said. 'You haven't heard this?'

'I can't say I have. I don't listen to music as it does nothing for me. There are just sounds and people screaming or yelling loudly.'

'You serious?'

'*Yeah.*'

'Then I guess you haven't danced before as well, right?'

William laughed. 'You're not going to catch me dancing at all. And I don't think I have ever, if I remember correctly.'

'Well, you're going to, now.'

'What?!'

'Come on.' She reached for his hand.

'You cannot be serious?'

'This is me celebrating.'

William stared at her in disbelief as he hesitated to take her hand. His breathing quickened in anxiety, and his hand became clammy. He wiped his hand on his pants before taking her hand.

CHAPTER 17

'Relax. All you have to do is sway.'

William followed her instructions, holding her close to him with his functional left hand while she had her hands around his neck. He didn't know where to look so he stared at his feet.

'You can look at me.'

He took a deep breath and looked at her. To his surprise, he was calming down.

'Have you ever been with someone?' she asked.

'I don't know how to answer that question.'

'Zerya?'

'Among other stuff.'

'I used to dance with Charles. He taught me some moves so we could dance when the time was appropriate.'

'I'm beginning to think Charles was an all-round lady's man.'

They chuckled.

'How am I doing considering the broken arm?'

'You're doing okay.'

I hope so, he wanted to say. He swayed with the soft playing music as she rested her against his shoulder. The pair continued to dance until the song was over and Demi left to cook.

'Have a shower and clean yourself up,' she said. 'It'll do you some good for the morning.'

William nodded then watched her ascend the steps. He stripped naked and hopped into the shower. His cough returned with blood splattering everywhere, heavier this time. He dropped to his knees and continued to cough and cough until at last the moment passed. He pushed himself upright, digging his fingers against the tiles. Then desperation set in.

Not like this...

He washed the blood off, dried his body and wore the same clothes he'd slept in. He exited the bathroom and looked at the time. Twenty minutes had passed. Surprised by the time he'd spent showering; he wondered if Demi had come back at all while he was in the bathroom. He walked towards the safehouse entrance, when he heard a soft rustle from behind, thinking it was Ramses meandering.

He turned around to see a police officer launching a rifle's heel at his face. He blacked out upon impact.

'Hey... wake up...' a voice said.

'What?' William asked, speaking to the dark for a moment. His mind wouldn't function for him.

'Oi! Wake up.' the voice said, louder.

William's eyes shot right open to see a team of officers and Enforcers standing guard. The morning sky before sunrise illuminated the area clearly and he saw that they all faced him and Demi except for one who had their mask off. A puff of smoke blew away from their head as they smoked on a cigarette. Black grizzly hair hung down by their neck.

'Oh, you gotta be kidding me,' William said, fury rising. Fear no longer gripped him, maybe because he would be dead soon anyway. He didn't hold back anymore. 'You're still here? Man, I'm flattered you would come all this way for me but you got take a hint. I just don't like ya.'

'Shut it!' an officer said, as they struck William on the face.

William wasn't impressed. As his face moved left from the punch, he caught sight of Demi kneeling beside officers. Her lip was already swollen with blood dried along the side. 'You alright?'

She tilted her head and shrugged her shoulders as if to say 'what do you think?', but nothing more.

'You shouldn't concern yourself with her if I were you,' Ulyanov said, back still facing them. He puffed smoke again before turning around to reveal his face. His eyes bounced between the pair. 'You might be wondering how I'm still here?'

'Honestly, I couldn't care,' Demi said. 'Given the fact that you're still here gives me another shot to try the same thing again. You got a car around, so I can run you over this time?'

'No talking!' another guard said, kicking her stomach so hard, she seemed to retch.

'Leave her alone!' William said.

'If it wasn't for that suit I was wearing when we last met,' Ulyanov approached Demi, kneeling down to meet her eye level. 'I might have been dead. Technology has definitely served us well, especially the ability to hover. Anyway, I'm going to get straight to the point of this meeting.' He took out another cigarette and lit the tip. 'You may begin.' He said with an authoritative tone.

CHAPTER 17

William didn't know what he was talking about until three soldiers battered his face and body with punches and kicks.

'Will!' Demi said. She got up but was holstered back to her knees by the standing officer.

'A signal was broadcasted earlier this morning,' Ulyanov said, 'to an unknown destination. No response came back but history indicates there has been communication taking place here. Who was it sent to?'

William turned his face away, trying to find a different angle where he wouldn't get hit. He tried to fight back but his attempts failed him as another punch or kick came flying at him. Blood spilt over his body as one boot collided against his mouth. He groaned in pain and focused his attention on the conversation between Demi and Ulyanov. He took the beating yet their voices disappeared under the shuffling of feet and heavy breathing of the police officers hitting him.

'Who was it sent to?' Ulyanov asked.

Demi continued to watch Will get beaten up. Time wasn't helping him and he swelling on his body was mounting up.

'Your friend won't last much longer.'

'Please stop this,' Demi said.

'You need only answer my question.'

Demi stared at Ulyanov. Her face registered concern—clearly the idea of sharing the information would bring about severe consequences for others.

'Yes?'

Demi exhaled deeply. Her head dropped. She seemed defeated. 'It was to Gaia.'

Ulyanov went quiet with his cigarette still burning away. He walked away from Demi, taking the cigarette out of his mouth to expel the smoke. 'Enough.'

'Yes, sir,' one officer said.

William lay on the ground, beaten. His body burned from the bruises swelling up over the last few minutes. He heaved and coughed up blood.

'Will,' Demi said, trying to get to him. The officer standing beside her pushed her back on her knees. She yelled in frustration.

'Gaia...' Ulyanov said. 'This definitely changes things. If anything, it might work in our favour.' He looked at Demi. 'When are they expected to arrive?'

'Today,' Demi said, 'but there wasn't any time given on when or how they were going to get here.'

'Demi, what are you doing?' Will asked.

'We'll wait, then. Let this be the day that marks the beginning of the end of Gaia. How foolish they were to think they would be able to trust you to join their ranks only to be betrayed later on.'

'I didn't betray them,' Demi said.

'That's not what history will say; nor will anyone remember who you were. You'll soon join the ranks of the Archived Citizens. You should consider yourself privileged. You'll be known as nothing after this day.' He smiled, then with lighting speed, grasped his firearm and hammered the trigger. The shot echoed through the area as the bullet hit William directly in his right leg.

William groaned. The pain created a domino effect on his bruises. He tossed around, clutching his leg tightly. Yet nothing worked as the bullet seemed to dig further in as he moved around.

'Will!' Demi said.

Ulyanov approached William. 'Although your trip there will be monitored *thoroughly*. If you thought your death would be a swift one, you were mistaken. Your time is limited. And if you think that being a Contaminant would stop me squeezing every ounce of your life out of you, you'd be mistaken *again*.' He knelt beside William, speaking in a lower voice. 'Fret not, you will be joining your other friend when it's all over.'

William glared directly at Ulyanov. If he was capable of wreaking havoc right now, he knew the officer would be dead.

'Sir!' one officer said, pointing at something in the sky, some distance away from them.

William turned his head to see two helicopters flying over the ocean while approaching them.

'Take cover now,' Ulyanov said. 'Activate infrared blockers. This encounter mustn't end against us. Only shoot to stun. We need as many as we can take alive if we are to have a chance in finding where they are.' He looked at his subordinate. 'Take him away and keep him quiet.' Then he looked at Demi. 'As for you... you have the most important task of all.' He drew an item out of his pocket and walked towards her.

William tried to hear what Ulyanov was saying as he was dragged away, so he stared at Demi until he could only see a portion of her behind the bush. He tried to move closer but the firearm clicked, followed by the guard levelling their weapon at his face. Understanding the point, he stopped moving.

228

CHAPTER 17

Within minutes, the two helicopters flew towards the area with Demi on her feet with no one around as the police officers and Enforcers camouflaged themselves behind the bushes.

William watched as the first helicopter landed about fifty meters to his right on open land while the other one flew over. *I wager they're scouting the place.* He looked back at Demi who was limping towards the helicopter.

'Demitrova,' a soldier said, armed with tactical body equipment and an assault rifle.

'Yes,' Demi said, keeping her hands in the air.

'Orders, captain,' the guard spoke directly into his radio, who was watching William.

'Don't do anything yet,' Ulyanov said.

The pair fell silent as Demi started using hand-gesture signals as if she was using sign language. William chuckled. *Damn, you're good.*

'Quiet!' the guard said.

Demi and the soldier walked together into the safehouse while the pilot in the helicopter remained seated in the cockpit. There seemed to be another soldier in the helicopter but it was difficult to see inside through the tinted windows.

'Do we attack?' another officer asked through the radio.

'Hold,' Ulyanov said. 'Hold.'

William struggled with uncertainty. An attack was imminent but he had no means of informing Demi or the soldiers. His beaten body weakened with each passing moment. He grimaced at the wriggling pain around his leg as the bullet moved further inside. He checked his wound. Blood continued to seep out.

Heavy boots scraped across the rocky terrain as the Demi and the soldier emerged, carrying the energy emitter, tools, equipment, and Ramses.

Ramses?!

'On my mark,' Ulyanov said. 'When they approach the helicopter, we attack.'

William dug his fingers into the rocks from the stress.

'Now!'

A barrage of shots fired directly at Demi and soldiers of Gaia. A forcefield appeared around the pair ricocheting the incoming fire. The police officers emerged from their hiding spots and engaged in an all-out battle between the soldiers on the ground and the second helicopter flying around the area with a machine gun operator raining hellfire. Bullets whistled in all directions as a highly contentious battle ensued.

'Contact! Contact!' one officer yelled through the radio.

'Incoming fire from the helicopter,' another officer said. 'They are circling around to take—' Their voice disappeared behind radio static and an explosion.

William saw flames erupt on his right from an explosion. He continued to watch the battle unfold. His eyes landed on Demi as she rushed around the helicopter before her body dropped. Her body convulsed uncontrollably on the ground. 'Demi!'

William darted for cover as bullets whistled past. He kept his hand over his head, knowing it was futile against flying bullets. He remained low, watching the posted police officer beside him join in the gunfire.

Thud! Suddenly, the police officer jerked and slumped flat onto the ground.

'The hell?' William said. He approached the guard to see a hole on the front of the helmet. A puff of smoke rose from the black mark left by the bullet. He collected the magnum firearm beside the guard, and removed their ammunition, grenade and radio with his functional hand. He clicked on the trigger. *Bam!* The recoil rattled his body as he dropped back. 'Shit.' He looked back at Demi who hadn't gotten up yet as one of the soldiers tried to stop her moving. 'Demi...'

He remembered Ulyanov removing something from his pocket as he'd approached her earlier. He knew the tyrant officer was responsible and he turned around to find him. Time was against him. He looked at the radio and spoke in the best indiscernible accent he could muster. 'Contact! Contact! Unidentified parties emerging from the east. I repeat, unidentified parties emerging from the east.'

'Where?' one officer said.

'Still tracking,' William said. 'We've lost another member. The boy is dead. Looks like crossfire.'

'Focus efforts on the girl,' Ulyanov said. 'I'll handle those coming from the East.'

Gotcha. William noticed he wasn't shaking at all. He moved quickly towards the East, where a tall figure in full armour raced ahead through the area. He knew it was Ulyanov and threw a grenade. His poor throw landed the shell about five meters away from the officer. But he got closer before it detonated and threw another one this time closer to Ulyanov. The explosion sent the officer flying.

The attack seemed to catch the attention of nearby officers as William now came under fire. He stumbled away and approached Ulyanov who lay motionless on his back. His entire front guard and headpiece were cracked and singed by smoke. He turned around to see Demi sitting upright. She appeared weakened by the experience as the soldier carried her up. 'Thank god.'

'Don't thank him yet,' Ulyanov said.

With his remaining strength, he turned around to fire a shot but Ulyanov ripped the firearm out of his hand and front-kicked him. The force propelled him close to the battlefield. He groaned in pain on the rocky ground.

'You know, just for that... these last few moments of yours will be your worst but my best.'

William watched Ulyanov walk with malice and concentration in his stride. Half his headpiece was gone, revealing a burnt, fleshy wound across the face. Dread filled him as he scurried away from Ulyanov who unsheathed a large, charcoal knife.

He turned around to get up—a decision he regretted as a sharp incision struck his calf, cutting it to the bone. He yelled in agony. The pain almost knocked him unconscious. He grasped hold of anything he could find to get away. Instead, he found himself pulled back, coming face to face with Ulyanov. This time the knife struck his chest and body several times before Ulyanov dug it right back into his chest, moving the knife in circles. William groaned and struggled to remove the knife but was too weak to do anything.

'Remember this, Mr. Kepler,' Ulyanov said. 'Watch your body convulse. Scream, perhaps. There will be no one to save you and your friend from me. All will follow the rule that will prevail over the lands. You understand? No one will be able to stop everything that is to come from those who govern the law? You understand? No one! Gaia, simpleton protestors, no one will be able to—' Ulyanov murmured something inaudible as something hit his head. His eyes fluttered in confusion.

William watched as Ulyanov's body seemed to spasm several seconds before he fell aside. He still couldn't tell if Ulyanov was dead but there was a bullet hole in his head and blood now seeped through the mask openings. He remained still, taking in harsh breaths.

'Will?' Demi said.

Shuffling footsteps hit the rock ground above his head. He stayed on the ground as Demi limped towards him. She gasped for air, as if short of breath herself. Then her face froze. Shock and fear registered through her eyes and mouth.

'It's *that* bad, isn't it?' William asked.

'No, it's just—' She looked up. 'Help! I need help!'

'It's alright, Demi. It's *alright.*'

A Gaia soldier appeared beside Demi, carrying a medical kit in one hand, and their assault rifle in the other.

'Can you help him?' Demi asked.

The soldier cast a quick glance at the wounds on William, then hung their head. The soldier's sweaty, grave face said it all.

'Is there anything you can do?'

The soldier opened his medical kit and removed a silver cylindrical syringe.

'It's all pain management from here, isn't it?' William asked, chuckling.

He looked at William without answering and passed the syringe. 'Apply it where you need it most.'

'Morphine?' Demi said.

'Can I have a patch?' William asked.

William grabbed the syringe and stuck the needle where the knife remained fixed on his chest. After several moments, the morphine swept the pain aside, almost completely. He grabbed the patch from the soldier and placed it over the wound after removing the knife. 'If you could help me up. I don't want to be here.' He pushed himself upright with Demi holding him tightly.

'Where do you want to go?' Demi asked.

'Closer to the edge.'

He trudged over to an area where he could lay against the rocky face, and look towards the ocean as the rising sun appeared to set first light to Earth. He sighed in relief as he faced the sky for daybreak. He saw sadness on Demi's face.

'What's wrong?' he asked.

'I can't return the favour.'

'What do you mean?'

'You helped me get to Gaia. There's nothing I can do to repay my gratitude.'

'Sure you can. You can look after my cat.'

'I'm serious.'

CHAPTER 17

'So am I.' He paused and grabbed her hand. 'You're here. You've made it. Make it count, Demi... Make it count.'

'My name isn't Demi.'

'What?'

'My name isn't Demi... It's Amelia.'

Beep, beep! The soldier standing guard quickly reached for their radio. 'What's wrong?'

'We have another group,' the voice said, 'of unknown hostiles heading our way. They seemed to be doubled in numbers. With Enforcers as well.'

'Roger that!' He approached the pair. 'We must go, Demitrova.'

William nodded in affirmation. 'Look after yourself... Amelia.'

Amelia appeared reluctant to leave, then embraced William for a moment. She gave him a kiss on the forehead before walking away.

The soldier unholstered a firearm and placed it beside William. 'A failsafe.' He nodded and left with Amelia for the helicopter.

William stared at the weapon, wondering if he would use it or not. He looked at the rays of light hitting the rocky ground around him, then slowly lifted his gaze towards the sun creeping over the horizon. He marvelled at the view. These were experiences he had forgotten from his own life. He raised his hand to the sun to see the light pass through his fingers. He smiled in joy as his life energy drained away.

A helicopter came into view high over the water. He spotted Amelia looking at him by the window before it headed away from the cliff towards an unknown destination.

William hoped for the world to see a better life—a life he wished he could have lived—and knew would be achieved with Amelia in it.

Hopefully with Ramses, it might make it better. William chuckled as his life disappeared into the dark peace of the unknown.

www.ingramcontent.com/pod-product-compliance
Lightning Source LLC
Chambersburg PA
CBHW021233130626
46554CB00004B/1473